HOW I STRAYED FROM THE PATH TO STOP FALLING BY THE WAYSIDE

My Pilgrimage

EDUARD FREUNDLINGER

Chapter One

One of my earliest childhood memories is of an adventure trip, or, to be more precise, of a Sunday visit to my grandparents who lived two villages away. Although it was still much too early to set off, I was already whinging. After all I was dying to show my grandparents the tricycle I had been given for my fourth birthday. My mother, who was busy decorating a cake, her hair still in curlers, sent me ahead.

"But only as far as the main road. There you stay put and wait for us", she said and stroked my hair lovingly. Her next touch, however, was to be a hefty slap in my face but neither she nor I could have foreseen that.

So I struggled on my tricycle along the gravel path which led to the main road. There I stopped and waited for a while. Of course I didn't have a watch of my own then and so had no clue as to how long I stood waiting for my parents. Unfortunately in those days the concept of patience appeared just as strange to me as the term obedience and I was still inexperienced in dealing with both.

It wasn't my first Sunday outing to meet Grandma and Grandpa. Quite often the route had rolled past me when I had been looking out of the car window from my seat. Thus I knew I just had to turn my tricycle left and follow the main road for a couple of kilometres until it connected to a busy main road. I would then just have to cycle along this road, keeping close to the grass verge in order not to get run over. First, I would pass through a rather small village, then through a larger one. After that the route would lead downhill to reach the small town of Seekirchen shortly after. My grandparents' house was located at the beginning of the town.

Although I had never covered such a distance on my tricycle before - I had only owned my three-wheeler for a few days - I was convinced I could manage the distance with my short legs. Without thinking of my mother's admonitory words I pedalled off and dared for the first time to exit my childhood comfort zone.

Around three hours later I was ringing the bell at my grandparents' house. Apart from an anxious lady at a bus stop who had tried to hinder the little hero from cycling any further, I had achieved my objective without major incidents. I was jolly proud of myself. My Grandma, who had already been notified about my disappearance, was speechless and pressed me so tightly against her bosom that I – anyway out of breath – almost suffocated. A little later my hastily informed parents arrived. They seemed to rejoice at seeing the young adventurer again, even though my mother expressed her delight in a slightly strange manner – namely in the form of the earlier mentioned slap.

Forty years later life had struck me with quite a number of slaps in the face and my childish, self-confidence had long since disappeared. Fears and worries accompanied my way through life. I couldn't even listen to my mother's advice any more as she had long since passed away. Voluntarily departing from life.

Many years ago I had left my homeland – with winters far too cold – in order to move to a country that is far too hot in summer. I had pursued various careers without feeling any personal calling or even satisfaction. I had married a beautiful woman and divorced her again - because this beautiful woman had found another man. I had travelled more than fifty countries on all continents and shot countless photos on the way, which afterwards I never looked at and whilst taking them had hardly noticed a thing beyond the camera lens. And anyway my thoughts had seldom been in the present but rather in yesterday, in tomorrow, in the last quarrel or the next appointment. Or I was engrossed in soliloquies, in which I ruthlessly gave someone my opinion, something I quite certainly would never do if that person was actually standing in front of me.

I could be agreeable if I wanted to, but these occasions became increasingly rare. I could be humorous, although I myself had nothing to laugh about. I could appear self-confident, doubting at the same time whether I would succeed. I even had admirers, some of whom wanted to be like me. On the other hand I longed to be someone else, desiring to be more successful and wealthier or slimmer and more sporty or wiser and better educated or rather more carefree and happier.

I was actually happiest whilst dreaming. In escaping from my everyday life into an imaginary and in creating new realities. I dreamt of further journeys to distant lands, dangerous adventures which only tough guys survive, of romances with beguiling women, having an athletic body, financial liberty, a villa in the mountains and a yacht in the harbour. Some of my dreams I was able to fulfil, but more often than not I noticed afterwards that I – as quite often before – had pursued false dreams and in doing so had only burdened myself unnecessarily.

Moreover, my life was just heading into an abyss – financially, emotionally and socially. I hadn't the faintest idea how I was going to change course at the last moment – it was too late to put the brakes on now anyway – and I was terrified of the final descent into chaos.

Over and over again I searched for solutions to my dilemma. I was constantly preoccupied by questions whose answers could not be found on the Internet. Like the question of 'happiness'. How did one attain it? How did one recognize it? How did one hold on to it? How did one define it in the first place? I had once read that happiness stood for the desire of recurrence. But was that really true?

I had already suspected that happiness was unlikely to just walk through the door. Obviously it had to be invited. But shouldn't one tidy and clean up the mess at home first of all? Perhaps by learning how better to deal with worries, to be more relaxed, more attentive, become more sincere and more grateful and how to get to grips with pain and disappointments? Perhaps one should also invite long-lost contemporaries such as joy, enthusiasm and love into one's home just to make happiness feel comfortable?

However, I was no good at tidying up and at home I used the services of a cleaning lady for this. I had no idea how happiness should find its way through my door, and that made me unhappy.

I did indeed ponder on such issues at regular intervals – but not for very long. Emails had to be answered, phone calls made, appointments kept. A whole bunch of problems were waiting for solutions. No time whatsoever for happiness or contemplating truly important issues in life. Other people didn't do it either. And surely if one followed the crowd there was no need for a guilty conscience, I thought. And from where should I gain the essential insights? After all I didn't happen to be a philosopher, an enlightened Buddhist or a neuroscientist.

I had lost my self-confidence, had forgotten how it had felt on the tricycle over forty years ago. The recollection of cheering when a giant truck had thundered by, its air suction lifting my tricycle onto just two wheels and almost but not quite pushing it into the roadside ditch had faded because then I had considered myself invincible, feeling like a super hero, long before I was even able to read my first comic book.

Chapter Two

One day I had an appointment with a business partner. The man had just returned from his vacation and seemed to have changed somehow. Calmer and more relaxed rather than hectic and nervous as before. He spoke at a slower pace and had lost some weight. His hands lay calmly on the table when he explained something. We had a problem to discuss but that didn't seem to bother my counterpart particularly. That must have been a relaxing holiday, I thought, and asked him where he had been.

I guessed the Maldives.

"I walked part of the Way of St. James – the historic pilgrimage route" he told me. Gosh! I would certainly never have thought him capable of doing something like that. During the following hour I listened intently to his coverage.

"One day I'm going to walk the St. James Way, too", I announced to my business partner when we said goodbye, although even while I was saying it, it sounded like a lie. Ever since I had lived in Spain – at that time for already twenty years – I had dreamt of it. Over the years I had sworn to myself again and again that one day I would walk the trail myself. After all, it was one of the unfulfilled dreams on my to-do list. I had been inspired by Paolo Coelho's novel *The Pilgrimage*. It had impressed me greatly that pilgrims had been wandering that path for hundreds of years. But I still hadn't walked along the *Camino Francés* (the French Way – the most popular of the

St. James Ways, leading from St. Jean-Pied-de-Port in the French Pyrenees to the stunning cathedral of Santiago de Compostela in Galicia where Saint James is believed to be buried). Of course not. Well, how could I have? I didn't have enough time! After all, this was not a Sunday excursion but a forced march of at least thirty daily stages, not including rest as well as arrival and departure days. I hadn't even considered taking the time. And thus it had remained a dream.

However, I couldn't get the conversation with my business partner out of my head for the rest of that day as well as the next morning. I asked myself: What kind of an idiot are you actually? Why don't you just take off and start walking? But my inner demon interfered: "Are you crazy? You've just been on holiday in Austria for a full month, you have to work, keep your small real estate company from going bust, finally write your fourth crime novel, you've been invited to attend two weddings in October and there are important business appointments pending. Also you've got hardly any money left. So just forget it and carry on dreaming."

However, this time round I did not let my demon give me a dressing down and countered: "I could still work on my fourth novel afterwards – and it would become an even better one because I could integrate the new experiences gained on the walk. And although I don't have much money, accommodation would only be five or ten euros per night and for just one month I would still be able to finance it. And as far as the pending 'important appointments' are concerned, my dear demon, what could indeed be more important than the fulfilment of a long-standing dream?"

So the discussion in my head continued for quite a while and finally the sceptical demon gave up. And so the decision was made. I was going to walk the St. James Way. Not next year, not next month but *at once*! That very same day I purchased the necessary items in an outdoor shop, the day after I postponed my appointments and re-organized an entire month, and the very next morning I drove a thousand kilometres from my home in the south of Spain to the French starting point of the Way of St. James.

While I was preoccupied with the hasty planning phase there was luckily hardly any time to think about my current state of fitness. Although I more or less regularly visited a gym, lifting tons of iron there, I tended to avoid anything to do with endurance, such as climbing stairs to the third floor! After twenty minutes of tread-mill exercise the mean device would throw me off like a rodeo rider; after half an hour of spinning, my hyperventilating and panting drowned the music blaring out from loudspeakers on the walls and after an hour's hiking ... to be quite honest I had no recent experi-ence at all to determine how my 18-stone body would react to one hour of hiking as I hadn't done it for ages.

During that first sleepless night in a bunk bed of a pilgrims' hostel in the rather sleepy French border village of Saint-Jean-Pied-de-Port, I began to wonder about the physical aspects of my project. The spiteful part of my ego gave me lectures that I would never ever achieve it. My alter ego, however, argued to the contrary that I would very well succeed given the necessary willpower. Particularly since 'learning by doing' happened to be one of my fundamental principles. I also slowly but surely tried to grow into my new role as a pilgrim, and after a few hundred kilometres I would turn out to be sufficiently fit – I thought.

Unfortunately the topography thwarted my plans due to the fact that the first stage of the St. James Way happened to be the most ambitious. Right from the hostel's front door the route led straight into the Pyrenees, only known to me from Tour de France TV broadcasts I had watched from the comfort of my couch. At the outset I was already confronted with the crowning stage – and that even undoped. A fact which during that first night – in combination with the snores of half a dozen fellow pilgrims – disturbed me and helped keep me awake.

Chapter Three

Saint-Jean-Pied-de-Port – Roncesvalles

E ven before dawn I donned my far-too-heavy backpack – and set it down straight away. I repeated this procedure four times because first of all I had to dig out my hiking jacket, secondly reposition the water bottle, thirdly, in order to capture the historical moment, I had to pull my mobile phone out of a side pocket and the fourth time was for controlling whether all pockets and pouches were tightly closed so that no items could fall out during my upcoming march over the Pyrenees. This activity made me run out of breath and brought me into such a sweat that I had to unbuckle my backpack for a fifth time to stuff my windbreaker back inside.

During my first breather I experienced my first apparition on the St. James Way. Unfortunately it was not the Virgin Mary whispering into my ear that I would not have to walk eight hundred kilometres for her to forgive all my sins and that one Lord's Prayer would do sufficiently. No, it was a Belgian woman with curves comparable to a mountain road in the Pyrenees, who wanted to know whether there was a fruit shop open nearby. I doubted it and offered her some fruit from my backpack megastore. I had kiwis, bananas, apples, pears, sandwiches and cereal bars with me. And two litres of electrolyte drinks. With abundant provision I was trying to make up for my lack of fitness. The only problem that arose here was that I hadn't taken on a sherpa to carry my backpack and had subsequently to carry the additional weight myself.

The Belgian woman smiled at me in a way that made the sun seem to rise one hour before time but refused my offer with thanks and departed into the opposite direction to look for a fruit seller. I found it a pity for I would have liked to have walked alongside her for a while – of course only to distract myself with small talk from the virtually insoluble task of having to drag myself along on foot for almost eight hundred kilometres to Santiago de Compostela, carrying this 'intervertebral-disc-massacring' backpack.

After taking one last deep breath I finally set off. As of now my task was to be a pilgrim for at least one month. While my hiking sticks clattered over the cobblestoned alleyways of Saint-Jean-Pied-de-Port I reminded myself of what being a pilgrim meant to me. I didn't look at the Camino Francés as being an athletic challenge as, for example, a marathon, in which one has only to cross the finishing line within a couple of hours, but as a rather spiritual steeplechase.

My intention was to benefit from the long hiking hours by using them to deal with new thoughts for which I had had no time during my everyday life. Thereby I was hoping to gain new insights which could point the way towards fundamental changes in my life – for these changes were damn necessary. That was the actual reason for my decision to walk the Way.

In order to not deprive myself of the opportunity right from the start, I had to walk the route with full awareness. No music from earphones or other distractions. Furthermore I intended for the most part to hike alone. Trivial small talk with other pilgrims would only needlessly interfere with my flow of thoughts, I told myself. The very next moment the Belgian woman with her angelic face sprang to mind, who obviously the Apostle James had rubbed right under my pilgrim's nose as a kind of welcome gift. Of course I would have made an exception to the rule for her as, after all, there would be enough time for reflecting and pondering during the coming month.

Furthermore another detail had to be considered. Just a couple of weeks ago, on my forty-fifth birthday, I had held a book presentation in Salzburg in front of numerous guests, friends as well as family members. At the end of the reading from my latest crime novel, *Im Schatten der Alhambra*, I had addressed some emotional words in Russian to my partner, with whom I had shared the past five years. After that speech I had placed a ring on Tatiana's finger. We had both had to cry. Since then we had been happily engaged.

I thought of her (and not of the Belgian woman) when I reached the Porte d'Espagne, an archway which marked the unofficial starting point of the French Way of St. James. I hadn't seen Tatiana in three weeks as she had gone to Russia to visit her parents. I missed her dearly. But this was the wrong point in time for sentimentalities. Now it was essential to become fully aware of the moment, to do some soul-searching, to be at one with oneself and to watch carefully for signs. After all, I had resolved to do just that. Hence, after taking a photo with my mobile phone I strode piously through the Porte d'Espagne.

After the first ten metres on the trail, I paused to reflect and listened to my inner self. What was I feeling right now? And lo and behold – my first insight on the Camino didn't let me wait for long: I had to urgently relieve myself.

Right after that I eventually found my rhythm. By daylight the grim wall, as the Pyrenees had appeared before sunrise, had lost its terror. Gently inclining dirt tracks led through lush meadows and autumnal woodlands into the mountains. After a few kilometres I was able to enjoy a fantastic view back down into the valley where the last wafts of mist were dispersing. Herds of sheep lined the path.

But sheep were in the minority. Besides myself dozens of other people had the same idea to hike along the St. James Way on this sunny autumn day. They came from France, Spain, Korea, Sweden, Germany, Brazil, Hungary and other countries. Whenever one overtook another or walked past another pilgrim there was a mutual "*buen camino!*" or "have a good hike!".

I felt like part of a community. I was fine, I felt free, light hearted, enthusiastic – and I had an objective in mind. I enjoyed this rare feeling of happiness being quite aware, however, that it might just be a nice illusion which would only last for a short while. I must keep a firm grip on this feeling, I thought to myself. The question of how to do so was worth contemplating for the rest of the day. And when a group of chitchatting Americans passed me, I let myself fall back behind their frequency range in order to be able to get lost in my thoughts in peace.

I wondered what had triggered off these positive emotions in me. I had just been panting up a mountain slope and my clothes were as wet as if it had been raining the whole day long. Did I need this from now on to get such feelings of immense pleasure? Would I henceforth have to climb a mountain a day? I hoped not as my back was aching, my knees hurt and my new hiking boots pinched although I hadn't even yet made it through half the first day's stage – of an estimated total of thirty, mind you.

This could hardly be the solution, but as I didn't feel quite as well now as before because of these worries, I answered the question myself: earlier I had felt so good because I *hadn't* been thinking about what part of my body had started aching, even though I had only walked the first seven out of eight hundred kilometres. Thereby I hadn't even covered one percent of the St. James Way and had already reached my physical limits.

Nevertheless, I had taken delight in the amazing autumnal landscape, had realized that I could keep up with considerably younger pilgrims and had forgotten my problems for a while. Basically my backpack weighed eight stones, but only just over two stones were luggage items - the rest of the weight seemed to be the feeling of my worries, which I carried with me all the time, no matter where I went.

During a break I realized that it had done me good for a while *not* to keep brooding over why my three crime novels had been selling so poorly that I couldn't even start to make ends meet with the royalties. I hadn't thought about my real estate company either, which had only been making a loss for some time, nor that I wouldn't be in a position to keep up the mortgage payments on my house as of next month. For a moment I had also forgotten that quite recently my application for an increased overdraft limit had been rejected by my bank, and that my savings had become so depleted that it was difficult to foresee if I would be at all able to pay for meals and lodgings by the time I reached Santiago de Compostela. And the question that now preoccupied me was whether the Camino would really offer me the fulfillment of a long-cherished dream – or, rather, would amount to an escape route from all these sad truths.

Now that all these negative thoughts were buzzing around in my head my mental well-being was over and done with. No longer was I in the 'here and now', but clinging to the past and reflecting on how I had manoeuvred myself into this situation and what I could possibly have done differently. Yet just a short while ago I had felt better than I had done in a long time.

I ate a banana, ended my break and let the past be the past. Instead I thought of the future. What would come after completing the Camino? What would be the best way out of my misery?

What alternatives were there for me to avert the catastrophe at the last minute? What could I do to improve my situation? Was it absolutely necessary for me to wait for the future?

The track now rose steeply through a magical-looking forest. Colourful foliage rustled beneath my hiking boots. But I wasn't paying much attention to my surroundings. I felt melancholy and wanted to return to the blissful state of mind I had had before. At least for the remainder of this stage of the journey. Or even better: for the rest of the St. James Way! And all of a sudden I got my first true insight on the Camino.

I unbuckled my backpack and sat down on a tree stump. With my hiking stick I drew circles into the forest soil. A passing pilgrim asked me in English whether everything was in order. "Yes, now it is!", I replied.

I had made a decision. For the remainder of the St. James Way – no matter how far I got – I would not let my thoughts influence me. I decided that the past should best be left in the past and I wasn't going to waste any more thoughts on the future. The only reality was that of *today*. The *here* and *now*. As of now I would just concentrate on overcoming each stage of the route as it came rather than contemplating all the further stretches in advance. And if I shut out all other thoughts and only took delight in my surroundings, I would regain the sublime feeling from the start of today's stage and, hopefully, be able to hold on to it.

I opened my backpack and pulled out a pair of socks. The left sock symbolically was to typify the past and the right one the future. After I had filled both of them with leaves, I loudly told my left sock that there was nothing I could change about it anyway and let the right sock know that I was no longer interested in it because I had no idea what it could have in store for me. Then I assured both socks that for the rest of the the Camino I would not think about them any more and tossed them away in a high arc. As I did so I yelled aloud "Yesss!" and stretched both arms into the air.

A German woman pilgrim who had obviously followed my ceremony enquired whether I was all right or not. I smiled and nodded. This didn't seem to convince her and all of a sudden she seemed to become aware of having encountered a lunatic whilst all alone in a patch of woodland. In any case she wished me *"buen camino"* and hastily went on her way. As of now I'm sure of having a good pilgrimage, I thought to myself.

For the rest of the first stage of the route my body was busy dragging itself over a never-ending Pyrenean mountain, while my mind tried to put my ambitious aim into practice: to relish the moment, shutting out the rest. I managed both better than I had expected. Early that afternoon I had stood on the peak of that mountain and felt like Reinhold Messner on an 'Ecstasy' trip.

According to my smart St. James Way guidebook there were two alternatives for the descent. The recommended route led down into the valley on a paved road, with a second, a bit more demanding track, leading straight to the hostel and running down a steep and rather stony path. The latter option, however, was not advisable the guidebook argued, as after hours of trekking uphill one would have tired feet and probably be suffering from poor concentration. Therefore there was quite a risk of tripping and falling on the way down.

Such nonsense. I should have bought a different travel guide, I thought. After all I was a born Austrian, even though I hadn't been living there for ages. What they called 'mountains' here would best be accepted as 'gently undulating hillocks' in my old native country. As a small lad I had climbed mountains with my father that had been three times as high compared to this

Pyrenean pipsqueak.

Together with my newly acquired self-confidence, a rather unfortunate amount of cockiness arose in me. Of course I would choose the "dangerous" woodland track and since it could not be much further I set off towards the hostel, spurred on with thoughts of the chilled beer that would most probably be waiting for me as a kind of reward. It didn't take even ten minutes before I had to change my mind about my smart booklet. I stepped with my right foot into a damp wheel rut, slipped and sprawled onto my hip and shoulder. I could hardly curse for pain. As I was obviously the only one to have chosen this route alternative there was no help in sight. I lay motionless and feared for the worst. Then I unbuckled my backpack, tried to get up – which required a number of attempts – and ventured a self-diagnosis. My hip ached and my right foot was trembling, but that was probably for reasons of shock. The shoulder, which had anyway been suffering from the backpack strap, throbbed as if my heart had just slid there. But I could still rotate my arm, even though it hurt. Limping, I carefully continued my descent.

Around four o'clock in the afternoon I arrived at Roncesvalles. In a bar I came across hard-drinking Irishmen and Canadians with whom I celebrated my first stage victory. Afterwards I attended a pilgrim's service in the chapel of the monastery guest house. Later on this was followed by a free-of-charge concert: the 'orchestra' was playing in the dormitory – where a hundred people slept – and entertained the occupants with a 'symphony' of at least fifty snorers from all over the world. The conductor was obviously located in the lower part of my bunk bed. He and his ensemble snored as if it was intended to scare off evil spirits. I shoved my ear plugs so deeply into my ears that I had great difficulty the next morning to pull them out again.

Chapter Four

Roncesvalles - Larrasoaña

The second leg of the Way stretched for twenty-six kilometres to Larrasoaña – through woodland and meadows, through hamlets consisting of only a handful of stone houses, over centuries-old Roman bridges and through sunny alluvial plains. As this route happened to be slightly shorter than that of the previous day and the topography seemed rather reminiscent of the Netherlands, I didn't need to worry about not surviving this day.

The first stage according to my guidebook had been the most difficult of the entire St. James Way. And I had mastered it. Even better than some of the other fellow-pilgrims who had reached the lodging very late. This strengthened my newfound sense of confidence. In only one day quite a bit had changed in me mentally. I quarrelled less and less with my past and didn't care two hoots about the future. My mental barrier was about to disappear into thin air. I was able to think freely and take pleasure in small things along the wayside, e.g. a praying mantis, a particularly old tree in autumnal splendour, a beautiful cloud formation, pleasant conversations during a break and even a signpost into which "Santiago de Compostela 765 km" had been engraved, made me smile. I was pleased about the thirty-five completed kilometres and did not think about what lay ahead of me.

As I walked through a forest my thoughts circled around the term 'self-confidence'. The previous day in the Pyrenees had taught me something important: no matter what I should encounter, either today or in the forthcoming days and weeks, I would overcome it. If you can master the most difficult leg, I thought, you should be able to manage the whole stretch.

I began to ask myself why I hadn't always drawn such intriguingly simple conclusions. Even though I had never been to the Pyrenees before I had already overcome some obstacles in my life in the form of hard strokes of fate, seemingly hopeless situations and financial difficulties. In my early twenties I had turned my back on Austria and chosen a life at the limit – without any substantial collateral.

For a year I had travelled the South American continent, sleeping in hammocks and together with a pal and without the necessary knowledge and experience had sailed across the Atlantic and later in the Caribbean for a couple of years. Using a machete I had battled my way through the Colombian jungle, swum with piranhas in a cholera-polluted arm of the Amazon, survived a train accident in Ecuador, a crash-landing with my paraglider, a severe car accident in Austria and a motorcycle mishap in Serbia. In the Straits of Gibraltar I had almost slammed our sailing boat into a super tanker and in the middle of the Atlantic Ocean was nearly slain by a gyrating boom. Every five years I had set up a company, sold it again or had gone bankrupt, only to try once more in a different line of business. I had to cope with the death of my beloved mother but, on the bright side, fate had given me a wonderful daughter. I had married and got divorced. There was hardly anything I had left out. Life went up and down. Riding high or back down into the depths of despair. Permanently.

Even though my life had changed directions every couple of years, over the past two decades one thing had never altered: no matter in what mess I had found myself, somehow I had managed to get out of it again. And right now, in the magical atmosphere of this forest that the Way of St. James was now taking me, I wondered why on earth all this should suddenly change. Why shouldn't I continue to trust in this strength – no matter whether it be called a guardian angel, God or something entirely different?

I noticed a stream flowing along just off the track. I sat down next to it and threw pebbles into the water.

"You're an idiot!", I scolded myself aloud.

"There's something that has been protecting you for most of the time and instead of accepting this free life insurance gratefully you are in fact questioning it and worrying about whether it will also function the next time."

I fished my notepad out of my backpack and noted the second important realization I had made on the St. James' Way: *If after a nine-hour hike over a mountain you have gained enough self- confidence to master the rest of the Camino, you should also draw sufficient self-assurance from your personal history for your further life.*

Pleased with this perception I continued walking. Along the way I came across a Swede with a big bushy beard and nickel spectacles. As we continued our pilgrimage together along the remaining stretch to the hostel, Mats told me that back home he regularly undertook hiking longer distances. He also used to cover the ten kilometres to work on foot.

"Well, in that case you are optimally prepared", I said patting him on his back, at the same time thinking of my own training which had consisted of walking to the baker's twice in order to break in the hiking boots.

"There's nothing that could prepare you for this walk", Mats responded meaningfully. "I only hope that I'll make it to Santiago this year", he went on. "On my first attempt last year I had to give up after a hundred and seventy kilometres."

I beg your pardon? I sized up the guy. He was roughly fifteen years younger and at least three stones lighter in weight than myself - backpack included.

"Huhh! ... Why that?" I dug deeper.

"Last year I started off a little too fast and optimistically. En route I contracted an inflammation of the ankle which worsened so much that at some stage nothing worked any more."

Oh dear! My newly-discovered self-confidence suddenly became more scuffed than the soles of my hiking boots. Until now I had only thought of three factors that could prevent me from the successful outcome of my pilgrimage: my fitness, my willpower and my rather frugal money reserves. After this enlightening conversation, worries about joint complaints, slipped discs, hip damage and other physical wear and tear of all kinds were added as the fourth horror scenario.

Chapter Five

Larrasoaña - Pamplona

After completing the two longer stages of my walk, I decided to heed Mats' advice and walk the mere fifteen kilometres to Pamplona as 'joint-friendly' as possible. I tried once again not only to keep my feet on the trot but also my head. In keeping with my current trains of thought, I resolved to address the term 'problem' as the third leg of my spiritual pilgrimage. That morning I had been confronted namely with a major problem. After my arrival the previous evening I had hand-washed my laundry and hung it out to dry on a clothesline in the sunny garden of my hostel.

Afterwards, together with Mats, the two heavy-drinking Irishmen and some other pilgrims, I had visited the only bar in Larrasoaña. A pilgrim's menu usually cost ten euros. There was a starter comprising of either salad, pasta or soup with bread, followed by a main dish of meat or fish and finally a dessert, accompanied by as much 'pilgrim's diesel' – as I had accustomed myself to referring to wine whilst on the Way – as one could drink! The red wine carafes were refilled many a time and the round became correspondingly cheerful. I made many new acquaintances and just about got back into my bunk bed before the hostel's gates were locked at 10 p.m. And of course I had forgotten to take my – by now dry – laundry off the clothesline.

In the morning every piece was clammy from dew, especially the socks. And even as a 'hiking dyslexic' I knew that damp socks resulted in blisters. And blisters on both feet could, in the worst case, jeopardize my entire project. Until a short time ago – when the day-to-day problems had bombarded me like a meteorite shower – I would never have thought that wet socks could become my most elementary concern. I finally solved the problem by attaching them to the top of my backpack and walking in flip-flops until the socks had dried.

As the magnificent autumnal landscape slid by, I thought about this new angle to my personal problems. When the socks had dried and I could put on my hiking boots I was carefree. But why, actually? Well, I had dealt with my current problem but had a lot more to worry about that was far more serious and more complicated to resolve.

Were there actually two dimensions of problems or rather two dimensions of worries resulting from them? The most recent one, which had to be dealt with *right away*, and another, a more abstract or even illusory kind – one that could not be solved here and now because it lay in the future and might possibly have resolved itself when the time came.

This had indeed happened to me in the past. Then I had worried about matters that had never actually occurred, had needlessly burdened myself with wild notions and had suffered from them at the decisive moment, namely the present. On the other hand, my current problems were not at all just in the imagination. They were quite real. By the time I returned home chaos would be waiting and I didn't have the faintest idea how to cope with the unfortunate situation.

In the distance I could vaguely make out Pamplona. Soon I would be reaching the city's outskirts. My thoughts would be distracted by street noise, shop windows and crowds of people. But before that I wanted to follow my train of thought through to the end. So I sat down just off the path in a woodland clearing. What kind of "current problems" did I actually have – at *this* very moment? My socks had dried. It was not even noon, and a hike of approximately one hour lay ahead of me. This morning I had booked a bed by telephone in the *Paderborn* hostel managed by Germans and therefore had no worries about my night's lodging. I carried provisions and water with me, I was neither too cold nor too warm, nothing hurt, the weather was marvellous, nobody threatened me, there were no dangerous animals in this forest and natural catastrophes didn't seem imminent either.

Should I perhaps only adjust my temporal focus? However intensely I pondered on the matter, not even the smallest problem sprang to mind which I actually had to face this very moment.

I found it worth noting this insight. I pulled out my notepad and wrote: *Problems fade away into illusory constructions if one only focusses on the present, on the here and now. However, if one concentrates on a problem that has to be solved at a later stage, one needlessly burdens oneself with worries in the only real time, namely the actual moment.*

Chapter Six

Pamplona - Puente de la Reina

I reached Pamplona early that afternoon. After three days of solitude I was looking forward to the hustle and bustle. Ernest Hemingway had spent quite some time in this city, especially in the Café Iruna on the main square, to which I now headed. His spirit could be felt so strongly here, as if he had only just left for a moment or two. In this place, where a Nobel laureate had found inspiration for his literary work, I had a few drinks in honour of the author I so much admired and for the first time during my journey I made an entry in my diary.

After that I wandered through Pamplona just off the St. James Way. After three days of spartan life the city with its numerous bars and restaurants came just at the right time. At last I could once again enjoy fine tapas, good wine in the party atmosphere of the local fiesta – the famous

'San Fermin Festival' – which was just in full swing.

But once again there was a bit too much hustle and bustle for me here. Even though the culinary offerings of the countless bars were utterly tempting, they were unfortunately unaffordable for a frugal pilgrim. Thus I had to make do with just one tortilla and invested the balance of my daily budget in additional drinks before I returned to my hostel.

The cost of eight euros fifty cents for one night at the Paderborn hostel including breakfast comprising German black bread was quite fair. I only had to share the room with a pleasant Canadian couple. At first they were nice to me. But the following morning they didn't even cast me a second glance. The evening before we had begun chatting before going to bed and they had told me that they hadn't had a wink of sleep the previous night as somebody in the hostel's dormitory had been snoring so loudly.

This information really set me under pressure. After all, I didn't want to be the cause of yet another sleepless night for the two of them. Unfortunately I was aware that I sometimes did not exactly glide soundlessly through the night. Moreover, the volume could indeed be doubled with every tenth of a millilitre of alcohol and in order to follow in Ernest Hemingway's footsteps through Pamplona as authentically as possible one had to get really canned. So as I had already guessed that my respiratory tract could mutate into a tractor engine with chronic backfiring, that evening I gave the Canadian couple a tip about the invention of earplugs. Just in case ... The two of them eyed me suspiciously and said that they didn't have any with them. I offered them some of mine but they rejected. Well, I thought, it's your own fault and snuggled up in my sleeping bag without another word.

Not even ten minutes later a loud "Stop snoring!" came from the Canadian woman, almost causing me to fall out of the upper bunk bed with shock. Was I the reason for her complaint? Had I already dozed off? I mumbled "Sorry!" but the situation had become so embarrassing for me that I decided to postpone my own slumber until they had both fallen asleep. Therefore I carried on reading in my e-book until I was certain that the Canadians were sleeping. However, he started snoring so loudly that I thought to myself that perhaps his wife might have been referring to him some moments ago. I replaced my own earplugs and tried to drift off to sleep - which I was unable to do for quite a while.

By the time I finally succeeded, a renewed "Stop snoring!" penetrated my auditory canal and woke me up again. As my earplugs let hardly any noise pass through, the sensitive woman must have yelled out very loudly. Now I had had enough. I took my sleeping bag and looked for somewhere else to sleep. The other dormitories, however, were fully occupied, so I relocated my night's lodging to a couch in the entrance hall of the hostel. During the day it could comfortably seat two people next to one another but for lying down it was far too short. I spent the next two hours trying to compress my body from 188 cm (or almost 6' 2") to 120 cm (or 3' 9") in a variety of positions. In the end I looked like a pregnant caterpillar praying towards Mecca. The idea that I could have dragged the mattress from my bunk bed into the entrance hall had sadly dawned on me only retro-spectively – namely whilst writing these lines.

As I was packing my backpack next morning the Canadian guy came up to me complaining that because of me he hadn't slept a wink the entire night, and his wife eyed me as if I was a child abuser. I had to bite my tongue to keep it in check and forego the tasty breakfast with fresh German black bread in order to hit the road before them. I had left my first bad experience on my pilgrimage behind me and felt miserable.

Overtired and rather bad-tempered I followed the St. James Way scallop shell sign through the city, still dirty and littered from yesterday's Fiesta. When I paused at a signpost on the outskirts not far from the university three young ladies approached me. They introduced themselves as Colombian exchange students whose wish was simply to walk one stage of the Camino, and asked me whether they might possibly join me as they obviously didn't know the way.

Without enlarging upon the looks of the three students in greater detail – each one of them could have been Shakira's cousin – such a situation could have been defined as a rare stroke of luck for any heterosexual. That was probably what the three Colombian girls must have thought themselves; and they appeared all the more astonished by my response. I explained that they did not need a companion – all they had to do was to follow the scallop shell sign or the yellow arrows and there would be no danger of getting lost. The three Latino girls were obviously not used to meeting with such a rebuff from a species from the male world. They goggled at me dumbfounded and wandered off without looking back. One of them was wearing pink coloured high-heeled boots that made me doubt whether she would make it at all to Puente de la Reina. I also wanted to dedicate this day to my insight project, which the company of three chattering female escorts would have definitely hindered.

However, today it would be rather difficult to achieve fresh insights. I had hardly slept at all last night and in my thoughts was still in dispute with the Canadian couple whom I would hopefully never ever encounter again.

Ahead of me lay the wide barren landscape of the Province of Navarra. The path led through harvested fields and farmland on to a hilltop bearing a pilgrim's memorial from where one enjoyed a magnificent view. Ten kilometres short of the day's destination I once more caught up with the Colombians. The girl with the pink boots was hobbling in stockinged feet over the now unpaved path, carrying her new footwear. I offered my help even though I was not quite certain what I could do, but they anyhow refused even to look at me again.

As I had set off soon after sunrise that morning and the leg of the route was only twenty-three kilometres long, I arrived at the hostel by early afternoon. I did my laundry and relaxed a little, thereby feeling a certain dissatisfaction as, after all, the only insight I had attained was that I snored and obviously annoyed other pilgrims. The fact that most of the other male pilgrims also snored and didn't let it bother them was of no particular comfort to me. I suppressed this line of thought and had a long telephone call with my fiancée in Russia. Afterwards I felt considerably better. How lucky I was to have her. How wonderful to be in love with such a woman and to know that I was going to spend the rest of my life with her.

"Hey, nice to see you again!", said Mats, the bearded Swede on his second try at the Camino trail, and shook my hand. He had been allocated the bed next to mine. At least this coming night I would be able to fall asleep with a clear conscience – this guy himself snored like a Viking suffering from bronchitis. He pulled something out of his backpack that looked like winter socks which had been stuffed into a thin protective cover. The object measured roughly ten by twenty centimetres. Mats removed the cover and spread out his sleeping bag onto his bed.

I couldn't believe what I saw. Didn't he freeze to death inside this piece of thin rag? When I showed Mats my sleeping bag he had a fit of laughter and took the trouble to repack his, put it next to mine and took a photograph of the amusing comparison. My sleeping bag was roughly as bulky as two pillows stacked one on top of the other and kept warm up to minus twenty-five degrees Celsius. With it I could have spent a cosy night in the Mount Everest death zone, but in the frequently heated dormitories of the hostels along the St. James Way I was definitely over-equipped. I perspired so profusely that I had only once used the expensively acquired piece of high-tech thermo equipment that the crafty salesman in the sports store had talked me into buying. In most of the lodgings there were blankets available anyway.

I then lifted Mats' backpack for the fun of it and afterwards my own. The Swede did the same and had another laughing fit – his weighed hardly a third of mine.

Now I knew what I had to do. If I was going to make it to Santiago I still had seven hundred kilometres ahead of me. I decided to not burden myself with even a single gram too much. I emptied the contents of my backpack onto the bed and started to sort out my belongings. First of all, I cast aside as surplus ballast everything which I had not used during the first four days and had only carried around with me after having followed recommendations on a "what to pack for the St. James Way" list I had discovered on the Internet. My reasoning told me that I wouldn't miss these items for the remainder of the Camino. Among them were a pullover, one pair of slacks, one pair of shorts, sun lotion, clothes pegs, ointment and cutlery. I even flushed half of my toothpaste down the toilet bowl. Only with my sleeping bag was I a little reluctant. After all I had just bought it for ninety euros. But it kept me far too warm and filled half my backpack. Tonight I wouldn't need it as there were blankets on every bed – as in most of the hostels before. So out it went. I had three pieces each of underwear, socks and t-shirts with me which meant that I only had to do my laundry every third day. I removed one set of them and convinced myself that I could also wear the pieces for two days in a row, meaning that I would only have to wash the fewer items of clothing every fourth day. Finally I threw my spare bottle of water into the waste bin. One litre of drinking water had to suffice. There were more than enough wells along the way – or so I thought at the time!

Satisfied I inspected the ballast that I had been needlessly carrying around with me up to now. I took the lot and put it into the lost & found box, which was provided in every hostel. Maybe my things could be of use to other pilgrims.

When I had packed the rest back into my backpack and buckled it around me I was amazed at the difference in weight. The prospect of only having half the former weight on my back for the remainder of the St. James Way filled me with deep satisfaction. Completely forgotten were the Canadian couple or the fact that I hadn't achieved any exceedingly clever insight during the day's stage of the route.

I stepped outside the hostel where there were a few deserted wooden benches and tables in a field. The sun was just about to set and my gaze wandered off towards the horizon. In the far distance a low mountain range loomed up, apart from which no building disturbed the panorama. I had just realized that new insights did not necessarily have to manifest themselves during the hike. These could just as well become evident in a hostel in the way I had experienced moments before with Mats, who was so amused at the sight of my luggage. It now became all the more important to keep alert and look out for clues. And just now I had received a strong sign.

To go one's own way with less ballast more light-heartedly and happier does not only function on a pilgrimage – like all the other things which I had learned from the hike so far and which could have been applied to my daily life. I recalled one-week vacation trips on which I had dragged a three stone suitcase along with me. And all the bits and pieces of junk which had accumulated in my cellar over the years and which I had thought at some stage that I just had to own.

The insight about lightweight luggage did not only apply to

consumer waste accumulated over time, but also to various seemingly great and important issues like work, relationships, friendships and real estate. Was it really necessary to live in a house providing beds for up to fifteen people, with a garden and a swimming pool? Didn't this house represent my sleeping-bag in everyday life, which I had just given away because it was of no use to me and more of a burden? And what about my profession? My company gave me a great deal of work and still didn't function properly. Why then did I hold on to it? The answer was as plain as sad: because it had always been like that and in my daily routine I had never found the time to think about these matters.

Meanwhile the sun had sunk below the horizon and it was slowly starting to get chilly. Time for dinner. With the firm resolution that immediately after my return home I would make an inventory and clear out the backpack of my life, I mingled with the other pilgrims.

Chapter Seven

Puente de la Reina – Estella

Last night I had slept through for the first time since the start of my pilgrimage. At sunrise I set out for Estella carrying my backpack that by now weighed not a lot more than my daughter's school satchel. Right behind the Roman bridge that had given the village of Puente de la Reina its name I encountered Alison from Belgium. Yet again. She had been the very first person I had run into on the St. James Way at Saint-Jean-Pied-de-Port asking me where fruit could be bought. Ever since then our paths had crossed with such regularity as if the Apostle James himself was endeavouring to pair us off – as a kind of reward for going on the eight-hundred-kilometre-pilgrimage to Santiago de Compostela for his sake. Unfortunately, the good man hadn't considered that I was getting married soon. But for an Apostle he actually had quite a fine taste in women – one had to give him his due.

After all the spiritual insights I had attained on the first days of my walk, I decided to let my brain enjoy a little break and hiked for a few kilometres side-by-side with Alison. But soon enough a crowd of French and Spanish pilgrims, whom Alison had also run into during the first few days, began forming around us. I had had no idea how attentive my peers of the same sex could be. At least towards attractive ladies. They would have probably carried Alison's backpack all the way to Santiago, whereas as far as I was concerned they would hardly have noticed if I had suffered a sudden stroke. Quite amused I watched the courtship display for a while, then stepped up my pace and passed the group surrounding Alison.

The landscape didn't have much variety to offer. I crossed some centuries old bridges, whose purposes had long since become redundant since the rivulets beneath them had all run dry, followed dirt tracks through abandoned farmland and ate grapes from the first vines I encountered. After all, I was getting closer to the province of Rioja. I walked through tiny villages, went into small churches, filled up my water reserves at the local well, had a chat with some elderly residents who sat on benches on the main square and wrote a loving message to my fiancée, Tatiana, before continuing on my hike.

Today I was in a joyful mood. I swaggered along the Camino like a Russian General during a military parade and even whistled for part of the way, first having to learn how to do it again as I hadn't done so since my school days. Instead of just enjoying my high spirits until a lousy thought from the quagmire of my everyday sneaked in and spoiled my private endorphin fiesta, I endeavoured to analyse why I was feeling so good today.

I was en route for the fifth day today and meanwhile quite a bit had happened: my attempt to suppress past and future as best as possible did not work out all the time but was still better than anticipated. My awareness of not having any problems to brood about right now combined with the fact that I was now hiking through the Northern Spanish Pampas quite a few kilos lighter than before, accounted primarily for my temporary high!

But that was not all. A word sprang to mind that was worthwhile thinking about for the remainder of today's stretch – "freedom". The Way of St. James offered the rare opportunity to be free to do virtually whatever one wanted – or not. I actually felt obliged to neither anything nor anyone, could determine the length and speed of my daily stages according to desire and mood, as I did not have to be the fastest, best, most efficient, most productive, most successful or the best dressed pilgrim. As opposed to some other areas of my life there was no competition along the Camino. I was under no pressure whatsoever. And that meant sheer freedom.

Part of that freedom certainly took place in one's head. It was all too easy to burden oneself with artificial pressure if that was one's intention. I could have set a goal for myself such as having to walk the entire St. James Way within three weeks or to be at the hostels before two o'clock in the afternoon every day, as later there might not be a bed available any more as well as queues for using the showers or doing the laundry. During the summer months this situation apparently took on excessive dimensions. Thus some of the pilgrims hit the road at 2.00 in the morning in order to reach their destination for breakfast. I, however, always had faith in somehow being able to find shelter, even if my hiking guidebook wrote about possible bottlenecks. So far the universe had not let me down. I indulged in the liberty of following my own rhythm and not having to comply with the pace set by situations or fellow human beings. That was one of the main reasons for my feeling of elation today.

While taking a break at the side of the trail, I decided to intensify this feeling of liberty. For me freedom and time were closely linked. How often did I catch myself looking at my watch? Most of the time out of simple reflex action. And a few minutes later again. Now it showed just after 12.46. But what did that mean? Should I end my break? Did I have to hurry up or should I feel hungry as time suggested?

I took off my wrist watch, stowed it away into my backpack and decided I wouldn't take it out again until Santiago. As a result I now had no sense of time. How lovely. I stayed at this resting place for quite a while, contemplating – after all I was facing an intellectual challenge.

So far the insights I had gathered could all be integrated into my everyday life. But what about freedom? Did this only function along the St. James Way? Back in the office I would be confronted with the omnipresent competition again – would have to be faster, more productive, more efficient and less expensive than my rivals. I would have to sell and rent out real estate in order to be able to pay my bills. And do so "*rapido*". On top of that thousands of female and male readers were waiting for my fourth crime novel, which I hadn't even started yet.

I would be under permanent pressure once again, look at my watch every other minute and rush from one appointment to another. So how should I sense freedom in every situation in life? The answer to that seemed of such utmost importance to me that I, sunk deeply in thought, didn't notice Alison sitting down next to me. Apparently the pretty Belgian girl had managed to get rid of her companions.

I resolved to postpone my enlightenment in terms of freedom to the next day's leg of the Way and mentally logged into the social environment of my pilgrimage again. Alison and I walked the rest of the stretch to Estella together. I estimated by means of the sun's position that I could have easily managed another ten kilometres from Estella to the next village. But in that way I would have virtually taken flight from some nice people, all of whom had been walking the stages of the route in the same rhythm as myself. Very much in keeping with the Spanish saying: "Nobody is lonelier than the leader." I thus stayed in Estella.

However, this time round I avoided the municipal pilgrim's hostel Alison was heading for, claiming that I was in search of a cash machine, and headed straight for the tourist information office. There I asked for the cheapest single room in town.

A little later I was sitting on a worn-out bed in a small, windowless, filthy room. Even before I had unpacked my backpack the first signs of a depression set in. The room was located right above a restaurant kitchen and correspondingly smelled of fried fish. At twelve euros per night the room was also much more expensive compared with the hostel at a mere five, and a real comedown in terms of star category. But I was afraid to have been allocated a bed next to Alison. Nothing was further from my intentions than to disturb her with my snoring.

But now I felt miserable, lonely and for the first time off the beaten track on the St. James Way – and all because of a Canadian couple in Pamplona whom I should never encounter again.

Once more it became quite apparent that quarrelling with the past could have a powerful influence on the present. It would be advantageous to put an end to some of the 'construction sites' of my past, so that they could not catch up with me in moments of weakness. But I would rather ponder on this on one of the following hiking days, of which I had quite enough before me. Now was not the proper point in time. And the gloomy, stuffy, cramped room was most certainly no adequate breeding ground for new insights. I had to get out of here. After I had so unfortunately extracted myself from the pilgrim community, I decided to cut my losses as quickly as possible. I went out and bought plentiful supplies of pasta and three bottles of wine in a nearby supermarket and entered the local hostel as if I had been a regular guest there. That I wasn't, didn't strike the receptionist at that moment because she was busy checking-in another pilgrim.

The kitchen as well as the common room were packed with cheerful pilgrims. I sighted Alison and a few other familiar faces, opened a bottle of wine for my *amigos* and cooked a pile of pasta for all those who wanted to try it. It turned out to be a pleasant evening in an illustrious circle comprising of Americans, Brazilians, Hungarians, Germans and Swedes. So far I had not run into any fellow countrymen from Austria on my Way of St. James.

The Camino community slowly started to take shape and it felt great to be part of it. However, I was reminded that, strictly speaking, I wasn't really a part of it today by shaggy-bearded Lars when he asked me to which dormitory I had been allocated. As 'the crazy guy from Austria' I had already acquired a certain level of recognition amongst the Camino pilgrims. On the one hand this was due to my constantly well-filled 'bota', a leathery, boot-shaped wine receptacle normally utilized by shepherds or peasants, which made the rounds to the pleasure of everybody at various resting places. On the other, this was also due to my quirky sense of humour as well as my clumsiness.

For example, a Swedish girl had told everyone who was willing to listen, that I would stuff earplugs so far into my ears that the next morning I could pull them out of my nose. Obviously the good woman had believed the nonsense I had told her. A Mexican lady –

fortunately travelling without pepper spray – related that I had paid her an unplanned visit one night, as after a 'pit stop' I had confused the dormitory doors. Drowsy as I was I had approached my bed – as I thought – climbed the ladder to the upper part, shaken my sleeping bag straight and thereby tossed her feet into the air. Both of us were so severely frightened that I almost fell backwards onto the floor. Henceforth she used this episode as a thematic anchor for any pilgrim's small talk.

Furthermore the others encountered me far more often than a standard pilgrim. Before noon I galloped so agilely along the St. James Way that I overtook most of my fellow pilgrims. A little later they all strolled past me as I started to dawdle or, taking a break, lay spread-eagled beside the trail only to resume my hike after a short rest and spurt past the rest of the field of pilgrims from the back once again. This procedure could recur up to five times during a longer stretch. Thus I was no stranger to the pilgrims' scene. Accordingly everyone was staring at me as I had obviously not been allocated a bed in the dormitory.

I felt extremely embarrassed but resolved to stick to the truth and to out myself as a militant snorer who would rather stay overnight alone in a worn-out guest house room than disturb the sleep of his fellow pilgrims. I described my snoring trauma of Pamplona and those around me thought it quite exaggerated that I had decided to separate myself from them for that reason. Someone said that he had slept above me the previous night and had heard nothing of the sort. Another fellow pilgrim had assured me that my snoring was not at all that bad. Alison even said that she liked these kind of noises as they reminded her of her father and gave her a feeling of comfort. If I hadn't been engaged I would have pondered longer on the deeper meaning of her statement.

My new friends on the Camino were right. I resolved not to think so much about such things any more and not to detach myself from the group for a second time. However, there was one advantage in the private accommodation: I did not have to be back there by 10 p.m. sharp. So I treated myself to a Champions League broadcast with the FC Barcelona in a bar and subsequently hung out in others until 3.00 in the morning simply because I was not that eager to return back to my dismal accommodation too early. When I finally arrived back, I typed a long declaration of love to my fiancée on my mobile phone and went to sleep.

Chapter Eight

Estella – Los Arcos

That night in the boarding house was catastrophic. Next morning my back as well as my head were aching. Why on earth had I gone on a pub crawl last night! Outside, for the first time since the start of my pilgrimage, it was raining cats and dogs. Moreover it was cold, and my warmest piece of clothing was a rather thin windbreaker. Fortunately after lengthy consideration I hadn't yet disposed of my rain poncho. The sports' store salesman, with whom I should definitely have to have a serious conversation on my return, had assured me that this one-size poncho would certainly fit me. I slipped it awkwardly over my body and backpack but it only just reached my navel. Whilst putting it on it had also got torn and I didn't waste much time before throwing this bad investment into the waste bin. Another three hundred grams had been 'economized'.

Wet through and freezing I endeavoured to resume my yesterday's thoughts on freedom. As long as I was on the Way of St. James I was as free as a bird, but in my everyday life I felt like a parrot in a cage. I had become a slave to the circumstances of my life, servant of the email and mobile phone, lackey of market economy and devoted minion of the consumer society. But wasn't everyone of my age – the so-called 'rush hour of life'? At least along the Camino I had switched my mobile phone to silent and when on the Way used it just for taking photos. Only news from my fiancée reached me with a characteristic signal sound. Just now I had received such a message. Since I hadn't been in touch with my dearest for three days I was looking forward to reading her news. Surely it was the answer to my last message. But I wanted to read it at a somewhat quieter place and not whilst walking in the pouring rain. Furthermore it would only distract me from my thoughts as, just for a split second, a vague new insight had flashed into mind.

What is the real meaning of freedom? To put in a nutshell it is the possibility of making a choice from various options without constraint and deciding on one devoid of repression. In many countries of this globe, unfortunately such choice was not possible. As a blogger one was not allowed to criticize the regime, got locked up or even whipped. In many countries a woman was not allowed to drive a car or marry anyone of a different religion. And in a dictatorship there was hardly any choice at all.

I, on the other hand, had the privilege to live in the south of Spain. Why then did I still not feel as free as I would have liked to? Why did I have to hike eight hundred kilometres to achieve the feeling of sheer liberty? The answer was exactly as simple as embarrassing: in reality I was free. Only my mind wasn't. It was tightly stuck on a treadmill and reacted to circumstances of life instead of questioning and changing them. It rejected letting go, rejected being free. In order to attain real freedom one only had to bring one's mind under control, disengage oneself from it and show it the way to freedom by following the holy scallop shell. In fact I had all the options available that were necessary to achieve this.

Freedom is not only based on various selection opportunities, but also on change and the ability to consider it as necessary. I could hand over the keys of my much too large house to the mortgage department of my bank and move into a smaller flat. I could give up my real estate company and with immediate effect commit myself solely to my career as an author. From then on I would be free – with hardly any worries. And, best of all, nobody could forbid me this free choice: no dictator, regime or boss – only my reasoning. My mind would then instantly summon up its heavy artillery to counter the choice: Give up your house? Are you insane? Lose all the money that you have already put into the pad! Besides that your retirement provisions would then go down the drain. And how do you imagine giving up your real estate company? All the work you have already invested in the firm would have been in vain, the more so as you cannot live off the royalties from your books. You eternal dreamer!

On this day, my sixth on the Way of St. James, a further insight emerged. For a moment I was afraid it might be paranoia – a disorder, which would have to be treated in ten sessions with a psychiatrist. But after the rain clouds had disappeared and the sun came out this particular thought felt increasingly sensible. It had become clear to me that I wasn't necessarily identical to my mind, which anyhow seemed to be bossy and work against me all the time. I identified my own mind as being a dictator, an enemy in the head, who, from time to time, under the disguise of rationality restricted my freedom, limited my well-being and torpedoed my dreams.

There had to be a revolution. I had to become the Che Guevara of my spirit and to topple the oppressor from his throne.

"*Viva la Revolucion!*", I yelled more euphorically than intended. Regretfully I had not been as alone as I had thought.

"*Viva! Viva! Viva!*", replied three Spaniards in chorus, who – something really unthinkable for a group of Spaniards – had caught up with me from behind without a sound. If I myself had been afraid that my latest insight could be a case for the psychotherapist, the Spaniards must have been absolutely certain in this respect. The guys wanted to know for which country I intended to instigate a revolution. One of the three had served in the Spanish navy for many years and could therefore support me, they wisecracked. Embarrassed I murmured that I had rather meant the revolution that was just taking place in my head, and let the three pass by.

I perched myself on a Camino sign and noted today's insight:

It is your decision to be free, because freedom starts in your head. You can change anything which is restricting freedom. In doing so listen to your inner self and not to your mind. Learn to let go. Free yourself from burdens.

Satisfied, I put my damp notepad back into my backpack. Originally I had intended to read my fiancée's message once I had reached the hostel, but as I had completed only half of the stretch so far, I didn't want to wait any longer. I pulled out my mobile phone and opened the message.

"Hello. Today I'm afraid I don't have good news. My parents are getting older and older and have problems. My mother lost her job and my father is ill all the time. I feel that I should support them and so I'm going to look for work in Russia and won't be returning to Spain. I'll send the engagement ring back to you. I'm very sorry and I wish you all the best! Tatiana."

Chapter Nine

Los Arcos – Logroño

The following morning I could hardly recall how I had made it to the hostel, arriving long after sunset, after having received such devastating news. I had suffered an emotional blackout, couldn't walk even two hundred metres in one go, squatted by the wayside snivelling, infuriated and hurt, undertook various attempts with trembling fingers to type an answer into my smartphone and cast all of them aside. I had to fight to get her back, had to abandon my pilgrimage on the Way of St. James, had to fly to Russia and persuade Tatiana that she could only be happy at my side. All my clever insights of the first days were forgotten and worthless: *Let go. Accept change. Live in the here and now. Indulge in pain.* No way! This woman meant the world to me and was it now all going to be over, just like that?

Her message had hit me as unexpected and unprepared as had years ago my father's call to tell me that my mother had thrown herself in front of a train that morning. At that time I had been driving the car and, blinded by tears, had run into a garbage container and driven the wrong way down a one-way street.

In the hostel in Los Arcos with the rather alluring name of "Casa Austria" I met up again with my fellow pilgrims who were obviously interested in why the same route had taken me seven full hours longer than the rest of our group. I was tempted to mingle with them and get drunk but that would not have turned out well. Thus I had just curled up into my bunk bed and moaned myself to sleep.

Next morning my plan was to walk thirty kilometres to the city of Logroño. Yesterday I had only just about managed a distance ten kilometres shorter, therefore I started to wonder whether I would make it at all. Surely there would be a travel agency in Logroño who could advise me about getting to Moscow as quickly as possible. But... did travel agencies still exist? I hadn't been to one for ages.

I split the day's stage into two mental sections of 15 kilometres each. During the first half of the stretch I wanted to think about how to react to Tatiana's decision and throughout the second half to start getting to grips with the situation.

I asked myself why this message had to reach me just when I was walking the St. James Way, where I was hoping for insights and inspirations of various kinds. Was Tatiana possibly angry with me for tackling the Camino without her? She had hinted at nothing of the kind and, on the contrary, seemed happy for me.

Could there possibly be another reason for her leaving me, apart from her parent's problems? Since our engagement party, not even seven weeks ago, our relationship had been as harmonious as hardly ever before. On top of that, until three days ago, we had sworn our mutual love for each other. Had she fallen head over heels in love with someone else or had she unearthed an old love of her youth in Russia? I couldn't and I didn't want to believe it.

Either way I was stuck in the past once again and thought back to our wonderful years together. But hadn't I stuffed the past into an old sock on the very first day and hurled it symbolically away from me? The past could not be changed, so it was pointless to brood about what I could have done better to avoid her leaving me. *Now* I had to cope with this situation and make a decision.

Fight or accept? Cling or let go? Run after or look into the future? Hope that she would change her mind in a couple of weeks or months, or not? To fight, cling and hope meant suffering for me – and also for Tatiana. After all I didn't have an exclusive right to the freedom of choice. The same rights also applied to Tatiana. Was this a coincidence? Only yesterday I had been thinking about freedom, and shortly afterwards it had entered my life in such a way that I felt quite misunderstood by the gods.

I let these thoughts sink in, concentrated on today's stretch and paid attention to changes on the trail. I passed the border dividing the provinces of Navarra and Rioja. Where, during summer, ears of wheat swayed, now, in autumn, the fields lay empty, freshly ploughed. Coloured leaves fell from the trees. Vines were harvested. All in all it became colder, the days shorter, the nights longer - everything was subject to change.

Why was it such a struggle for a human being? Why was it so hard to cope with change or loss? Because one's ego identified itself with a workplace, a relationship status or the possession of certain consumer products? If one should lose them, one also lost one's identity. One minute Head of Sales or Manageress of the Advertising Department, the next regarded as jobless. Weeks ago family father, now divorced. Only recently a proud Mercedes owner, now driver of a small second-hand car.

Basically it was as if a tree were to define itself through its leaves and mourn their loss in autumn and winter and demand them back. Even though the trunk and roots form the permanent basis of the tree and the leaves are merely its decorative accessories, similar to our circumstances of life.

To compare myself with the trunk of a tree and Tatiana with a green leaf was certainly a little far-fetched and perhaps not quite appropriate. All the same this allegory supported me to immerse myself into more comforting thoughts. From the St. James Way I had hoped for signs and insights that would positively change my life. And now this! At first glance it seemed as if the Camino had given me the wrong sign. But how should I know? How could I assess it *now*? Maybe it was the proper sign even though it didn't serve my purposes. Perhaps Tatiana was not the right woman for me? Maybe it was better that she left me now instead of in a few years' time after we might have founded a family. Until now everything which had happened to me since the start of my journey had turned out to be positive.

Why should I therefore judge this very incident as being negative? Very simply, because it hurt me. But why did it hurt me? The answer was also evident: because my ego had classified it as a disaster, as a stroke of destiny. It wanted to remain committed to the relationship. Conversely that meant: if I were to assess Tatiana's message *now* as something which, in retrospect, would prove to be a good sign at the right time, for whatever reasons, I could not possibly feel hurt.

I began to brood over which reasons these might be. On the one hand I planned to change my life radically after the St. James Way and this upheaval would be easier to put into practice as a single person than with a partner or as a family father. On the other hand it was actually a lucky coincidence that this message had reached me on the Way of St. James. Had Tatiana left me in the midst of everyday life, I would have reacted differently, would have fought and suffered. Perhaps on the Camino, too, I would get out of step for a while, but at some stage I would come to terms with it.

As I passed through a tiny little village I sat down on a bench in front of a church and typed a short message into my mobile phone. I assured Tatiana that I respected her decision and found it great that she wanted to support her parents as they were in need of help. I wrote that she could of course keep the engagement ring and wished her and her family all the best for the future.

Adiós mi amor.

Then I put my phone away, filled my water bottle at the village well and beamed myself back into the present. In a bar at the village exit I met some familiar pilgrims and joined them. I ordered a sandwich and tried to distract myself with small talk, but failed. The group had hardly left to continue on its way, when I delved into my backpack and fished out my mobile. Had Tatiana replied to my message in the meantime? Did she feel sorry now? Or had she even changed her mind and longed to get back into my arms? *Nada.* How many hours was the time difference between Russia and Spain? Two, three or four? Had we already switched to wintertime? Was she still asleep? I realized how I was making myself go crazy about it. No way would this encourage letting go and looking ahead.

It became obvious to me that open communication channels just kept hope alive and obstructed my further spiritual path. I had to burn all bridges behind me. And I did just that by blocking my ex-fiancée on WhatsApp, deleting her from my friends' list on Facebook and cancelling her telephone number. That might – from an ethical point of view – have been rather questionable but was the best chance for me to end our relationship once and for all.

I paid for my sandwich and tried to think positively. At some further stage another woman would step into my life. And right at that moment, there she came around the corner on her pilgrimage. The gods along the Camino seemed to be working very effectively – one had to give them their due credit here. However, considering all the exertion, uncomfortable beds and monotonous pilgrims' meals one might reasonably expect a minimum service level in return.

"Hello", the familiar voice of a dear pilgrim sister greeted me.

"Hi. Nice to see you, Alison", I responded and offered her the chair next to me.

As Alison's hip was aching she had set the village of Viana as her day's target, which was only a few kilometres' hike away. It wasn't even eleven o'clock in the morning and my intention had been to walk on to Logroño. Well, originally. But I had discarded my plans in the past for far more trivial reasons compared to this surely outstandingly effective Belgian antidote for love-sickness. And so we marched on together.

When we came across a pharmacy Alison, who didn't speak Spanish, asked me to enquire about a sports ointment. Even though we went in together, the helpful chemist grabbed her by the hip in a way just short of sexual harassment and recommended tackling the root of the problem. With that he meant her feet, which he immediately began to massage gently. Alison didn't need any ointment but insoles, he said, and led her into the corner of the pharmacy displaying

Dr. Scholl's products.

Meanwhile I scrutinized as inconspicuously as possible the large selection of condoms on the shelves. Although I couldn't imagine how serious Apostle James was about his heavenly appearance in the shape of the sweet Belgian girl, a little preparation on the worldly level wouldn't do any harm. But then it crossed my mind that one should pay attention to the signals one transmitted oneself. If I left the pharmacy with an economy pack of condoms with tutti-frutti tastes, that could well be interpreted by the suffering Alison as the wrong indication.

In addition my daily budget had sufficiently been burdened by the high-tech insoles that the business-minded pharmacist had also talked me into purchasing. Thanks to that I was now skipping along the path like a kangaroo on a trampoline. Nevertheless we made slow progress. I accompanied Alison to her hostel at Viana, but said good-bye to her there and continued on to Logroño, knowing full well that our paths would not cross again. Though I could have adjusted my pace to hers, my heart told me that I had to cope with the separation from my fiancée myself and should not count on the support of a Belgian girl with hip problems.

Two days previously I had made a first acquaintance with Rain-hard. The man from Nuremberg was seventy-two years old and was right now on the Way of St James for the fourth time. This man was incredible. I met him again when I checked into the municipal hostel in Logroño at

5 p.m. That evening we strolled through the city's tapas bars together, enjoyed excellent *pinchos* and a few glasses of white 'pilgrim's diesel' and chatted about the Camino. In spite of the rather dramatic change in my relationship status on Facebook, I discovered a reason to celebrate: today I had completed the first full week of the Way of St. James. By now I had been hiking for one hundred and fifty kilometres with no major physical problems, not even blisters on my feet. Bearing in mind that ten days ago I hadn't even known that I would walk the Camino, things hadn't worked out too badly, I thought, and ordered another two glasses of white wine.

Pilgrim brother 'Bonehard', as I called him henceforth, was a wandering St. James' Way encyclopaedia in the light of his experience. He knew most of the monuments, hostels, forks in the path and had a lot of stories to tell. I could have joined him, could have let myself be pulled along by him as by a locomotive all the way to Santiago whilst leaving my clever booklet in my backpack and entrusting myself entirely to my new private guide. But the most convenient path is not always the best – so much had my life experience taught me in the meantime.

Chapter Ten

Logroño – Ventosa

F or the first kilometres of the next day's stage I hiked with my pilgrim brother Rainhard. At first the route led out of the city through an industrial quarter, thereafter through a local recreation area and along an idyllically-located dam. As we walked Rainhard fed me with the latest pilgrim news: this year a murder had taken place for the first time along the Way of St. James. Being a crime story author I immediately pricked up my ears.

On 5th April a forty-one-year-old American woman had been reported missing without a trace near the city of Astorga. Hundreds of policemen had searched for her and even the FBI had intervened. She wasn't found until mid-September, but then in an unfortunately very different state. Her murderer, a poor local peasant, had diverted her to his dwelling by means of a fake signpost, then killed and buried her. He had revealed himself by trying to change a thousand dollars in the bank in his home village – a transaction which the bank clerks regarded as being highly suspicious. The FBI had managed to assign the bank notes to the American woman through a highly elaborate process and thus the file was closed.

Murder on the Camino. Along a trail which attracted two

hundred thousand peaceful pilgrims each year from all over the world. There was clearly obvious potential. I would only have to equip the protagonist with substantially more brains and promote him to a serial killer. I would transfer my unconventional Andalusian police inspector to a dusty northern Spanish backwater town for disciplinary reasons (which, after the hijacking of a police helicopter at the end of his last case would have happened to him anyway) and subsequently assign him with the search for the phantom of the Camino. And my fourth crime story would be complete. The idea was tempting. Up to now I didn't have the faintest idea about a topic for my new manuscript, which I intended to tackle after the Way of St James.

I let pilgrim brother Rainhard hurry on ahead and continued planning the plot of my new murder mystery. By the time we had reached kilometre ten I already had four corpses in my backpack and three kilometres further on the motive and context. Had I only known that hiking inspired creativity so much, I would have started walking with a dictaphone in my hand when writing my first three detective stories instead of hatching out my ideas at a desk.

When I again surfaced from the depths of planning my thriller, I encountered Gandalf from *Lord of the Rings*. At least that's what the man looked like with his long grey mane and record-breaking beard who, from inside a wooden lean-to, was offering fruit, religious pictures as well as a stamp in the pilgrim's pass in exchange for an "optional" donation. I recalled that this guy was even pictured in my hiking guidebook. And not only there – his picture was also hanging in many hostels and bars along the Camino. In his cowl and with pilgrim's staff, dog and donkey he smiled down benignly from the wall in many dining halls and bars – next to the king's portrait. His name was Marcelino, the permanent pilgrim, a living legend of the Camino.

I definitely wanted to exchange a few words with him and got some astonishing information: he had first walked the St. James Way in 1971 as one of thirteen pilgrims. Since then he had repeated the French Camino two to three times a year. He wasn't sure how often he had actually made it as he had never counted. Marcelino lived for the Camino. And when he wasn't walking he earned his money at the roadside. I was fascinated by this man who seemed to like me as well. At least he answered my questions obligingly while hordes of pilgrims walked by taking no notice of him. For example, the three American women who had already shouted from afar:

"Oh my god, look at him! Doesn't he look weird? Let's take a photo, grab a stamp and keep on going …"

I, however, decided to shorten my day's stage if necessary so that I could continue talking to Marcelino for a while, as even around here one didn't encounter such an interesting conversation partner on every corner. This man must have had walked close to a hundred Caminos. I was sure I would soon gather new stories for garnishing my planned thriller.

But 'Gandalf' preferred to go on about the questionable development of "his" St. James Way into becoming a commercial mass event. Most of the present-day pilgrims just listened to music from their earphones or chatted incessantly about trivial issues. Nobody seemed to want to listen to the Way's 'stillness', he lamented. "Listen to the silence of the Way", he would advise anyone who lent him an ear.

I gladly agreed with him. For some hikers it wouldn't have made any difference spiritually whether they covered the same distance on a sport treadmill in a gym or here. On the other hand everyone was free to experience the St. James Way as they saw fit.

But permanent pilgrim Marcelino didn't want to hear of it. In closing, he told me about an interview he had given an American outdoor magazine. The reporter had asked him the question about what kind of personal characteristics a good pilgrim should have. His answer was that: "he or she should be hard drinking, smoke like a chimney, snore like walrus and be as stubborn as a donkey".

Disillusioned I said good-bye to Marcelino. In the process of becoming an exemplary pilgrim, I was unfortunately lacking one attribute – but just for this I didn't intend to start smoking.

The trail now led me through the sparse expanse of the Rioja region. The terrain became increasingly flatter and the path extended in a straight line towards the horizon. A mentally challenging area. Hardly anything served as a reference point by which one could measure one's progress. I satisfied my hunger with grapes from the vines along the wayside and thought back to my conversation with Marcelino. *Listen to the silence of the Way …*

The monotonous region was quite perfect for doing so. During the first week I had encountered many a pilgrim who was quite hooked on the Camino. Some of them had walked the Way of St. James two or three times already. Others had chosen alternative routes such as the *Via de la Plata*, running from Seville to Santiago de Compostela, the *Camino del Norte* which ran along the coastline or the *Caminho Português* through Portugal. Some of them had 'forewarned' me that one could get addicted to the St. James Way, but there was no danger of this happening to me. I was definitely resistant to sweat-inducing physical activities of any kind. I went to the fitness studio with about as much desire as a visit to the dentist for a root canal treatment. I was determined somehow to make it to Santiago, but thereafter I would nail my hiking boots to the wall for some time to come. At least that was my intention at the outset of the Camino – not knowing then just how mistaken I would be.

I was sure that Rainhard, with whom I had set off that morning, must surely have already reached the hostel. Thus I had enough time during the remaining kilometres to the village of Ventosa to reflect on the insight of this day. I had already sensed that it would have to do with the highlight of today's stage – my chat with Camino celebrity Marcelino. "*Listen to the silence of the Way*" echoed in my head like a mantra.

Of course I knew what this guy had meant. And for precisely this reason I was walking the pilgrimage trail. That was exactly what gave the Way its special appeal: the unlimited time one had for thinking and meditating, being focussed on one's own thoughts and feelings and the signs one received along the Way – both the real as well as the metaphysical. These were the factors which contributed to making the hike a unique spiritual event – as long as one did not consciously look for distraction through iPod, mobile phone, Internet or just small talk, as many pilgrims did. When did one have such time at home to reflect for hours? And that for an entire month.

A further aspect made the Camino unique: the exchange of information with co-pilgrims. In everyday life one usually communicates with an established circle of people consisting of family, friends, work colleagues, acquaintances and relatives. For the most part, the same day-to-day subjects are discussed over and over again and one often fights shy of bringing up any new or even contrary topics. After all one wants to remain being 'normal' in the eyes of one's friends and relatives and not suddenly to be out on a limb and considered as a weirdo. Furthermore in everyday life one usually socialises first and foremost with service providers such as taxi drivers, hairdressers or sales assistants, with whom one at best engages in some small talk. This way it's hardly ever possible to gather any new input from fellow human beings – which is actually a great shame.

Even on the trail the fruitful exchange of information and ideas with interesting people from all over the world is not necessarily automatic. One big advantage of the Camino, however, is that it's easy to get into conversation with other pilgrims. At home I wouldn't dream of joining others at a table without being asked and even start a conversation, or of exchanging at least a few words with almost anybody I ran into on the street. On a pilgrimage, however, this is quite normal.

But in order to receive worthwhile answers one should, however, ask proper questions: "what's your destination target for today?", "how was your lodging yesterday?" and "have you heard about that crazy Swede, who ...?" are all questions that do not really belong in this category. I began to avoid superficial chats of this kind because slowly but surely I became aware of the importance of my undertaking.

It was no longer my ambition 'somehow' to manage the St. James Way and afterwards hang a certificate on the wall. On the contrary, I intended to use the unique opportunity to change my way of living with the help of experiences I had gained on the pilgrimage. I realized that this had become necessary and that there wouldn't be a second chance just around the corner. If not now, then when?

I now determined to take in everything my co-pilgrims had to offer in terms of support and advice. And so I started to bombard them with partly unaccustomed, if not commonplace questions such as "Have you already learned something along the Camino that you might be able to make use of in your day-to day life back home?" or "Why are you walking the pilgrim's trail?", "What are your expectations?" or "Has the Camino already given you a sign or a signal? Possibly one of a spiritual nature?"

I was actually surprised what valuable conversations evolved from these types of question and what a difference it made whether you shouted an indifferent "Hello, how are you?" when passing somebody or posed more profound questions because one was truly interested in the respective person and his or her opinion.

In the distance the church tower of Ventosa rose into the sky. Time had gone by almost too fast. On an open space between the rows of vines I stretched out on the grass just off the track, clasped my hands and closed the eyes. I meditated for a while which worked out surprisingly well as, for the first time, my mind was not permanently drifting off. Afterwards I rummaged in my backpack for my notepad and took down my thoughts.

Satisfied, I ended my break. Due to my encounter with permanent-pilgrim Marcelino, I had gained another insight which I could apply to my everyday life. *Listen to the silence of the Way* – that could probably work in any place at any time.

And why shouldn't I be able to make time in my daily life for reflecting and meditating for at least a couple of minutes on a regular basis. I wanted to be less distracted and devote myself to more essential matters, fill my body, my mind and my soul with positive energy instead of allowing myself to be swamped by a tsunami of useless information from the entertainment industry.

As a next move I decided to challenge all activities and obligations that seemed to steal valuable time from me and had never contributed to my happiness. In future I wanted to chat less about trivial issues in my daily life and instead make sure to communicate more sustainably with my fellow men.

The opportunity to do that arose just now. From the start of my journey I had been keeping up a blog on Facebook, posting nice pictures and reporting on the respective stages of my pilgrimage. Although I certainly didn't have as many fans as Justin Bieber, quite a number of people were following my progress. As of now I would maintain a new quality of communication towards them. I no longer wanted only to report what I experienced on the St. James Way, but to write openly about what I really felt and what insights and lessons I could draw from the Camino.

To expose myself publicly and emotionally on the Internet had never been my thing to date and surely carried certain risks, but now I was very much looking forward to the reactions.

Chapter Eleven

Ventosa – Santo Domingo de la Calzada

Now the longest stretch of the route as yet lay ahead of me: over thirty-three kilometres. Following yesterday's day of dawdling, this time I set off at a brisker pace. To avoid walking for too long in the scorching midday sun, I started before 7 a.m. and after activating my Santiago 'turbo booster' managed to cover half the stretch even before eleven o'clock. During a breather, pilgrim brother Rainhard caught up with me. He had somehow changed his appearance today. Oh yes, he wasn't carrying a backpack.

"You're not getting senile, are you Raini?" I welcomed him.

"Have you forgotten your backpack?"

By now Rainhard had got used to my loose tongue and muttered briefly: "Camino Trans".

Ah, yes. For only five euros one could have his or her backpack transported by courier to the hostel at the end of the day's trek. A most appealing service which was made use of by many pilgrims. Others, on the other hand, took short cuts wherever possible or, even worse, they covered some monotonous sections with little variety of scenery by bus or taxi.

This was not for me. I was quite determined to walk the Way of

St. James in its entire length carrying my luggage myself according to the regulations on the back of my pilgrim's pass. If I swindled myself once, I'd do it again on other uninteresting stretches. In this way my inhibition threshold would steadily drop and I would lose sight of my goal – well, there wouldn't be a goal any more as the initial intention of walking each and every single kilometre of the Camino would no longer be attainable.

Admittedly honesty now took on somewhat disconcerting proportions for me, about which Rainhard could only shake his head. Once the trail led in a wide curve around a field. Straight across the middle of the field ran a path trodden by thousands of pilgrims' feet. Rainhard and, needless to say, all the others shortened the track by around fifty metres in this way and it was only myself who tenaciously stuck to the signposted route.

Or else whenever I had to leave the official route in a village in order to reach a hostel, the following day I didn't take the shortest way back to the Camino but returned to exactly the same spot at which I had left it the day before. In everyday life I was by no means that meticulous and pedantic – a fact my tax advisor could confirm – but now I had set myself the goal to walk each and every metre of the Camino. All the same I couldn't help casting a slightly envious glance at Rainhard's backpack-free back.

I had developed the habit of marching through the first half of the day like a sergeant major and by contrast dawdling in the afternoons, taking breaks, calling my daughter and drinking wine from my leather 'boot'. A bit of alcohol in my blood made it easier for me to wander through the dusty, dreary and endless steppe.

Whilst taking photos I detected an incoming SMS. Apparently my bank had rejected the monthly telephone bill debit. But there should have been enough money in the account to cover the paltry sixty euros telephone costs. A check of my company account, however, showed a remaining balance of a mere fourteen euros and seventy cents. After this stretch of the Way there wouldn't be much wine left in my *bota* in the evening.

The subject of alcohol had in fact gradually started to worry me. I didn't smoke, didn't take drugs and for over two years now had adopted a vegetarian lifestyle – even living vegan for eight months. But on the other hand I drank too much. Originally I had planned to take advantage of the time on the Camino for drastically reducing my alcohol consumption or even waiving it completely – thus complementing the mental cleansing with a liver flush.

Unfortunately up to now I had failed miserably with this undertaking. After the many hot and dusty hours in the prairie, dehydrated like a mummy in a sauna, one rewarded oneself afterwards with a cool beer before dinner. A wine flat rate was included in the price of a pilgrim's menu, something that was exploited to the best of everyone's ability.

Months ago I had come across a self-test on the Internet for determining where one's own hazard level of alcoholism lay. In retrospect I found it alarming that I had taken the five minutes' time at all to answer the dumb questions. The evaluation began as follows: "Your test result implies that at least one of your answers is considered to be 'code red'. Your information given in the test therefore indicates that alcohol already plays a significant role in your life. The strong advice: please endeavour to change your alcohol consumption habits."

An utterly sobering revelation, I thought at the time. However, I still hadn't done much about it as it wasn't as bad as all that. At least in this way I tried to appease my conscience.

An insight like "I shall drink less in future" would have been welcome but not suitable for the Camino. After all a Spanish saying read: "Con pan y vino se hace el Camino", which roughly stood for: "With bread and wine one's pilgrimage is fine". As this motto had worked out superbly for me so far, I had no intention of endangering my project by forgoing wine. Moreover in this endless vastness there had to be more significant findings than the rather mundane insight of drinking less in future. That I could safely postpone until New Year's morning – which I had been doing anyhow for many years.

Today my findings up to now had been regretfully of a very rudimentary nature: my feet and knees were hurting, as did my hip, and my heart was aching with grief in any case. On top of that I was broke and there were still six hundred kilometres to complete until Santiago, as a discouraging signpost had indicated. This caused me to venture into making some forecasts that resulted in a balance sheet as similarly disastrous as the bookkeeping of my real estate company:

a) I had covered approximately 200 kilometres. That sounded like a lot but represented just about one quarter of the entire route. Thus three quarters of the Camino lay ahead of me.

b) As I had taken eight days until reaching this point, there were twenty-four strenuous days to come.

c) An average of eight walking hours per day left a further two hundred arduous hiking hours until Santiago.

If, a few days ago, I had raised the likelihood of conquering the St. James Way in one go from ten to fifty percent – now, given the infinite stretch of steppe before me, I cut that back to twenty percent. I wouldn't be the first to have failed. After all I had heard about a few who had given up, such as an American couple on their honeymoon for whom the Way did not seem romantic enough. Or pilgrims with such serious blisters and infections on their feet that that they could hardly walk at all.

With a quarter of the total route behind me, the initial euphoria ("Hurrah, I'm walking the Saint James Way!") had long since faded and given way to a certain pilgrim's daily routine. The mind became more and more important and my body ran long with it as on autopilot. I wandered through a mental Azores low-pressure area and sensed that I had to rethink in order to ensure a spiritual weather change.

The term 'patience' came to my mind. Though it was recommendable to aim one's sights high and keep focussing on the targets, I should not only concentrate on one final target – Santiago. Otherwise I might run into the danger of becoming desperate due to the incredible distance I still had to cover. In addition such a strong focus could blind me to the nice little achievements of each stage of the route.

For me, as a writer, this was an important finding. As in this respect, too, I had set myself a sheer unattainable objective: my 'literary Santiago' would be the bestseller list of Germany's leading news magazine, *Der Spiegel*. That's where I intended to end up with my books even though the way there would be a long and stony. That target seemed to lie in the infinitely distant future – in spite of being backed by a reputable publishing house and the acclaim of my readers. This fact had stifled my motivation and was the reason why I hadn't written a line in a year. I was on the brink of giving up.

A further analogy to the St. James Way was that in view of my literary career my only ambition was to reach the great final goal as quickly as possible. Maybe I would achieve my own special target with my books – but probably I had only managed a quarter of the track in that direction as well.

This theory provided me with a totally new motivation. I had to think in stages. Today there were still eight kilometres to the end of the stretch. These would be easy to accomplish. But would I be able to get down to writing another crime novel of four hundred pages once back home? I doubted it. But then it crossed my mind that I could certainly imagine writing five pages each on five days a week. And thus the fourth novel would be complete within only four months.

And once again the Camino had taught me something for life: motivation was a matter of great targets and small steps to achieve them and then the enjoyment of each successful step.

I decided to follow my passion and continue writing books – no matter what the outcome might be. I would begin writing again as soon as I got back home. Having made this resolution the storm clouds in my mind disappeared and were replaced by the 'high-pressure area Eduard', which would hopefully stay for a couple of days. This decision called for a celebration this evening. But wasn't alcohol necessary in such case?

A damned vicious circle.

Late that afternoon I reached Santo Domingo de la Calzada. Joined by pilgrim brother Rainhard, I passed through the village that had become famous by a legend.

The story has it that once a couple from Germany had set off on their pilgrimage to Santiago with their son. In Santo Domingo they had stayed overnight in a hostel and the landlord's daughter had fallen in love with the young German boy. But apparently he didn't want to have anything to do with her.

Those must have been good times, I thought. Centuries later things happen just the other way around in my experience.

The girl had taken offence at being rejected by the young lad. She therefore hid a silver beaker in his luggage and subsequently accused him of theft. The young man was convicted and sentenced to death by hanging. When his parents approached the place of execution after it was over they found their son hanging from the gallows but still alive. Saint Dominic – or, in Spanish, Santo Domingo – the patron saint of the town, was supporting the wrongfully convicted lad by the legs. The couple told the judge about the miracle that had proven the innocence of their son, but he was not convinced. As he was about to have lunch he said to the couple that their son was as alive as the two chickens he was just about to eat. Thereupon the two birds flew off! Ever since then a white rooster is kept along with his hens in a cage in the Cathedral of Santo Domingo.

Rainhard said that according to the legend one should stay inside the cathedral until the cock crowed. That would bring luck for the remainder of the Camino. However, if it didn't crow that meant that one mishap after the other would follow. I thus spent a full hour in the church. Of course the stupid bird was on strike – just like Ryan Air pilots at that time. Having inherited my latent superstition from my mother, I didn't put any loose change into the offertory box but rather threw it in the direction of the silent cockerel. It was possible that even roosters were corrupt in Spain. After twenty years' experience with Andalusian local politics it wouldn't have surprised me, but that didn't help either.

Laden with ample bad omens I left the church and, if I hadn't been a vegetarian, out of pure vengeance I would have consumed two roast chickens for supper.

Chapter Twelve

Santo Domingo de la Calzada – Belorado

The mood in the hostel lounge was at its best. Peter from Hungary, who had had a hard time with the dormitory's short beds being over six-and-a-half feet tall, was playing the guitar. There was singing and dancing and laughter all around. Nevertheless I was in bed by ten o'clock and slept through until six in the morning. My Camino record so far.

A Canadian who had gone partying outside the hostel didn't have as much luck with his night's rest. At all costs, one had to be sure to be back in the hostel by 10 p.m. at the latest. Thereafter the doors were locked without mercy. The Canadian who had arrived back at 10.30 had to spend the night in a rather small hut located on the local children's playground.

After a short morning ritual – brushing my teeth, washing my face and vowing to drink less wine in future, I buckled on my backpack and hit the road. Around this time it was still dark and as I – since the invention of the electric light bulb – was probably the first pilgrim not to carry a torch, I had to wait until a better equipped colleague passed by so I could follow him in the beam of his headlamp until day broke. Until now this method had seemed to work outstandingly well. It was only in Roncesvalles where I had come across an American Navy Seal type with close-cropped hair who had marched on as rapidly as if enemy ground troops were pursuing him. I had rushed after him along a gloomy forest path until at a curve I had almost slammed into a tree.

In my estimation three quarters of all pilgrims had initially made a start on the Camino alone. Meanwhile, however, groups had formed: the French walked with the French, the Spaniards with *compañeros* from their own country, Swedes with Swedes, Americans with Canadians, Koreans with their fellow countrymen and also the Germans stayed amongst themselves. Even on the tenth day I had not yet met a single Austrian and thus had no reason to feel pressurized into joining a patriotic party and continued on my own.

I only felt rather committed to pilgrim brother Rainhard but had agreed with him that we would meet up at the hostel in the evening whilst hiking mostly separately during the day. There was still quite a lot to think about which I could only do on my own. On top of that it seemed important to me to follow my own rhythm. If I walked in a group I could only take breaks, detours to churches and bars or choose lodgings and daily targets in accordance with the others.

Today's leg of the trail offered as much diversity as a pilgrim's menu. I passed the border between the Province of Rioja and the autonomous region of Castile-Leon and walked between farmland and harvested fields through the proverbial 'nothing'. Some scrubland along the wayside and a couple of gnarled trees remained the only forms of vegetation. But that was OK with me. Here there was no danger of distraction and I was able to meditate. At any rate that's what I thought.

Unfortunately it didn't work out so well. I at least tried to nurture positive thoughts. But then whenever I passed a bank in one of the villages en route I immediately started thinking about my disastrous account balance. In the same way a pilgrim couple walking in front of me holding hands made my shattered wedding plans spring to mind. Or else I walked past a signpost for Santiago that showed seven kilometres more than the one the previous morning. Well, that would have even thrown the Dalai Lama into despair.

Today it was going to be difficult to get a new insight. Apart from sheep's droppings there were no signs along the way from which one could have gained any spiritual revelations. Yet there was still a diversity of burdens inherited from the past that I intended to ponder on at a more suitable moment in time than in that dreadful room in Estella, where I had segregated myself from the rest of the pilgrims. There and then I had figured out how even mundane past experiences could affect the present.

The complaint of the Canadian couple about my snoring had led me to feel uncomfortable in communal dormitories. I neither wanted nor could afford chic hotels, so I chose lodgings according to the size of their dormitories. The larger the better. I preferred those with thirty beds or more, of which the noise level at night resembled a carpenter's workshop. There I could anonymously carry on sawing logs as part of an orchestra. But how about the other 'construction sites' of my life?

As I walked through the solitude of Castile I realized how much my personality had been shaped by a multitude of individuals from childhood to the present — namely by people considerably more important than a Canadian pilgrim couple. I thought of my parents, teachers, friends and life partners, of superiors, business partners and other companions. In many respects my life had been following St. James Way scallop shells or yellow arrows that others had laid in my path. Was it not high time to break away from these entanglements and to refocus on my true self? If not now on the Camino then when?

However, if I intended to reveal my true inner self I had to ask myself: who was I at all? Some kind of stalagmite that had been shaped by the opinions and advice of fellow creatures dripping down on to it over decades? How could these layers be removed — and above all what would remain? Theoretically my true self, my prototype so-to-say. But what exactly was that?

Dios mío, today I was addressing the really great issues of mankind. In answer to the question of what would be left of me if all external influences were to be removed, one three-letter word spontaneously sprang to mind. However, this theory seemed so bizarre that I had to walk for quite a number of kilometres to allow it to subside.

I decided in the first place to think about how I could release myself from yesterday's entanglements in the same way as the famous magician Houdini. At the beginning of my hike I had chosen the easy way out by symbolically tossing away my old socks. It had worked quite well at first but unfortunately not all the time.

I'd have to go a step further. I wouldn't be able to dispense with the unhappy moments of my previous life by stubbornly clinging to the present, but come to an arrangement with them afterwards. Furthermore I should have to detach myself from judgements about myself that had been implanted in me since my childhood. How often in the past, when I hardly knew how to defend myself rhetorically, had I heard the words: *You won't be able to do that, you're good for nothing* and *you'll never make it.*

However, in some cases those judging me were right. As a matter of fact I am not, for example, particularly talented when it comes to the technical field. In other areas, however, I seem to be all the more successful.

I urgently had to overcome old thinking patterns and forgive some people by whom I felt I had been unjustly treated. Furthermore I now had to reassess negative key moments of years ago positively. Looking back, the 'disaster' had nearly always turned out to be a stroke of luck – or at least as a little nod of destiny in another direction.

In my early twenties, having already been infected with the travel bug, I had applied for a job as a flight attendant with Lauda Air. The airline served Asia, Australia and the Americas. I could have travelled and would have even been paid for it. My dream job at that time. I had been one of a hundred candidates and had to pass an aptitude test in Vienna. On the first day eighty applicants were filtered out. I was not among them. On day two only ten of the remaining twenty candidates were actually offered a job. I thought I had done quite well, but nevertheless I didn't rank among the lucky ones who henceforth would be flying all over the globe and being paid for doing so.

At the time I had been devastated about it. Today, however,

whenever I am served on board by flight attendants with artificial smiles that scarcely conceal their bad mood, I come to think of how lucky I was in those days not to have got the position. What sort of turn would my life have taken if I had been offered that lousily paid job?

Another example had been the Spanish real estate crisis. Until then I had made good money together with my business partner, Thomas, from Hamburg. However, without that crisis I would never have begun writing detective stories – which gives me much more pleasure than selling property. Thomas, who was also my former mentor, numbered among the people who had had a lasting impact on me over the past years. Unfortunately our partnership did not survive the real estate crisis, but afterwards I had enough time for writing and only by opting out of the joint company was I in a position to realize projects such as walking the Way of St. James. In retrospect that, too, had proved to be a great stroke of luck as well as many other things.

With a good feeling that someone was guiding me in the right direction at most of the crossroads of life – even if I had to accept detours every now and then – I entered the hostel Cuatro Cantones at Belorado. Who my 'guide' actually was remained a question I decided to leave until the next day to think about, because pilgrim brother Rainhard was already waiting for me with a beer in his hand. Regrettably I had to put him off for a while as there was still something I had to do.

I searched for a quiet corner, tore some blank sheets out of my diary and for the following hour wrote down all that was burdening me from my past, why it did and how I could come to an arrangement with it. Some issues could very easily be dealt with, others, on the other hand, were deeply ingrained – very deeply, such as the question of my then seven-year-old daughter, which repeatedly caught up with me and saddened me. She had asked me how old she had been when her mother and I had separated. I told her that she had been 5 years old. Thereupon she had said with tears in her eyes: "At least I had five happy years in my life then."

While I was making a note of that phrase on the sheet of paper, tears began rolling down my cheeks again. Of course I wanted to see my daughter happy, but on the other hand it was impossible for me to re-establish the basis for it any more. Although I got along very well with my ex-wife we would never become the happy family again that we had been before. On another very emotionally charged occasion, my daughter had confided to me that exactly that had been her wish to Santa Claus each year when she had still believed in him. Another trauma I had been struggling with until that day. Little girls should wish for dolls for Christmas but not a happy family – then that should be the normal course of events.

But in spite of all that hadn't Paula become a happy and cheerful child? At least she made this impression on me and her surroundings. However, at the same time she also played her roles in the theatre group she belonged to very convincingly. I decided to tackle this problem of coming to terms with my past immediately and dialled her mobile phone number.

"Hola, Daddy," she answered the phone after a while.

"Hola, cariño. How are you?"

"*Bien, gracias. Y tu?*"

"Also well. May I ask you something?"

A short break followed. "Well, it must be important if you're asking me in Spanish."

Caught! Usually I speak to her in German. She understands it almost perfectly but doesn't really like to speak it. But whenever I want to make sure that she gets the message I automatically switch to her mother tongue.

"Hmm … I wanted to ask you how you are …"

"But you just asked me that."

"Well, what I really meant was whether you are … hmm … whether you are happy?"

Another short breather. "Daddy? Are *you* all right?"

"Sure, I am, but I'd like to know whether you are really happy. Because … well, you know, because you asked me quite some time ago how old you were when your mum and I separated …"

"Did I, really? I can't remember."

"Pardon! How come? After all, you were seven years old at the time. I told you that you were five when we split up. In reply you said that if that was the case then you must have had five happy years in your life."

Another pause followed during which I sniffled into my mobile phone. Constantly getting closer to my physical and psychological limits made a sensitive soul like myself even more sentimental.

"But I don't remember saying that at all", she repeated.

Well, I never! "It worried me a lot at the time. And it has kept on bothering me until today. Well, now please tell me, *are* you happy or not?"

"Claro que sí, Papi. Muchísimo!"

"Seriously? And why if I may ask?"

"Well, because I happen to have a fabulous dad and a great mum, even though you are not together any more. Maybe I said something like that years ago, but then I was a little child and probably didn't mean it. So please don't worry any more. And now tell me – how are you progressing on the Camino? How many kilometres have you still got to walk?"

I went on chatting with her for some time – with my daughter who, for her age, was quite grown up – and whilst talking I ticked off this very important point on my to-do-list for coming to terms with my past.

Chapter Thirteen

Belorado – Agés

This morning the insight of the day manifested itself shortly after leaving the hostel. There were two different routes to choose from and – as in real life – I had to make a decision. Which path should I take? The two routes were identical on the map. It was only in my head that there seemed to be two different alternatives. The path on the left appeared to lead in heavy rain, strong winds and cold temperature. Without any waterproof jacket, I would surely get drenched after only a short while and probably also catch a cold or even slip on the wet path and injure myself. Most of the pilgrims followed this track. And so did I – even though I didn't have the slightest inclination to do so.

However, after a couple of hundred metres I decided to reverse my decision and turn back because, luckily, there was another path – the one on the right. Here one could delight in the sight of a rainbow, take deep breaths of clear air, freshened after the heavy downpour, listen to the wind rustling through the leaves of the trees, gaze in wonder at the heavy thunderclouds and actually enjoy fighting the elements to reach one's goal.

While on the track of my first choice, the more arduous way of reaching my destination, I had been subjected to fighting against adversities. On the other path, however, the one on the right, it was the beauty hidden behind these difficulties that was the main focus. I therefore made up my mind to take the path on the right – a choice that resulted in my spending a wonderful day despite rain, wind, cold and wet. I was happy about this insight because not only could it be applied to a short stretch of the St. James Way, but also to many other situations in life.

In future, in order to master an awkward situation or an unpleasant task I would always favour the more pleasant alternative – the path on the right – instead of sullenly lumbering over the one on the left. I just had to be aware of the choice and seek out the more beautiful track in my mind.

A genuine highlight of today's stage of the Way was Julia, a very wise young German woman for her age from Düsseldorf. She was a gardener, was alone on her pilgrimage – like most of the women – and had only two single-use cameras with her, each taking twenty seven pictures, to cover the entire St. James Way. Julia had no Facebook account and also no TV-set at home. It wasn't so long ago that I had also thought of sending my TV into 'exile' in the cellar, but decided to think it over first. In any case the set was as large as half a cinema screen, just a few months old and much too expensive. Talking to Julia, however, I started regretting this investment.

We also conversed about our worst experiences on the Camino to date. Mine had been the 'snoring trauma' in the Pamplona hostel and hers when she almost had to use the pepper spray she carried on her. She had felt stalked by a Canadian. This guy had turned up with uncanny regularity always somewhere near her, had harassed her and followed her through whole towns until she had finally confronted him in a dark alley with her spray can. I felt that at times it was indeed quite advantageous to be a man weighing over 18-stones and almost 6' 2" tall who, for these reasons alone, would be spared from these kinds of situation.

Our paths parted a little later but were to cross again quite a number of times. But luckily these encounters always arose quite obviously by chance so that Julia never had to pull out her pepper spray!

Early that afternoon the clouds cleared away and a fantastic rainbow appeared. I had originally intended to let my mind rest for half a day after my latest groundbreaking insight, but this weather phenomenon literally called out for me to resume my train of thought from yesterday. I had asked myself what would be left of me if I were able to liberate my inner self from all external influences, mental conditioning and expectations. What was my archetype? Who was I actually? And, above all, who was this someone who had continually set me on the right path at crucial junctions in my life?

One theme which inevitably sprang to mind on the St. James Way and necessitated closer examination was my relationship to God. After all, the route was full of impressive churches and cathedrals and I entered each and every one of these buildings as long as they were open and requested no admission fee.

My attitude towards God was comparable to believing in Santa Claus as a young boy or the faith in true love as a teenager: at some stage I had given up hoping that such things existed. Having said that I would have loved to have believed in God. After all, it must be a comforting and reassuring feeling to be protected everywhere and at all times by a higher power – and without the cost of an expensive insurance premium. If I were honest with myself my 'belief' in God was mainly based on the fear *not* to believe in him. During religious education at school or when I, little sinner, had to attend church services on Sundays with my parents in the small, very Catholic village of Plainfeld in Austria, freshly bathed, combed and full of childish awe, one was vividly warned of disbelief. The only way to be spared from purgatory, hell and worse was to believe in the divine saviour and obediently observe the Ten Commandments. Otherwise ... woe betide you!

However, I had hardly outgrown my confirmation suit when all infernal threats by God's faithful 'ground troops' were forgotten. In my youth I did not implicitly interpret the Ten Commandments – in particular "Thou shalt not commit adultery" and "Thou shalt not covet thy neighbour's wife" – in accordance with the clergy. However, inherently it was my intention to be on good terms with God – if he existed at all – rather than bad. To collect a couple of bonus points for a possible afterlife couldn't do any harm as an ascent-into-heaven strategy, I thought. But I had never really dwelled intensively on the subject of God and my last visit to church had been on the occasion of my daughter's christening, twelve years ago. So what about my belief in God? And Jesus? It was high time for a religious inventory. Needless to say the Camino was the ideal place for doing so.

In my debut novel, *Pata Negra*, the protagonist Joana answers the question whether she believes in God as follows:

"No, not at all, especially since I lost my entire family. And, what's more, faith often leads to war and misery. That was the case five hundred years ago when we Spaniards invaded the new world and tortured the Indios until they believed in the same God as we did. Even today mankind fights each other under the guise of faith in God. It's just that today we call it terrorism rather than a crusade. So why believe in something? However," she argued, *"I do think that there is some power which judges good and evil and I also don't doubt that Jesus Christ existed. But I think he was a kind of Che Guevara – a revolutionary who was mystified only centuries later by the Catholic church in order to make big business out of him."*

As Joana is a fictitious character, I, as the author, had put the words into her mouth, of course. The comparison between Jesus Christ and Che Guevara, however, did not originate from me but from my ex-wife, Virginia.

Rationally speaking, I could certainly acquire a taste for such a comparison. Both of them wanted to free their people and failed. Both of them were murdered and, with their long beards, even resembled one another. That Jesus had actually existed I didn't doubt – even though I regarded his miracles as being symbolic. If he had really been able to convert water into wine I would love to know the trick! He probably merely intended to demonstrate how, with enough willpower, something simple and ordinary could be enhanced and refined. Sometimes even I was able to perform such a transformation – namely in the kitchen – when, without any alchemistic prior knowledge or divine ability, I turned avocados into guacamole. And the many people who were able to transform strawberries into jam performed similar miracles every day. Even though nobody would probably be talking about it in two thousand years to come.

But where did God come in? This quite abstract Creator whom no mortal has ever set eyes on? Google's image search shows for the most part an old man with long curly grey hair and a big bushy beard wearing a voluminous gown and stretching out his hands graciously over mankind.

As I was resting beneath the most beautiful rainbow with the most vibrant colours I had ever seen, I realized that I simply didn't want to believe in a grey-haired man in heaven who meticulously audited his 'flock' all over the globe and kept a record of their sins. Was I an atheist after all or did I just feel uncomfortable with the way the Church imparted God's form of appearance? Indeed, it might have been helpful for the bishops over the centuries simply to frighten sinners and collect taxes from them if the name of the top 'boss' was known and, with the help of holy statues, he could be visualised.

But nowadays? What if the biblical forecast came true and Jesus actually returned to Earth? Would he then proclaim his doctrines via Facebook and Twitter and trigger off one shit storm after another?

What did I believe in, if not in a grey-haired figure named God? Good question. To date I hadn't been able to find an answer in any of the impressive Houses of God along the Way of St. James. I didn't feel any closer to God when in monumental cathedrals in towns and villages with only a few thousand inhabitants which had been built in decades of cumbersome labour than I did right at this moment, sitting under a rainbow between fields of barren landscape. This confirmed the theory of my belief – which is admittedly based upon a high level of speculation and merely my personal approach towards dealing with the subject.

Since time immemorial, according to my way of thinking, what we call God is not located in heaven but long since exists on earth. And not somewhere far away or on another continent but very close. *It* is amorphous, *it* is more of a nameless matter. *It* is with me – even in my inner self. It's what is left of a stalagmite after the decades-long effects of continuous dripping from external influences are chiselled away to expose the original form, the archetype, the true inner self.

I imagine God as an inner fulfilling force, a kind of organ which cannot be recognized through X-rays. This organ already has a name and everyone has heard of it. It's the soul. For me, God is identical to my soul. God is my soul. Even the ancient Greeks spoke of an inner God. Their term for it was 'enthusiasm'. Therefore whenever I feel enthusiastic about something – it is in fact God who is speaking to me.

I can even prove the existence of this divine matter in my inner self. After all it granted me the unforeseen power that allowed me to walk the Camino. It also lent me the creative force to convert water into wine when I come to think about my three novels that emerged from blank sheets of paper. And actually I am a kind of creator myself, able to make new life when I think of my adorable daughter.

Wouldn't it be appropriate in the light of all this to re-baptise what we have been calling God since primeval times into Eduard, Brigitte, James, Roberta, Mustafa or whatever names we might all have? Our soul is godly – no matter what nationality or denomination we are and what we call this force within us. Consequently in essence we are all equal.

I realize that this is a somewhat unconventional approach which will cause many a head to shake. But if all of us were to apply the same basic thoughts would there still be grounds for war, terrorism, expulsions and misery on earth? Hardly. Nonetheless, should the Lord actually be seated on a cloud up in heaven he certainly wouldn't have approved of all this. We have to take responsibility for the manifold tragedies on earth ourselves because we are not aware of our divine inner force and – when taking action – follow ancient dogmas with which we were indoctrinated in a way depending on the prevailing culture and which divide rather than unite us.

Chapter Fourteen

Agés - Burgos

W hereas the day before I had felt like the godly pilgrim brother Eduard, this morning everything looked quite different again. The Way of St. James gradually seemed to me more and more like a temperamental sea – one day a wave carried me up to an emotional high and the next it pushed me under water. Today low pressure was clearly prevailing.

Even the theory about water was not so farfetched. It was pelting down with rain and, of course, once again I was the only pilgrim far and wide who set out on the twenty-four-kilometre stretch to Burgos without any rain gear. I tried to implement yesterday's exercise and opt for the prettier track, but today it just didn't work.

After having walked for fourteen kilometres along a busy country road, I had not gained anything positive other than not having been run over by a skidding car on the wet road, although there was still a chance that this could happen.

I passed through a rather dingy suburb and an industrial quarter with car dealers displaying vehicles which I could never afford, furniture stores full of furniture I had no room for, fast food restaurants in which I couldn't eat anything anyway being a vegetarian and a bank whose cash dispenser was unwilling to disgorge any money. With only thirteen euros and seventy cents left in my wallet that was alarming. I tried my luck asking for a smaller amount but the stingy machine wouldn't negotiate with me. *Accounting process terminated. Please contact your bank.*

That had to be a mistake. I gave it a third chance, begging for fifty euros. But it wouldn't even issue that amount. I briefly thought how one could convincingly attempt to rob a bank brandishing trekking poles but, considering my luck in financial aspects, this bank branch would almost certainly have just gone bust. I re-pocketed my bankcard and dragged myself on, which was even more painstaking given my additional burden of worries.

I had calculated that the balance of the company account would by now be zero. But my private account should still hold a few hundred euros, shouldn't it? It had actually been a while since I last checked it. The noise of the trucks thundering by hardly two metres away from me plus the worry that completing the Camino might fail due to lack of money, of all things, destroyed any kind of pilgrimage spirit.

I entered a trucker's bar in order to warm myself up over a cup of tea. A celebrity show droned from the TV, a crowd had gathered around the counter, paper napkins and olive stones ended up on the floor. In a corner I spied a computer with the sticky dirt of thousands of fingertips on its keyboard that made the letters underneath hardly readable. I took off my soaked slouch hat and switched on the PC, which gave the impression that it had been sitting there since the times of the Cold War. Then I did what I had long postponed as I suspected what the outcome would be: I logged into my daily life.

The mystery of my non-functioning bankcard was rapidly solved. The Spanish social security had seized a monthly instalment that had remained unpaid since March, the revenue office had debited taxes which I had calculated would not be collected until the year's end and finally three hundred and forty euros had been withdrawn for the online marketing of my real estate portfolio. The actual account balance: forty-three euros and sixty-eight cents. Well, at least that amount was good enough for another two days on the Camino, I thought. "Don't lose your black humour!" I told myself. On top of that I still had my Austrian credit card with me that should still function to some extent. I had no idea how much money I could withdraw with it, as I had left the access codes for the online banking website at home.

I carried on with my self-mortification. In my mail server there was a potpourri of unpleasant news, final demands and client's queries that I couldn't deal with from here as well as problems I couldn't solve from afar. I logged into the publishing house's website where I could find the accurate daily sales figures of my books, only to learn that my novels had been selling badly for weeks, or not at all. Why write a Camino crime story if nobody is interested anyway, I thought embittered.

I had had enough. Within only two hours my inner peace of mind tediously gained over the last twelve days had completely vanished. When I left the bar, a bus showing the sign "*Burgos Centro*" pulled up at a bus stop around the corner. Three women pilgrims who wanted to spare walking the last ten rainy kilometres through industrial areas and suburbs got on.

Who could blame them? But that was no option for me, I thought, as I crossed the road. I was a genuine pilgrim who didn't take short cuts and who wouldn't take a bus even for one kilometre. Although...

I stopped right in the middle of the road and turned around. My journey was over anyway. From Burgos I would have to return home. I could only continue the St. James Way when I had some more money and less problems. In this rather precarious situation it was impossible for me just to walk on and pretend nothing had happened. What difference would it make to discontinue the journey *at* Burgos or ten kilometres *before*? None whatsoever.

I ran towards the bus and jumped on. A woman pilgrim in front of me fumbled in her purse for money. So that was it – end of the story. What a shameful end to my pilgrimage. To get on a bus in a forlorn industrial area in the pouring rain. I had been making steady progress on the St. James Way, had gone to considerable lengths and had to weather many highs and lows – and my body had fought bravely against all odds and would have done so till the very end.

I handed the bus driver money for the fare into town and sat down in the second row. The doors closed and the bus pulled off. Now it was official. The journey was over. I would walk the remainder of the Camino from Burgos in one or two years' time. After all, quite a number of people whom I had met along the trail had done so.

Nevertheless, it was not the same. My eyes were burning. What would my pilgrim amigos say, whom I had promised to meet at the Burgos hostel - Rainhard, Mats, Julia and all the others? I wouldn't see them again as I wouldn't be sleeping there tonight. After all I was now no longer a pilgrim.

The bus stopped. Some locals got on and a somewhat elderly Spaniard sat next to me and asked whether I was a pilgrim. I felt ashamed of my tears and wiped them away. "*Sí*" I answered. At least up until now, I added in thought.

The bus started again. The man next to me said that although he had always had the intention to walk the Camino he had actually never done it and by now he was too old. I mumbled a rather trivial answer and stared out of the window hoping the old fellow would leave me alone. I didn't want to speak about the Way of St. James any longer. I had failed. All of a sudden the Camino had thrown me from its saddle, unexpectedly, like a rodeo horse would do to its cowboy.

In strong contrast I had been in such cheerful spirits yesterday, had partied in the common room with fellow pilgrims until late in the evening and agreed to take a group selfie photo of all of us in front of the Cathedral in Santiago de Compostela. It would never have entered my mind that I was going to quit the pilgrimage only one day later.

Again my eyes filled with water. The bus stopped. And in a flash I knew what I had to do.

"Let me out! *Rápido, por favor!*" I urged the old guy next to me. I squeezed past him and the passengers who had just boarded. The doors were about to close. I shouted out to the bus driver that I had to get off urgently.

"Didn't you want to go to the town centre?" he asked.

"Change of plans" I explained and jumped out onto the road.

No way should it all end like this! Because of a couple of problems I wasn't going to throw in the towel. Meticulous as I was with the interpretation of the rules, I walked the stretch back in the opposite direction to the point where I had got on the bus in front of the trucker's bar. There I turned on my heels and walked back in the direction from which I had just come.

Now I was officially back on track and hadn't made a shortcut – not even for one metre. After a quarter of an hours' break I had become pilgrim brother Eduard again. As I walked through the bleak suburb for the second time I tried to analyse my pilgrim's blackout. My inner demon – assisted by the cold and the rain, the dreary stretch of the route, the cash dispenser on strike, the distressing virtual excursion into my daily grind as well as the unexpected arrival of a bus – had bundled its total power and dealt me a massive blow to the solar plexus.

Whilst hiking through picturesque landscapes devoid of banks or internet cafés along the route, the idea would never have entered my head to terminate the walk out of the blue – not even with cloudy and rainy skies. Yet again it had been my mind that had tempted me. Although my body ached during longer stages it had endured all physical strain without any complaint. Never would my feet have taken over on their own and led me to the bus stop.

I could rely on all parts of my body and they obeyed my each and every whim – at least the ones which had bones. Unfortunately it seemed to be different when it came to my mind. It had let me enter the bus like a marionette a little while ago – and once again the discussion in my head was in full swing.

My inner demon gave me a good scolding: "Why on earth did you get off the bus? You've been hiking through the Pampas for long enough! Forget about it all and see that you get home and tackle your problems. Alternatively you might as well jump off the church tower in Santiago."

However, during the last few days my true inner self had acquired more self-confidence and thus answered my demon quite cockily: "You might as well forget it, amigo! I shall hike the Camino to its very end, after all it's the journey of my life – though at times not the most comfortable. And as far as your problems are concerned, consider yourself lucky that you only have manageable ones. Obviously you haven't been watching the news for quite a while? And you should know something else: you might be able to solve some of the problems by throwing in the pilgrim's towel now, but new ones will follow. Because they always do – for each and every one of us. So we'll carry on with our pilgrimage and try to learn how to cope better with problems, anxieties and worries. This will help you much more in the long run rather than quitting the Camino in order to get rid of some minor problems in the short-term. *Capito?*"

This didn't really soothe my demon because he kept on trying to make me stop my pilgrimage by providing further arguments, but then I simply disconnected him.

Two hours later I reached the city of Burgos. Sunshine beamed through the clouds and dried my clothes. Once again I stood in front of a cash dispenser. This time I inserted my Austrian credit card into the slot, entered the code and answered the question concerning the desired amount for withdrawal with a confident "three hundred euros". The machine rattled for a while then it spit out my card and subsequently the required amount of cash. I felt as if I had just hit the jackpot! The following ten to twelve days were now safe. By then I would be within the calculated last third of the total Camino and was certain to be able to manage that as well, somehow.

Spurred on with this really good feeling I set off in search of a lodging.

"And afterwards, you damned idiot, comes the deluge or what?", my inner demon interrupted.

"Just shut up!", I counter-attacked in my mind and entered the huge hostel, not even a stone's throw from the cathedral. I paid five euros for the night and in turn received a voucher for bed number three hundred and sixty-eight on the third floor.

The dormitory was subdivided into booths of eight beds each. I shared mine with a French couple, three already tipsy Hungarians, a petite Korean woman as well as a red-haired Norwegian girl. I had met none of them on the Camino so far. The nearer one got to Santiago, the more crowded the route became. Quite certainly a large number of pilgrims had joined at Burgos. Anyhow, all of the one hundred and fifteen beds in this 'pilgrims castle' seemed to be occupied. Also on my exploratory walk through the other dormitories and the lounge I hardly came across any familiar faces.

However, when taking a short walk around the town, after a mere three hundred metres I bumped into pilgrim brother Rainhard. He had already arrived at Burgos four hours ago, the old nerd. Together we visited the impressive cathedral after which I met my amiga Julia from Germany again, as well as Peter and Ludwig from Hungary. Together we went for dinner. As usual we had a lot of fun chatting about a number of different topics – but one I kept to myself: that today I had been on the verge of failure.

After several glasses of wine I imagined for a moment how sad it would have been now to be sitting on the night bus home. Luckily I had managed just in time to get my pilgrim's act together and hit the road again.

Chapter Fifteen

Burgos - Hontanas

The night before we had taken full advantage of the hostel's opening hours and slipped through the doors at exactly 10 p.m. just as they were about to close. Everyone in my dormitory booth was already peacefully asleep. I was also ready to turn in if it hadn't been for my obligatory Facebook status report. There was not a lot to write home about this time as, as far as my Facebook community was concerned, I preferred to leave out my moment of weakness and the short bus ride.

The exchange of news with friends and fans on Facebook had steadily increased over the past few days. In the meantime it occupied a large portion of my leisure time on the Camino. Normally, compiling these reports on a laptop wouldn't have taken me more than half an hour but on my smart phone it could easily take two hours or even longer. Nevertheless I began to appreciate this new way of writing. So far each crime novel had taken me one and a half years, during which time the only feedback had been the meowing of my greedy cat whenever he was hungry. Now this direct dialogue with my readership meant breaking fresh ground for me and was a source of great pleasure.

But the whole thing also put me under enormous strain. Meanwhile, a few hundred if not thousands of users were following the daily travelogue that I complemented with cell-phone photos. However, as the case would be for a daily newspaper journalist, it also meant supplying suitable texts every day, which, as a novelist, I was not at all used to. Overtired and after several glasses of wine this was often rather toilsome at a late hour.

Sometimes I asked myself whether it was a good idea at all to discuss my St. James Way project in public. For then, if no-one had known about it, the moral inhibition threshold to flee the pilgrims' scene on the quiet would have been quite a lot lower. Well, I might have even stayed on the bus if it hadn't been for my Facebook community. After all, the large number of people who were following my daily highs and lows and sharing my hopes and fears, believed in me in spite of it all and would have been disappointed to read that I had suddenly abandoned my pilgrimage. Fortunately I had been spared this Internet disgrace, I thought to myself, as I finally finished my blog entry for the twelfth stage of the route at around one o'clock in the morning and switched off my phone.

Next morning I set off before 7 a.m. The route led me first out of Burgos. The storm clouds over the track had cleared away and so had those in my head. Before me lay a stretch of more than thirty kilometres – and I was in good spirits.

An Australian woman, Melissa, had asked whether she could join me as she was afraid of getting lost in the dark, particularly as the section through the town was not really well signposted. Of course I agreed and slowed down my pace. Melissa told me that she had to cope with her husband's death. She had first learned about the Way of St. James through an article she had read in a women's magazine in her dentist's waiting room. It had intrigued her so much that she had told her grown-up sons about it who, in turn, had kept on urging her to walk the Camino until she had finally set off for Spain.

Together we walked on for an hour or so until we had left the town behind us and the sky had brightened up. As of now it was impossible to lose one's way. The route led right into the middle of Castile-León's barren steppe. Although Mongolia was one of the countries I hadn't travelled to so far, in my imagination this distant country seemed somewhat comparable with the landscape that now spread out endlessly in front of me.

Infrastructure here was kept to a minimum. In a small dusty dump of a town, a delivery van rolled, hooting, along the only road and stopped next to the village well. Women in dressing gowns swarmed out of small brick houses and formed a queue in front of the vehicle, that turned out to be a mobile supermarket. I bought two bananas because my guidebook announced the imminent start of the infamous Meseta, the part of Spain's high central plateau stretching from the town of Rabé de las Calzadas onwards. The Meseta is a vast, sparsely populated, shadeless plateau with a barren landscape and little or no vegetation, particularly at that time of year – autumn – and I was approaching it.

According to my hiking guide, as well as in the opinion of several other pilgrims I had met on the route, this area was feared for its monotonous landscape which posed a psychological challenge for some. Many a pilgrim tended to skip this part of the St. James Way and did not re-join until León.

I looked at it quite differently. Around here there were no cash dispensers, Internet cafés or bus stops to throw me off-track again. The Meseta offered almost the perfect backdrop for recovering from the mentally strenuous stretch the day before. I tried to adapt my thoughts to these surroundings and proverbially not think about *anything* – thus creating my own Meseta in my head.

Of course this didn't even work for the first hundred paces and soon thoughts were dancing hip-hop around in my head again. Well, as long as I couldn't turn them off at least I intended to steer them into disciplined and orderly channels.

After my pilgrim's blackout the day before, I was now firmly determined to walk all the way to Santiago. Only a major disaster would stop me this time – such as falling off my bunk bed as had almost happened to me last night without the influence of too much 'pilgrim's diesel'. At some time during the night I had felt the urge to visit the W.C. and in getting out of bed had completely forgotten that after a couple of nights in the lower bunk, tonight I had been allocated the upper level bed.

I was quite proud of the fact that I had been hiking six to nine hours a day so far and my body had held out pretty well, apart from a tiny blister on my right heel. Although I felt tired, it was the rather pleasant sensation of fatigue that one gets when having achieved a great deal. However, the purely athletic aspect had long become secondary and the valuable insights I had gained along the Camino had become all the more significant.

As there was still a good few hours of walking until reaching my destination for the day – the 'metropolis' of Hontanas with its two hundred inhabitants – I decided I should add another important insight to my list. However, the only one that sprang to mind was that no such thing would manifest itself at the touch of a button.

Whilst enjoying a break I met Melissa again whom I had accompanied through the dark city of Burgos early that morning. We exchanged a few nice words after which we both set off again alone. Meanwhile I was convinced that absolutely nothing happened by chance along the Camino. Also meeting Melissa probably had a deeper significance for me or should at least provide me with food for thought along the last ten kilometres through this wasteland.

Melissa had joined me this morning, as she had been afraid of getting lost in dark. Even though I didn't know my way around in Burgos any better than she, I did, at any rate, have the advantage of speaking Spanish and could in case of doubt have asked the locals for directions.

While at almost every turn of the St. James Way one passed either a scallop shell sign or a yellow signpost showing the right direction to take, in real life, however, things were not so clearly signposted. More often than not one took the wrong path, on other occasions, however, the right one. Sometimes one was led in the wrong direction through the influence of others and, far too often, one ignored a sign only to realize much later that at a crucial cross-road in life the wrong path had been taken and that it was too late to turn back.

Along the Camino the signposts generally all looked alike. Although some of them were a little larger than others, some weather-beaten and some quite hidden, they always showed the same scallop shell symbol or the same yellow arrow. But how was one to recognize a signpost in one's everyday-life? What were the signposts for chances in life? I decided to spend the rest of the day's stretch of the route reflecting on which easily recognizable but also insignificant and 'weather-beaten' crossroads of my life I had so far passed by. Which ones had I accidentally overlooked and which ones consciously ignored?

The more I pondered on this issue the more fascinating I found the 'scallop shell' which had influenced my biography and made me walk the Way of St. James instead of sitting in a nameless office in Salzburg - as my education and training had intended. At what point had I actually left my predefined path?

Much in life is predestined by birth, and in my case that happened to be a major stroke of luck: I was born into a typical middle class family who lived in a comfortable house in the country-side on the outskirts of the city of Salzburg in Austria. My parents were neither alcoholics nor did they regularly give me a thrashing – apart from just the one hefty slap from my mother at our happy reunion after my tricycle excursion. I had a nice and sheltered child-hood. When young one tends to take these fortunate circumstances for granted, only fully appreciating them much later in life when things could have turned out a lot worse. Fortunately my dear mother had delayed taking her life until both her sons, at least on paper, were halfway grown-up – which, however, didn't make our loss less painful.

It is said that you cannot choose your family but your friends. In my case most of my best friends today had been more or less assigned to me by the school authority. Between the ages of ten and fourteen all of us were together at the secondary school in the neighbouring village of Hof near Salzburg. Instead of losing sight of each other in later years, we often had great nights out together in the many Salzburg bars and nearby country discotheques. We met almost every Friday night at Fritz's home with his exceedingly hospitable parents and at the weekends shot our own road movie riding around on our mopeds.

I shared my years of adolescence with my friends – from my first love followed by the first bouts of love-sickness, from the first self-earned money to the first vacations without parents.

It wasn't until some years later that I really got to appreciate the value of these friendships, which my friends and I have maintained to the present day. Even after three decades we regularly meet – despite living in different places with different family circumstances and careers.

I also have my friends to thank for getting my first detective novel, *Pata Negra*, published with a small publishing house. The publication was only possible with a pre-order of one thousand copies – such was the deal with my publisher at the time. So all my friends, together with quite a number of acquaintances and relatives, bought the first thousand copies themselves, which, given a sales price for the first edition of sixteen euros and ninety cents, represented quite a considerable financial effort on their part.

If, in addition to my eight school friends, I were to count a handful of people I had only got to know in Spain much later, I would come to a total of more than ten really good pals. A unique privilege. For how easy was it to go off the rails with the wrong friends, especially in one's unstable youth? If there was just one thing I could wish for my daughter, then it would be to have the same sort of luck with her friends as her father has had.

During my teens and as a young adult my friends had kept me on the right track. They themselves remained on their chosen career paths and were mostly successful in their fields of work – one of them as co-founder of an international software developer with hundreds of employees and another having created his own jewellery label.

It was only me who had broken away from the norm, starting a career as a *bon vivant* or artist of life in my early twenties. After all, according to my maxim every hamster wheel looks like a career ladder from the inside in the rat race of life. At that time I had already sensed that it would have been the wrong choice for me to remain in Austria and tinker around my career ladder. And having once got onto the wrong track, it was pointless to make fast progress.

But, I asked myself in the scorching heat of the Meseta, at what point would the 'scallop shell' have appeared to me to lead me on to my very own path two and a half decades ago? I began to realize that it had been one of those banal signs that usually one wouldn't have noticed, not even under a magnifying glass. Ultimately, if you like, it had been a night spent with another man that had steered my life into a completely different direction.

During my national service with the Austrian army, which had been obligatory at the time (unfortunately, as I had never had any interest whatsoever in all this military rigmarole), I was on guard duty one night whilst taking part in an army exercise. As my superiors had not entrusted me with the responsible task of patrolling alone in front of an empty ramshackle ammunition depot, another comrade had been assigned to me. I had found him quite likeable as, after all, both of us had the same fighting spirit to protect our fatherland and therefore, almost immediately, fell asleep.

I had probably already had the habit of snoring at that time, as it wasn't long before someone noticed us and woke us up roughly. Fortunately Austria was no military dictatorship, but the man with the important stars pinned to the collar of his uniform looked as if he wished it had been exactly that so that he could have had us court-martialled and shot. He warned us not to fall asleep again as otherwise we would face curfew on all weekends until the end of our service and instead of spending time with friends and family would be cleaning the company's washrooms and lavatories. That worked. We promised to guard the imaginary ammunition depot as of immediately as if it were the crown jewels, saluted him and suppressed a yawn. As energy drinks had not been invented at the time, we had to do without them for staying awake all night. We succeeded by chatting about travelling until dawn.

Up until then my travels had been restricted to such exotic destinations as a four-hour car trip to the distant northern Italian Adriatic coast, to nearby Croatia and the Greek party island of Ios. I announced to my guard comrade, however, that I was planning to travel to Australia right after my service.

My comrade lived with his parents in one of the best areas of Salzburg, and while I was reeling off the list of my exciting vacation destinations he almost dozed off again. He was definitely more worldly wise and widely-travelled than myself. He had already been to Australia, also to South East Asia as well as everywhere throughout Europe on 'Interrail' tickets anyway. He thought the

USA was awesome. However, the best, the ultimate, the unmatched highlight of all his travel destinations to-date had been Venezuela.

Slowly this guy started becoming less and less likeable for my taste. And, after all, wasn't I carrying a loaded gun? – even if loaded with blank ammunition only. Blathering, pretentious upstart, I thought at the time, not yet being resistant to envy and resentment, and I fumbled in the dark for the charging handle.

Yet my curiosity had been aroused and I asked him what had fascinated him so much about Venezuela. And so it happened that he kept me awake with detailed descriptions of his experiences which could be summarized as follows:

- beaches in Venezuela were as white as paper
- one beer didn't cost even five Austrian Schillings
- Venezuelan women were absolute blockbusters.

Forget Australia, I told myself at change of guard early the next morning. I have to get to Venezuela, and fast! But didn't they speak Spanish over there?

As I dragged myself over the last remaining kilometres through the Meseta, it dawned on me that the seemingly trivial chat with my army comrade at that time had been the scallop shell that had most influenced my path of life. Shortly after the end of my army service I had boarded a plane for Caracas.

Thereafter nothing would ever be the same again.

I was in my early twenties and hardly spoke a word of Spanish. My first Spanish conversation took place at Caracas airport when I asked a taxi driver roughly the following question: "You want me very cheap lodging recommend to Caracas?" Without a word the man nodded and drove me straight into the Caracas slums. There I discovered a slight variation of what my army comrade had raved about. I gained my initial language skills playing billiards with tooth-less locals in one of the numerous dives.

Three weeks later in Caracas I had already survived two muggings. I bought a American Dodge Dart for four hundred US Dollars, the sales sign for which I had spotted whilst waiting in front of a red traffic light. The deal which was concluded by handshake was sealed faster than it took the signal to turn green. Of course there were no documents to go with the old banger. It had most probably been stolen anyway. But I didn't care as I planned to conquer the country with it. Unfortunately the vehicle conked out after only two hundred kilometres, right in the middle of a rain-forest dirt road.

I hitch-hiked a ride to the ferry port of Puerto La Cruz, where I met a man called Jesus. Jesus spoke quite good English, pretended to own shares in a gold mine and invited me to his fancy apartment located on the party island of Margarita. Of course I was instantly impressed by my new 'amigo'. After being subjected to countless attempts to rip me off in the most ramshackle parts of Caracas, I had finally come across someone who meant well for me. At least that's what I thought at the time in my boundless naivety and treated Jesus to a few drinks on the ferry. After arriving at Margarita we didn't, however, drive straight to his apartment but contacted a woman who handed a key over to us. Jesus claimed his own apart-ment had apparently just been rented out for the time being and therefore he had to switch to another one for a while. He handed the woman a few smaller bank notes in local currency, whereas I had to contribute a couple of one hundred dollar bills – allegedly as a deposit which was to be refunded to me very soon.

As it turned out afterwards, it had not been Jesus inviting *me* to *his* apartment, as he didn't own one, but *I* letting *him* sleep in *mine* as I had actually just paid the rent six months in advance. Jesus' sympathy rating fell rapidly. Nevertheless I now had a flat at my disposal that, in the long run, was less expensive than a hotel room.

What was far more annoying, however, was the fact that shortly after our relocation, *my* apartment became frequented by a hoard of prostitutes who didn't at all look like the women my army comrade had raved about to me. These females visited Jesus with increasing regularity, also exchanging a smattering of Spanish with me that I slowly began to understand. Thereafter they disappeared with my flatmate – to my amazement – into the bathroom rather than the bedroom. Also a few shady-looking male characters, alleged busi-ness partners, came by at regular intervals.

It wasn't until a couple of days later when I was inspecting the bathroom a little more closely whilst searching for a new tube of toothpaste, that I came to the conclusion that the prostitutes weren't offering their usual services but it was the other way round instead and they were taking advantage of Jesus' very special service. There was more cocaine to be found in our bathroom than washing powder in a laundry. This became far too hot for me. If a police raid were to take place in our flat, I would be prosecuted as a potential accomplice and sent to jail as well.

I confronted Jesus and demanded the repayment of my deposit in order to be able to move out as soon as possible. But my flatmate informed me that only the woman who had handed over the key would be able to make a refund. And unfortunately she had died the week before.

I searched in my exceedingly meagre treasure trove of Spanish vocabulary and dug out the full set of Spanish abusive words that I had learned over the past six weeks from slum dwellers, whores and drug addicts and hurled them at Jesus. "Then you'll have to refund my deposit!" I shouted. But he just laughed at me and declared that he was broke at the moment as there was a problem with his gold mine. Sure thing.

Just as I was packing, somebody knocked on the apartment door. Jesus peeked through the spy hole and whispered something I didn't understand. Then he unlocked the door and three police officers in uniform came in. It took only a few moments to realize the full implications of their visit. Three heavily-armed policemen entered *my* apartment with *my* bathroom full of – at least hidden – cocaine. Never before had I felt so scared. I hoped they hadn't yet noticed me and disappeared into my room. The apartment was located on the fourth floor. I opened the window and looked down. Damn it. There was no fire ladder I could have used for my escape as in an American B-movie. Trembling with fear I waited for the worst to happen and envisaged myself growing old in a Venezuelan jail. I listened to what was going on behind the door but could hardly understand anything. The police officers' voices, however, didn't sound particularly harsh. There was even laughter. Carefully I removed the old fashioned key from its hole and peered through. Now I understood. Two policemen were rubbing their noses as the third handed Jesus a few bank notes. Then they said good-bye and left.

I waited until my heartbeat had slowed to a normal level and the coast was clear. Then I grabbed my backpack and set out in search of a completely new start in this country, one that in almost all aspects was totally different from my Austrian homeland.

Slowly but surely I began to master the Spanish language. Instead of the planned three months I stayed for a full year, during which I travelled to all the countries of Latin America. As I had hardly any money I hitch-hiked or took buses. I lived on empanadas, hot dogs or *arepas* – the tasty, filled tortillas bought from street vendors. I slept in my hammock on palm fringed beaches or in the wilderness, whereas in cities I stayed overnight in cheap guest houses or with young ladies who sometimes gladly granted me shelter.

I could fill three thick volumes of stories about the diversity of impressions and wonderful adventures I experienced during my one-year journey between the Andes, the Amazon, the Atlantic and Pacific coasts, through salt deserts, tropical rainforests, ancient Inca sites and modern metropolises. They broadened my horizons to such a lasting extent that upon returning to my hometown of Plainfeld, I felt just as lost as I had done when I arrived in the mega city of Caracas a year before.

"What took you so long?", asked pilgrim brother Rainhard bringing me back into the present. As usual the agile seventy-two year old had arrived hours before me at our hostel. He now sat in front of the entrance together with three English women of his age, drinking a large beer which, after the long stretch of the Camino through the hot and dusty Meseta, seemed to me like pure liquid gold. I postponed checking-in, showering, doing my laundry as well as my Facebook report for an indefinite time and joined the lively group of seniors.

Chapter Sixteen

Hontanas – Boadilla del Camino

The next morning pilgrim brother Rainhard and I set out at the same pace for a change. Meanwhile we had both come to an arrangement: he had agreed to honour my wish to walk most of the way on my own, but we would discuss and agree together on such things as our daily destination targets, choice of lodgings, and other similar topics. After all he had become my key contact person on the Camino and I profited from the experience of the soon-to-be multiple conqueror of the St. James Way. As a *quid pro quo* I served as his interpreter and took care of the evening's entertainment, ensuring an abundant supply of pilgrim's diesel. It proved quite an advantage for me that I didn't have to bother any more about my night's lodging as Rainhard always arrived at the hostel at our agreed destination much earlier, booking a bed for me as well. Vacant beds could become a problem especially during the summer months. Fortunately the Camino was not so overrun in October and therefore I was able to take my time during the second part of each day.

However, to begin with we marched on at Rainhard's brisk pace through the Meseta. We passed a desolate monastery ruin and entered the village of Castrojeriz, where I topped up my provisions of bread, cheese and wine in a supermarket. Today I didn't want to take a rest in a bar along the way but rather find a nice picnic spot. Three kilometres out of the village we reached the table-topped mountain which Rainhard had been trying to make me afraid of for the past two days. Although the ascent was steep it wasn't very long and an obstacle such as this definitely didn't bother me any more. We climbed uphill so fast that we even outpaced two mountain bikers.

Once we had reached the top, a spectacular panorama opened up before us over the Meseta. Even in its monotony the landscape was once again picturesque. The view stretched as far as the Cantabrian Mountains in the north. After our descent Rainhard marched on ahead, while I chose a rather more leisurely pace. A good half of today's twenty-eight-kilometre stretch lay behind me and it was not even eleven in the morning. So there was no need to rush.

I strolled along so slowly that even Peter from Hungary overtook me. This 6'6" guy usually strode slowly and deliberately through the countryside. Perhaps his pace had been recently spurred on by his present company. For days I had seen him marching side-by-side with Julia from Duesseldorf. And yet 'pepper-spray Julia' had told me after she had walked for a couple of kilometres with me a day a few days ago, that she really preferred to hike on her own. I therefore assumed that a pilgrim romance was developing and didn't want to get involved in *Camino* gossip any further but was more interested in continuing yesterday's thoughts about the most important signposts of my life's journey.

Anyway, if it hadn't been for my Austrian army comrade I would never have spent a year in Latin America, where I had become acquainted with a new culture as well as a new language and had become more independent, more open-minded and just more mature. At the same time my attitude towards my old homeland had completely changed. After my return from South America I had initially thought that my old companions had meanwhile somehow changed, until I realized that I was the one who had altered.

I wrote countless applications addressed to local companies that had branch offices in South America, but only received letters of refusal stating that the respective branch offices decided upon matters of personnel only on the spot. However, I wanted to get back to Venezuela as fast as possible. That's what I had solemnly promised someone. Her name was Elizabeth and to me she was the most beautiful girl in the world and my greatest love at the time. I had assured her then that I would return to her arms within three months at the latest. If I wanted to keep my promise, then I had only two weeks left. But without a job and any money I stood no chance of seeing Elizabeth again.

Thus my first romantic drama took its course. Unfortunately at the time I wasn't as experienced in coping with heartache as I would be today - having just got over a broken engagement as easily as swallowing two pints of beer, one after the other, at the end of a scorchingly hot thirty-kilometre trek.

Back then I had had no other option but to take on work in Austria. Jeff, a local friend of my father, had employed me in his company that supplied furniture and toys to kindergartens.

I did my best, attended training courses and seminars and worked many overtime hours for which I didn't ask for payment. After one and a half years I had accumulated enough compensatory time in combination with all my saved vacation to be able to take four months off for travel. I bought a round-the-world ticket and in time-lapse mode toured Thailand, Malaysia, Hong Kong, China, Singapore, Taiwan, Australia, New Zealand, Tonga, Western Samoa, Hawaii and Los Angeles. Venezuela, however, was not on my list any more as around a year after my return to Austria I had received a letter from Elizabeth telling me that she wouldn't wait for me any longer and instead would now carry on dating a German.

Rather than struggling against my fate I decided to accept it and soon got involved in my next romantic drama in the South Pacific paradise of Western Samoa, where I encountered an enticing 'scallop shell' that I would have loved to pursue.

My travel schedule had planned a one-week stay in Western Samoa, but I had no idea where to spend it on the island. The capital, Apia, did not seem very inviting, but my travel guide mentioned something about a newly-built guest house adjacent to a heavenly beach in the South Eastern part of the island – which at the time had barely been developed for tourism. That sounded great. At the Apia bus station I asked around for the right bus to take me there, which wasn't at all easy as hardly anyone spoke English and nobody had ever heard of this holiday paradise. Eventually one of the locals – gesticulating wildly – led me to a bus that seemed about to leave. I jumped on and held my book under the driver's nose, who then spoke a few words in Samoan and nodded. I shrugged, accepted my inevitable fate and searched for a seat, which again wasn't an easy undertaking as the vehicle resembled Noah's Ark, the number of animals outweighing the human passengers: chicken, parrots, pigs and other small livestock surveyed me warily – this fair-haired and blue-eyed exotic from abroad. I stared back at them, equally sceptical.

The bus trip took us for more than an hour through the hinterland and over a volcanic mountain chain to the southern side of the island. The direction seemed to be all right. When we stopped near a village where most of the women together with their animals left the bus, the driver started a lively discussion with me. I didn't understand a word of what he was saying and assumed that I should get off the bus as well because his finger pointed first at me and then towards the bus door. According to my travel guide, however, the guest house was located much further to the south-east of the island.

I remained stubborn and refused to get off, after all this could not be the last stop. Three women, a dozen chicks in cages, three cute piglets and a parrot that continuously shouted what sounded like "F... you!" were waiting to get on. The bus driver blurted out a gush of Samoan words that probably were supposed to be an ancient curse and started his vehicle with a cloud of black smoke billowing behind as he drove off. However, not in the direction of the south-east but towards the south-west of the island.

The last few pages my travel guide dealt with the local language. There I found the translations for *stop, wrong, back* and *help* and subsequently shouted out my first Samoan phrase. The driver looked briefly into his almost blind rear mirror and ignored me in the same way as he did with the parrot on the backrest of the front seat that had seemed terribly agitated since the departure – most probably due to the lack of onboard catering. It was all in vain. I would have to get off the bus at the next stop and wait for the one going in the opposite direction.

Admittedly the local public transport did not seem to be as well developed as in my home country, and to be precise I hadn't seen any other bus or – as a matter of fact – hardly any car in this sparsely populated region since our departure in Apia. So I thought it best to stay on board until the terminus and go back all the way in the same bus. With Salzburg public transport I usually did the same when I had overslept my stop. I would chalk up the lost time as a cheap round tour of the island.

After a further hour's bumpy ride along craggy volcanic foothills and deserted beaches the bus finally stopped. The dirt road ended in front of a rocky cliff. I hadn't noticed any sign of civilization since our last stop. It didn't seem any different here, either, except for a few naked children dancing around our bus. The three remaining Samoan women picked up their small livestock and got off. The bus driver darted another furious glance at me and disappeared, leaving me on my own. I remained seated as at some stage the bus would have to return to Apia, I thought.

Smilingly I waved at the children who were jumping around outside pulling faces at me. Adult men wearing only loincloths and thereby displaying their typical traditional Polynesian Maori tattoos pointed their fingers at me and were probably trying to figure out what to do with this strange guy. Frightening pictures of a giant cooking pot above a crackling bonfire arose in my mind's eye.

After a while a young woman entered the bus. Immediately scenes from the film *Mutiny on the Bounty* came into my mind. She was wearing a flower in her long black hair, her body was wrapped in a piece of colourful cloth and her smile beamed like a South Seas' sunrise. Were the first passengers now boarding the bus for Apia?

The exotic beauty approached me and asked in English what I

was doing here. I tried to give 'Miss Bounty' a brief explanation on the geographical miscommunication and asked her what time the bus would actually be returning to Apia. "In one week's time", was her reply. I must have looked so perplexed by this information, that she carried on to explain to me that the driver was her uncle and that he was by no means a professional bus driver. He just used to drive women to market in the capital on Saturdays and take them back afterwards. The bus would now simply stay where it was until the following Saturday. One look through the windows told me not even to think of asking the young lady for the telephone number of a taxi company.

Well, I had never ever before been further away from any kind of civilization. A little further inland on an area of cleared rainforest a settlement appeared, laid out in a circle and comprising of a dozen oval-shaped huts, the largest of which was in the middle. The dwellings were built on wooden foundations with eight posts supporting a bamboo cane roof. As they had neither walls nor doors I could look straight in. There was not a single piece of furniture to be seen but only straw mats scattered across the floor.

Furthermore, nothing in this 'village' showed any sign that mankind had in fact been involved in various stages of the industrial revolution for quite some time: no electricity, no vehicles or technical equipment, no plastic or gas bottles, cola cans, cutlery or dishes, no shops, no pubs or bars and, of course, no hotel. The rusty bus seemed as much out of place here as a crashed spacecraft would have been. The most advanced utensil happened to be a machete carried around by a well-muscled Samoan.

After leaving the bus I squatted down on the beach, surrounded by a flock of children with whom I couldn't exchange a word. I felt like a circus attraction. The only option would have been to walk back all the way, but in those days, more than twenty years prior to my walking hundreds of kilometres on a pilgrimage, I didn't waste a second thought on this option, given the tropical temperatures.

The 'exotic pearl' advised me after a while that people from her village had thought about the situation and decided that I could stay until next Saturday when the bus returned to Apia. Well, yes, but …? How did they think this could work? Where was I supposed to sleep? What would I have to eat if there was no restaurant? Owing to a lack of alternatives I turned to the back of my travel guide and uttered in my best Samoan "fa'afetei" – "thanks!

This was greeted by a joyous howling from all around me and I thus introduced myself using the Samoan tongue twister: "*O lo'u igoa 'o Eduard.*" From then on and for a full week I became a fellow citizen of this Stone Age community. The village leader paid his respect to me by inviting me to his hut for the night. At the same time he happened to be the father of my English-speaking beauty. She translated for me and disclosed that she would also be sleeping there – together with her father and mother, grandpa and grandma, one sister, three brothers, two stepsisters and five nephews. "And a handsome Austrian" – she added smilingly.

My walking pace had slowed down through melancholy and heavy-hearted nostalgia. Looking back, those seven days had been some of the most treasured in my entire life. If a fairy were to cross my path along the Camino and grant me the wish to relive just one week of my life, I'd chose the one in Samoa. It was time for a rest, but I didn't want to take it in a noisy bar in the next village but continue indulging in my exotic memories.

At a Roman stone bridge I climbed down to the lazily flowing course of a stream. The spot wasn't quite comparable to the South Pacific but for the Meseta fairly idyllic. I took off shoes and socks, drank a sip of wine, lay down in a field and continued my journey through time.

During my time in Western Samoa I had learned a few of their tongue twisters by heart. With each of my words in their language the children had erupted with laughter. They had shown me how to climb palm trees to get to the coconuts as there was nothing else there to drink. Or how to fish using the most primitive techniques. Meals were of fish or chicken with breadfruit or plantains. Grain, rice or noodles were as unknown as cutlery. Dining took place together with all the community members, and one ate with fingers from wooden bowls. The first night I slept amongst the large family, but the friendly hospitality was a bit uncomfortable for me and so I relocated my quarters for the rest of my stay to the beach. During the day the village leader's daughter didn't leave my side and as of the third night she came to visit me on the beach after her family had gone to sleep.

Under a star-studded sky, the likes of which can rarely be seen in our northern hemisphere, and a full moon that shone through the palm branches on to the beach, we savoured the romantic togetherness which was impossible during the day as we constantly had a horde of kids whirling around us. By now I really felt like a mutineer from the *Bounty*, one who would renounce everything else if only he was allowed to stay in paradise. But she was doing something strictly prohibited. She was not allowed to be alone with me as she kept telling me again and again, but she couldn't bear to leave me and usually stayed until dawn. We didn't make love to each other until our last night - and even then we didn't go all the way. The tradition of her tribe required that she could only marry a man from her own cultural background and had to be pure and "untainted" for him. That night I tried to persuade her to break with the tradition and, although somewhat improvised, made my first proposal of marriage at the age of twenty-two. But it was all in vain. The price would have been too high. Her family would have outcast and outlawed her until the end of her life.

Next morning I got on the bus. The entire village population came to bid me farewell. The children put a garland of flowers around my neck. She was the only one who didn't come to my farewell. Probably because her tears would have betrayed her. I also let my tears flow freely as I was being expelled from paradise after having nibbled at the forbidden fruit. "Tofa", I stammered, "Good-bye. See you again". Yet I knew only too well that there wouldn't be a next time.

Had the exotic beauty, whose unpronounceable name I couldn't recall later, said "ioe" at the time, meaning "yes", I might possibly have become stranded for love at a place where there was no electricity, where one dealt with one's morning toilet in the rainforest, where one only drank coconut milk and had to wash in the Pacific.

This hadn't been quite such an insignificant St. James Way scallop shell along the track of my life, I thought, whilst resting next to the Roman bridge. Suppose I had stayed in Western Samoa – what would have become of me? A happier person? I doubted it. Soon enough paradise would have turned into normality and far away from any civilization I wouldn't have met with all the wonderful experiences of the following two decades and would have missed quite a few important signposts of life.

Back at Apia airport, where I was waiting for my connecting flight to Honolulu, I ran into Peter again, a German from Hanover whom I had already met in New Zealand in Auckland. He also had a one week stay on Samoa behind him. At the time I had asked him whether he wanted to join me going to the south of the island, but he had preferred to stay in a smart hotel in the capital. Now, one week later, I asked him how he had found Samoa.

"It was the worst location on my entire journey so far", he stated indignantly. He told me the hotel food had been disgusting, the city filthy and very noisy and somewhere around the market he had been mugged and his wallet stolen.

Well, I thought, as I sat by the stream sipping some wine and munching a cheese sandwich, such a small island and two such completely different opinions. I was often asked which of the countries I had travelled to I liked best. My answer was always the same: the countries themselves never actually played a major role but rather set the scene for the decisive factor – the experiences I had gained and the observations I had made in the respective countries. This also applied to the Camino. Quite a few people with whom I had set out from the Pyrenees were long since back home again – having given up their pilgrimages as a result of negative experiences on the Way of St. James or the non-fulfilment of exaggerated expectations.

I put an end to my break and started to attack the last few kilometres towards Boadilla del Camino. In doing so I asked myself what the exact appeal of the St. James Way was for me. The great scenery? Well, it was indeed an impressive and varied region, that is to say if one disregarded the Meseta. But to be perfectly honest: walking through the Salzburg or Tyrolean Alpine countryside would actually be more beautiful. Also the food would be, in the culinary sense, worlds apart from the soggy pilgrim menus prepared with the cheapest ingredients. And compared with the average pilgrims' hostels, Austrian guest houses seemed more like luxury hotels. So what was it that I appreciated so much about the Camino?

The answer was quite simple: because it represented an adventure and I happened to love adventures. Although, to be honest, adventures and comfort were incompatible to my mind. I hadn't had my most pleasant experiences in five star hotels but in hammocks, tents and on sleeping mats under starry skies – and also in five-Euro hostels along the Camino. If I had had a larger budget at my disposal, stayed in pre-booked comfortable hotels and had my backpack forwarded by Camino-Trans, the hike would no longer be an adventure for me and would have lost its appeal altogether.

What, apart from the above-mentioned, made the Camino such a unique experience for me? The fact that it made me become aware of the background noise of my deepest thoughts and heed them? Sometimes they came as silently as the surrounding countryside, at other times they rushed past as shrill as a six-lane Beijing motorway. To allow my scatterbrained thoughts to flow along in an orderly course was by far my greatest inner achievement on the Camino so far. In comparison, even my athletic performance to have travelled almost half the St. James Way without any serious injuries to my feet seemed insignificant.

In light of the refugee and immigration crisis which had been dominating the headlines in news from home at that time, whilst standing at the boundary between the provinces of Burgos and Palencia, I realized what the greatest appeal the Camino had for me: the good fortune of getting to know such a wide variety of people – from more than twenty countries on all continents, from all walks of life and religions. The spectrum ranged from Scotsman Tom, who financed his journey by performing handstands whilst playing the harmonica at the same time on the main squares of larger towns, to a rich Spanish factory owner with three mansions in Marbella. And all of them ate the same pilgrim's menu at night, slept in the same dormitory and snored in the same way. To cut a long story short, the Way of St. James was so far the only place for me where *all* people were equal, where *all* people followed the same path and where *all* people incurred similar privations and difficulties.

As I crossed the border between the two provinces I became very much aware of how unbearable it would have been if a barbed wire fence had been there only letting a few of us

pass ...

Chapter Seventeen

Boadilla del Camino − Carrión de los Condes

The previous evening had come to an end in a cheerful get-together. As I had held myself back on pilgrim's diesel and had slept through until seven o'clock in the morning, I felt fit and motivated and enthusiastic. As today's milestone, Pilgrim brother Rainhard and I had agreed on Carrion de los Condes which, however, with its mere twenty seven kilometres seemed to me a little too near. When I had started my hike on the Camino I had listened carefully to the advice of Mats, the Swede, to take it easy at the beginning. Meanwhile, however, my body had become accustomed to long hikes and so I was confident that I could trust it with stretches of more than thirty kilometres. But what was the point?

That morning I set out even before 7 a.m., without breakfast, because I intended to have one in the village of Frómista that was just six kilometres further down the road. The first few kilometres led alongside a canal that was praised by my travel guide as a masterpiece of eighteenth-century architecture and had originally been used as a transport route. Now it served as an irrigation system for the so-called Tierra de Campos. The fields lay shrouded in patches of fog, a haze billowed over the waters of the canal and all that could be heard were one's own footsteps and the chirping of birds. The air was cold and clear. I took a large number of photos of the sunrise and walked on slowly and awestruck with happiness.

Eventually I arrived at Frómista, which was at least big enough to have a supermarket offering the choice of two different pasta sauces. Instead of having breakfast in the village I bought picnic provisions and had a cup of tea in a local bar. As usual the TV set was so loud that no-one could ignore it. A news broadcast was just on. A young girl had been murdered. Distressed parents. Shocked neighbours. The motive. The suspect. Court trial. I was close to tears. I couldn't bear the pictures any longer and drank my tea outside in the cold. Adiós, peaceful mood.

The trail continued for some kilometres along a main road. My travel guide described this section as "pilgrim's motorway". I still couldn't get the TV pictures out of my mind. It would be difficult today to present any new insights to my Facebook amigos. After all, insights didn't lie scattered around like autumn leaves. After another eighteen kilometres there were two options: either to stay on the "pilgrim's motorway" or to follow a stream through autumnal woods and accept taking a detour.

After a short inner dispute with myself I decided to choose the more scenic route. Here I was alone, as most other pilgrims would rather devour their blister-plasters than walk extra kilometres. Around lunchtime I climbed down the embankment towards the creek, spread out my towel and took my picnic out of my backpack. While I was eating I stared at the clear water and asked myself whether the choice between two different tracks, both of which led to the same target, held a deeper significance for me than just the banal conclusion that the longer way is sometimes the more attractive one. But I couldn't figure it out. I took a nap and afterwards spent a while reading a book that I had brought with me, before walking on after two hours of rest.

The forest path joined the 'pilgrims' motorway' again and followed it for nine kilometres through endless stretches of farmland. The rhythm of my footsteps as well as the clicking of my hiking poles had something meditative about it. All of a sudden my heavy thoughts began to lift and I saw things in a completely different light and from a distance. At once I recognized an insight.

I stopped so abruptly that a Korean woman almost bumped into me from behind. In Frómista, without knowing it, I had stood at a parting of the ways where I had been spiritually confronted by an oversized 'scallop shell' which would have pointed me in a completely new direction. But I had passed by without noticing it. This time it had been about following the path to become a writer. It wasn't until now – quite some time later – that I realized what had actually happened then.

The whole thing had to do with the murder of the young girl I had learned about from the TV in the inn. The victim had been the same age as my daughter and the dreadful pictures had haunted me throughout the following hours of my hike.

I came to the simple and sad conclusion that I was writing the wrong kind of books, and since the beginning of my literary career had chosen the wrong path – namely the unpleasant instead of the nice one. I asked myself why, seven years ago, I had actually started to write novels on murder and manslaughter, agony, drama, injustice and tragedy. Why hadn't I opted for positive novels that would have delighted my readership instead of frightening them? I seemed to recall that my decision at the time had been based on a study that had found that crime stories were the genre with the largest target group. So I must have followed ulterior motives of a commercial nature rather than letting my writing be guided by the literary path which gave me the greatest pleasure.

I had never been able to deal with violence well – not in any shape or form. The saying "he could never harm a fly" applied to me literally. Whenever a bluebottle was getting on my nerves, whilst I was writing, for example, I swiped at it – but so hesitantly and gently, that even the lamest fly would have enough time to mate before getting hit by my hand. And I, of all people, who absolutely detested any form of violence had been writing books for years about it.

Thus I made up my mind to discontinue writing crime novels after my return from the Camino and change the subject matter. I would simply reprieve the five pilgrims whom I had meanwhile mentally 'murdered'. During the remaining kilometres I contemplated my new career path and with each step it felt better and better. Having said this, there was a problem: I couldn't post this news on Facebook that evening without making any further comments. How could I gently break the news of the sudden change of direction in my writing to my fans who – for quite a while now – had been waiting and longing for the fourth thriller in my crime series?

For one year now I hadn't produced a single page of my planned fourth Andalusian detective novel, most probably because it had already become clear to me – subconsciously – that I had been dealing with the wrong theme. This awareness had robbed me of any kind of motivation. I was about to stop my career as an author altogether. However, I now sensed that new energy was being generated in me. I wanted to think over my decision one night more and then promise my fanbase further books, which although they might not give rise to goose bumps any longer, would instead be written with more warmth, more profoundly and be spiritually more valuable. At the same time I wanted to retain my style of writing and also keep up a certain atmosphere of suspense and excitement. However, the suspense should no longer result from violence and intrigue. How exactly I was going to achieve this I hadn't worked out by the end of the day's stretch, but I was confident that a suitable solution would occur to me soon.

Whilst on the last third of the stretch, I had met Omar from the USA, Florence from Canada and Paula from Berlin. These three had set out independently of one another at Saint-Jean-Piet-de-Port and for a few days now had been walking together. I joined them until we took a rest in one of the next inns and ordered some wine. Paula seemed to have a rather loose tongue and was bombarding me with questions, so I told her about my mystery stories, my life in Spain and that my daughter's name also happened to be Paula. Ever since my ex-fiancée had downgraded me to single status, I hadn't merely kept an eye out for beautiful scenery but also for pretty, female fellow pilgrims. Paula walked around in clothes that looked as if she wore them as pyjamas at home and had obviously forgotten to pack her hair brush – still, I thought she was quite cute.

Regrettably she didn't only have the same name as my daughter, from her age she could in fact also have been my daughter. So no pilgrim's flirt was going to develop here – even more so as in this respect I had got rather out of practice in the meantime.

The group wanted to hike as far as Cape Finisterre – a plan that other pilgrims had also told me about. In the Middle Ages people believed that the earth ended at the most western tip of the Iberian Peninsula. In ancient times pilgrims from all over Europe, after having received absolution from all their sins in Santiago, also wanted to see where the known world ended. Even though today everyone knows that this is located in Washington, I resolved that I, too, would also try and make it to Finisterre. It would mean walking an extra one hundred kilometres and extending my pilgrimage by three or four days. My problems at home would certainly wait this long for me.

Omar had stretched out four fingers towards the waiter once again, but I declined. My three new friends were becoming increasingly more cheerful, but four glasses of wine during a break were quite enough. I rather wanted to get the remaining kilometres to the next lodging over and done with even though Paula was trying hard to persuade me to stay.

Pilgrim brother Rainhard had organized a room in a real monastery. It was the first time I had ever slept in a monastery and it turned out to be exactly as I had imagined it. The poky little room contained only two small beds and apart from a crucifix pinned to the wall there were no additional furnishings. At night we went out to dinner into the village. Heinz, a somewhat older likeable Swiss, joined us. As we were just having dessert Omar, Florence and Paula staggered, singing, past the restaurant. Five hours had passed since I had left them at the inn. They still wore their backpacks and were dead drunk. Paula saw me sitting by the window and came towards me, closed her eyes, kissed the pane of glass that was separating us, began to sway, stumbled and went sprawling to the ground.

Chapter Eighteen

Carrión de los Condes – Terradillos de los Templarios

Right after the town of Carrión de los Condes came to an end, an eighteen-kilometre section of the route lay ahead which led dead straight through nothing, always seeming to trail away to the horizon. Rainhard had set off earlier and I felt that I didn't want to walk this stretch on my own. Luckily the track itself sent me a suitable companion straight away. A briskly walking Spaniard caught up with me from behind and we started talking. First of all it was just small talk about the Way of St. James, but when I started asking the right questions the conversation deepened. At seventy-four years of age Elesio was walking the Camino to try to gain divine support for two of his daughters. One had become a widow under tragic circumstances not long ago, while the husband of the other daughter was suffering from leukaemia. He himself had lost his wife at a young age due to a car accident, leaving him with four children between the ages of six and ten.

Today he was in a happy mood because his two daughters together with four of his grandchildren were going to join him next day and accompany him for part of the route on their bicycles. A very heart-warming story. After eighteen kilometres our ways parted as he was about to meet his family. However, I had the feeling that I had got to know Elesio in the short time far better than a lot of other people I had been encountering for years, hardly getting any further than a curt "Hello, how are you?"

I walked the last part of this stretch on my own. The landscape didn't offer much variety so I tried to meditate for a while as I was walking. But fairly soon I stopped my attempt as quite associatively an incident sprang to my mind that had happened two decades ago in very similar surroundings and also had to do with walking. At the time I had been the responsible skipper on our yacht *Orion* sailing with a charter crew along the Venezuelan coastline. We had anchored just off La Blanquilla, a flat, uninhabited island approximately ten kilometres long. Our anchorage was in a cove located on the western part of the island, where three palm trees and a dream-like sandy beach served as a perfect photo backcloth. Other than that there were no signs of civilization, not even a wooden shack.

The island lay roughly two hundred nautical miles north of the Venezuelan coast and we were the only ship in that bay. There wasn't a soul to be seen. We'd been heading for La Blanquilla early that day coming from the Isla Margarita and intended to sail with direction Puerto La Cruz on the Venezuelan mainland that same afternoon. We had planned to spend the day diving and chilling out at the beach. So far the plan.

After having had breakfast on board, we took the yacht's dinghy across to the beach. Not long afterwards a green jeep approached on a dirt road that seemed to come – through cacti and

thicket – from the centre of the island. Two soldiers in uniform approached us. They pointed at the dinghy's outboard motor and asked if we would lend it out to them for a couple of hours. They claimed that there was a military base on the other side of the island and the motor of their military boat had busted. They were in desperate need of a replacement in order to be able to ferry goods from a supply ship to the military base. I didn't like the idea much, but the two left me in no doubt that they had authority here and wouldn't allow any argument. I surrendered – if rather hesitantly – our outboard motor to them but at least made them promise to bring it back at the latest by two in the afternoon as we were planning to set sail with the *Orion* then. *"Claro que sí, Señor"*, the uniformed men assured me and roared off with our motor.

"Claro que sí, these bloody idiots promised me!" I ranted and raved at half past three in the afternoon when our outboard still hadn't been brought back. By that time our ship should have long since been underway in order to arrive the next day, New Year's Eve, back in civilization. The charter guests didn't seem all that pleased about the change in plan and so there was nothing else for me to do but to start searching the island for the military base. This meant a march of ten kilometres through the desolate wasteland of the island under a burning sun wearing only bathing trunks and sandals.

With every metre I walked my anger at the soldiers who had shamelessly taken advantage of my readiness to help steadily increased. One-and-a-half hours later I couldn't believe my eyes. The military base was far larger than I had expected and the supply vessel in question was a fifty-metre-long cargo ship that was anchored half a nautical mile off the jetty in the bay. Going back and forth between the ship and the jetty was a fully laden barge about ten metres long, fitted with our already hissing and smoking and totally overstrained outboard motor, which had far too little power for this task and could hardly propel the wooden boat forward. There were around a dozen soldiers on the jetty carrying crates to the base. If this were to continue at that sort of speed it would take hours to complete the process if, however, our outboard motor didn't give up the ghost in the meantime. I had seldom been so furious. I ran on to the jetty where the barge, overloaded with supplies, was about to land and shouted: *"Alto! Alto! Alto!"*

The barge had hardly moored when I jumped onto it and quickly unscrewed the mounting of outboard motor.

"We aren't ready yet", yelled one of the soldiers.

"I don't give a damn, fuck you my friends!" I muttered in my native language, just to be on the safe side. Carrying the motor on my shoulders I climbed back on to the jetty and stood in sandals and trunks facing a squad of armed and grim-looking officers blocking my way.

I explained that I needed the motor back as we were about to set sail for Puerto de la Cruz. Could somebody please drive me back to the other side of the island? The soldiers, obviously amused by the bold behaviour of this gringo in bathing trunks, wouldn't dream of it. The presumably highest-ranking officer stepped forward, took the outboard motor away from me and shouted at me. "This is a military operation. The motor will remain in possession of the Ministry of Defence of the sovereign nation of Venezuela until this important mission has been completed. Then you may take it away with you."

No way, amigo! Completely exhausted and dehydrated from marching over the island and in addition foaming with rage and at the end of my patience, I wrenched the motor from the Commander under furious protests and a tirade of mutual insults. This impertinence could of course not be tolerated by the troops. They snatched the motor away from me again and 'accompanied' me to the military base. On the way, the Commander recited a list of my offences: violation of state authorities, sabotage of a military operation, obstruction of a senior official of the sovereign nation of Venezuela in exercising his duties. If I didn't cool down I'd end up serving a sentence of several years of imprisonment. I was pushed into a room and the door locked from the outside. For the first time in my life I was in prison. So that's what comes from being helpful!

Two decades later I realized that at the time I should have aimed for de-escalation of the situation. But instead I had hammered my fists against the door, bellowing all the bad language that I was familiar with in Spanish. No-one reacted to it. The soldiers had obviously returned to unloading the supplies and at the same time were ruining my dinghy's outboard motor. Buying a new one at this time just wouldn't have been financially possible. So the order of the day seemed to be to fight for it like a lion – which also happens to be my zodiac sign. Luckily the room was not a prison cell as I had known from TV films – in any case the only window was not barred. However, in spite of this, today the room would be escape-proof for me as, first of all, I would not be able to climb up to the narrow opening two metres high and, secondly, I certainly wouldn't pass through it. At the time, however, I luckily just about managed it. Covered with scratches and bruises on shoulders and hips, I plumped down head first on the other side into a thicket. My first jailbreak seemed to have been crowned with immediate success. Now only my getaway had to work out well, too.

I circled the military barracks and peered around the corner. The soldiers were still busy unloading crates and boxes from the barge. Once the barge had been fully emptied it stayed moored at the jetty. I peeped around the corner again and watched the goods being carried towards the military base. However, this time the soldiers didn't come back. Had they finished or were they just having a break? It didn't really matter. There was no-one to be seen right now. But for how long? And when would my escape be discovered?

My heart was pounding so wildly that I was afraid it would give me away. I checked my surroundings one more time, spurted towards the barge, unscrewed the motor, climbed back on to the jetty with it, had one last look at the barracks, took a deep breath and sprinted towards the island's interior.

I was afraid that I probably wouldn't get very far. It was already getting dark and I thought of tracker dogs, of armed search squads and of the possibility of getting lost in the darkness as I couldn't follow the dirt track on which they would almost certainly be searching for me with the jeep. Furthermore, I could flake out at any stage. I hadn't had anything to drink for hours in this blazing heat and was now faced with the task of hauling a bulky outboard motor weighing almost fifty kilos over rocks and rubble, through under-growth and cactuses to the other side of the island in the dark, where my charter guests were by now probably getting worried about my disappearance.

And if I should actually make it as far as the beach without collapsing under the weight of the motor, the military would most certainly be waiting for me, fuming with rage and without doubt put me in jail for years to come – if they didn't shoot me right away. One gringo less was of no concern to people in this country.

Towards the end of my route march I had to put down the outboard motor every ten metres. I carried it alternately on my shoulders or with both hands pressed to my belly. My shoulders were bloody with grazes, the inner sides of my arms sore and twice I had twisted my ankle on a stone in the gloom of night and had fallen over, but was able to get back on my feet again and carry on. A number of times I had thought, half in delirium, that I had got lost in the dark and once I walked straight into a cactus.

Some time after midnight I reached the western side of the island. I didn't care any longer whether the soldiers were still looking for me or not. With my last ounce of strength I re-mounted the motor on to the dinghy and crossed over to our sailing ship where the charter guests were anxiously waiting for me, having had to swim back to the *Orion,* and started bombarding me with questions. I simply ignored them whilst staggering towards the galley, where I grabbed a one-and-a-half-litre bottle of water and almost downed it in one go. "Let's get out of here", I told them when I had recovered my breath again.

At the time I had thought that I could confidently do without experiences of this kind. It had merely been one of the many borderline experiences that had happened to me during my adventurous journeys. Today, however, I strongly believe that, looking back, life is made up of such episodes that are worth telling or writing down. In retrospect I was even grateful to have experienced such situations that, at the time, I would have preferred not to have gone through. A dreary evening in front of the TV is, today, still something I can't even remember a week later. But this incident in Venezuela, twenty years ago, I shall never forget.

Isn't life basically made up of recollections? If one were to pursue this notion, then every single opportunity of being pushed to the limit should be joyfully welcomed. According to that, in future I should be happy about every opportunity where all my physical and intellectual strengths should be expended in order to succeed. It's only the memorable moments that make life unforgettable. To weather a severe storm at sea may be less comfortable than to rest at the poolside drinking a cocktail, but with which of the two options would I feel more alive? The answer is quite clear for me: in the middle of the storm. And what will remain deep in my memory in years to come? My battle against the elements, of course.

A travel agent offering adventure trips once formulated in his promotion slogan very appropriately, "Write down all your possessions and you'll hold a list in your hands. Write down your experiences and they'll tell a story."

My mobile rang. Damn. I would have preferred to continue following these thoughts. It was Rainhard. Of course he had already arrived at our destination for today long ago and had booked beds for both of us, as well as a table for dinner for Heinz, me and himself. I responded very briefly and ended the call as soon as I could. It began to annoy me that Rainhard, even though well meaning, had such an influence on my Camino. I wanted to follow my own path not just walk in his footsteps. Although he was organizing every aspect outstandingly, given all the experience of his four Caminos, I now felt more inclined to decide for myself where I slept, where I had dinner and with whom I sat at the table. So I decided to make a compromise this evening. I had the pilgrim's menu together with Heinz and Rainhard but afterwards joined Omar, Florence, Paula and Johanna from Bulgaria with a bottle of wine. Of course Paula couldn't recall kissing me through a window pane the evening before – which I didn't mind at all.

On this evening I chatted somewhat longer with Johanna from Sofia who was sitting next to me. She was good-looking and a great deal older than Paula. I would have really loved *her* to kiss me – but without a pane of glass between us! Nevertheless I soon retired to bed. I wanted to rid myself of my heartache because of Tatiana and not go through the same pain again – something that would undoubtedly happen if I fell for a pretty girl from Bulgaria and would then have to say good-bye to her for good at the Santiago bus station. So I took myself off to bed at 10 p.m. – and for a good reason: I had a perfidious plan, namely to leave pilgrim brother Rainhard behind and from then on go my own way.

But in order to be able to outwalk the old Camino hero it would take a marathon performance.

Chapter Nineteen

Terradillos de los Templarios – Reliegos

U nfortunately I hardly slept that night and, soaked in sweat, kept twisting and turning in bed. But before dawn Rainhard put an end to both our night's rest by switching on the light. He wanted to have breakfast with me and then set off together. I dawdled around and said that I would follow. I had dreamt of Johanna from Sofia and classified that as a clear and unmistakable sign. Hoping to have breakfast with *her* and walk today's stretch at *her side*, I entered the hostel's cafeteria. But no-one was to be seen except Rainhard and Heinz. Outside it was raining. The sky was dark and hung with clouds. I had tea and some bread and jam. Today it was quite an effort for me to step out into the rain and follow the scallop shell signs. But having said that, there was in fact a good reason to celebrate: today marked my having covered half of the total distance to Santiago de Compostela. This in itself was a reason to be happy, if it hadn't been for the conniving demon in my head that kept reminding me that I still had the other half of the St. James Way in front of me. Quite a horror scenario.

I strapped on my backpack and trudged alongside harvested wheat fields. As always at the beginning of a stretch of the Way my leg muscles were over acidified and my hip ached. My gait had long since ceased to resemble that of a super model on a catwalk. After thirteen kilometres I approached a hotel in the small village of Sahagún. A chalkboard outside offered single rooms for thirty euros inclusive of use of sauna and spa. A very special offer for pilgrims.

The clock had just struck 11 a.m. as I stood at the reception desk like a penniless teenager in front of an Apple store. A time-out for my tired body seemed very tempting. After two weeks of sleeping in 'snor-mitories' just the word 'single room' seemed like an excellent selling point. I tried to barter with the receptionists and get the price reduced to twenty euros, but in vain. For thirty euros I could have stayed overnight six times in a municipal hostel - so I walked on.

In the next hotel I came across I had tea and met Peter from Hungary. At the reception I asked the price for a single room. Forty-five euros. Come again? Disgruntled I continued walking through the rain. What on earth had gone wrong with my life over the past decade? At that time I had paid ten times as much for a family suite at the Venice Hilton without batting an eye and had stayed there for a week.

But then I reflected on yesterday's insight again. Even though my inner demon was yelling out at me until it was hoarse, I realized that the St. James Way would stay in my mind forever as a cherished memory if I didn't give up now – despite all the physical and psychological strains, pain, monotonous pilgrim menus, over-crowded dormitories and the missing privacy. The only thing I can recall now of the expensive trip to Venice was that my ex-wife and I had continuously quarrelled over trivia.

As I continued walking through the Meseta, slowly but steadily feeling better, I asked myself whether I was being really honest with myself or whether I was just trying to search for consolation for my current unfortunate financial situation. Would I really stay overnight in first class hotels if I had sufficient budget available? Such as in a Parador with soft and silky bedding, a lavish spa facility and an over-loaded breakfast buffet? I thought it over and the answer was a defi-nite "no".

The pilgrim community accounted for a large part of the flair of the St. James Way, something that could not be found in the restaurant of a five-star hotel but rather in the communal kitchen of a Camino hostel. During the past seventeen days I had come across lawyers, retired bankers, physicians, entrepreneurs and many others who could have afforded an exclusive hotel but preferred a simple hostel for little money.

Had I felt lacking in energy early that morning, my condition improved with every kilometre I covered from noon onwards. Around three o'clock in the afternoon I arrived at El Burgo Ranero. Rainhard had already called me and explained the way to our hostel. He had told me that at the village entrance I would have to turn left.

I don't *have* to do anything, I thought to myself, and recalled my ambitious plan simply to get away from Rainhard as I no longer intended to let him dictate the route. But for today I was tired of walking. Defiantly I looked for an alternative lodging in my guide-book. Preferably the one where the pretty Bulgarian girl would be staying overnight. But how could I find that out beforehand? I wandered aimlessly through the village and came upon a bar that was advertising a plate of pasta and a carafe of wine for only five euros. This offer was so convincing that I treated myself to it twice.

I had just left the bar when I met Elesio with whom I had walked together on the long shadeless stretch the day before. We greeted each other and I asked after his daughters, who were accompanying him on bicycles. Elesio told me that both of them had already arrived at Reliegos and therefore he would now have to hurry up. "Isn't it a little late for that?" I asked. The distance to Reliegos was roughly 13 kilometres. I asked him from where he had set off that morning. From Terradilla de los Templarios, he told me. Wow! Exactly like me. The only difference was that he was thirty years older.

Full up after two big plates of pasta and also a little tipsy from the wine, I decided to do likewise and hike on to Reliegos. This way I would be able to escape from Rainhard for a while. On top of that I would achieve the marathon distance of my life. At the end of the day I would have covered forty-three kilometres in all. This was noteworthy in as much as that in the past I had enrolled for three marathons: Berlin, Rome and Madrid. However, I never actually ran one of them as in all cases I had to give up the training period after only a short while due to problems with my knee. I was just too heavy for long-distance running.

Or had I just never had enough confidence in my body's ability to manage that kind of distance? For a little over two weeks now I had walked the equivalent of ten marathons in a row. Carrying a backpack. This was proof enough that with the proper willpower one could achieve almost everything, even if I had never dreamt of it before. What were a few bloodstains on my hiking socks compared to this insight?

I accompanied Elesio for the first few kilometres and then let myself fall behind. The seventy-four year old was in admirable physical condition. The last ten kilometres of this record stage led over a gravel track that ran parallel to a main road. It started raining again and after the single-room temptation for thirty euros, I was faced with the day's second true moral test. A Spanish woman of about my age with a child on the rear seat stopped her car beside me and asked which way I was heading.

"To Reliegos" I replied.

"Well, you're lucky. Jump in!"

That's very kind of you indeed, my inner demon said, holding the passenger door open for me.

"*Muchas gracias,* but I prefer walking" I said.

"But it's raining and it's still quite a long way to Reliegos."

She's damn right, amigo, my demon insisted. Apart from that you've hiked enough for today.

"Yes, I know, but I'm a pilgrim and have to walk" I explained.

"Rubbish! I've given lots of pilgrims a lift", the woman behind the steering wheel said.

I hesitated for a moment. The offer was indeed very tempting.

Just climb in, you stubborn idiot!, the voice in my head was ranting.

"It's very kind of you, but I really prefer to walk" I said and turned away.

Nutcase! My inner demon shouted as the woman drove away shaking her head.

"Just shut up!" I replied.

And then the sun came out. I pulled my mobile out of my pocket and took a photo of the rainbow. At that moment I saw that my best pal, Walter, had tried to call me. I called him back and we chatted for a while. Very proud of myself I announced that I had just managed half the total distance. I explained to him that the Way of St. James showed similarities to the first Atlantic crossing on our sailing ship, *Orion*, two decades ago – new, exciting and demanding. Walter wished me good luck for the second half of the Camino.

The conversation with my friend echoed in my head for a while. Walter was probably the most valuable 'scallop shell' on my path of life and I simply don't know where I would be today without him. I had got to know him after my one year sojourn in South America and my subsequent world tour. At the time I was twenty-three years old, worked for a company producing kindergarden equipment, lived with my parents, didn't have a girlfriend, partied with my pals at weekends and dreamt of the great wide world. One night at the Salzburg wheat beer brewery, my other great lifelong friend, Fritz, introduced me to his boss, Walter Daxer. At the time Fritz used to work for the Vienna branch of a Salzburg-based planning bureau for ventilation and heating technology that was managed by Walter.

Walter was a jeans, leather jacket and Timberland boots type of guy, held a well-paid position, had a BMW company car, an Arnold Schwarzenegger chest, a super apartment, was Austrian karate champion and, of course, dated a pretty girlfriend – he thus had everything a young Austrian could dream of.

But Walter dreamt of other things in life. One of his hobbies was sailing. Two weeks previously he had passed the sailing licence exam somewhere along the Adriatic coastline and was planning a world circumnavigation. I would give anything to be able to take part, I had thought at the time. Sailing around the world on the high seas had become my greatest dream – just three minutes ago!

After ordering my next beer I asked Walter on what sort of sailing craft he was going to do the tour, who his crew would be and whether he had planned his route already.

He didn't yet have a sailing boat, he said, but there were enough for sale. He also hadn't chosen a crew as none of his pals seemed neither crazy enough to join him nor had the time. The route would determine itself once he was underway – first going west across the Atlantic Ocean towards the Caribbean.

That certainly sounded like a well thought-out plan, right down to the finest detail. I told him briefly about my various travels and that I admired him for his project – and also envied him a little as I also dreamt of such adventures.

The following words from Walter were to turn my life into a completely new direction. "Well, why don't you simply join me?" he said.

"I beg your pardon? Do you mean … join you to sail around the world?" I stuttered.

"Sure! Two-man sailing is a lot more relaxed anyway because of the watch sequences."

"Great idea! Of course you must join him! It'll be really cool!" my pal Fritz shouted, who had been following our conversation in the noisy pub.

My pulse skyrocketed with euphoria but moments later it descended just as quickly. Sailing round the world was as realistic for me as a flight to the moon. With my office job I was earning just enough money to get by on and all my savings had been devoured by my travels. There were about ten thousand Austrian Shillings left on my current account – today, less than one thousand euros.

"I'd love to come along, but I just don't have the cash", I told him, totally frustrated. "A sailing yacht is anything but cheap and on the way I'd have to live off something."

"Well, the whole plan shouldn't fail because of that", Walter said. "I'll sell my apartment to my father and with the money we can buy a cheap yacht. You'll just owe me half. In the Caribbean we'll offer yacht charter and from the earnings we should be able to live quite well. You can pay me back your half of the cost of the yacht whenever you can."

"Really? Are you sure?" I stammered.

Walter nodded and stretched out his hand. Without further ado I accepted. I hadn't known the guy for more than an hour and had just decided to sail around the world with him. My father was going to be really delighted by his son's carefully considered decision! And likewise my boss and mentor Jeff, when I handed him my resignation the next day and he had to accept that all the training seminars he had funded for me had been for nothing.

At last the church tower of Reliegos came into view. Dusk had already set in. Although I had initially intended to stay overnight in a hostel in the village centre recommended by my travel guide, upon entering Reliegos I took the first one available. I had really just covered forty-three kilometres!

Upon arrival at the hostel I spread out my sleeping bag on my bed, greeted my fellow pilgrims but couldn't make out any familiar faces. The dining room was overcrowded but there, too,

I didn't know anyone. The afternoon's two plates of pasta had to last until breakfast and so I only ordered a beer. I sorted my thoughts and prepared my Facebook-post for the day.

Right now I'm thinking about acquaintances and friendships made on the St. James Way – and in general. Try and imagine the Camino as a train consisting of around thirty carriages. Each carriage represents one stage of the route. At the beginning you enter the last carriage and the train picks up speed. Usually you cover around twenty to twenty-five kilometres per day. The following day you have already been placed in the last but one carriage, as behind yours the new arrivals have been coupled on. The front carriage on the other hand has been un-coupled as its passengers have reached their destination – Santiago. In each carriage there are a few dozen travellers. Until yesterday I was just a little behind the middle part of the train, meaning that by now my fellow passengers and I had got to know each other quite well having come across one another regularly on the route and usually dining, drinking and laughing together in the various hostels in the evening.

Today, however, having set a personal walking record of forty-three kilometres in one stage, I left my carriage during the journey and progressed straight into the carriage in front of me. In my previous carriage I had known everyone and everyone had known me - 'Eddy, the Austrian guy'. Now, in my new carriage, I don't know anyone.

In retrospect I keep asking myself why I did that. Because of my action I had left quite a number of pilgrims behind whom I had got used seeing every

now and then on the track or in a hostel. Furthermore some pilgrims make use of the St. James Way as a kind of dating agency – and more often than not with considerable success. For a new 'single' like myself, having fallen out of love, this was indeed an interesting aspect. Also in my old compartment there had been two or three 'pilgrim sisters', just the sight of whom would have made many a priest protest loudly against the vow of celibacy right in front of the Vatican gates. I had even outrun these ladies today. Something quite new for me as usually it would have been quite the other way around.

There had actually been a reason for my intuitively walking two stages in a row today: because I want to walk and find my own way and someone from this group of pilgrims had begun to determine the way for me. An experienced German pilgrim, actually quite a pleasant guy, had all of a sudden started determining for me the destination target of each day's stage, where to take a rest, where to stay overnight, the inn for eating our pilgrim's menu, the sights and attractions to visit en route and so on.

After having hiked the Camino four times, he could be called the St. James Way Wikipedia.

A perfectionist, with a precisely-timed appointment calendar packed full for each stretch of the Way. I would rather regard myself as belonging to the flock of chaos pilgrims. Just to carry on following him would have been simple and convenient for me, as I wouldn't have had to take care of any organisational matters. But for someone who had come here to go his own way – and to find it – it's painstaking and demoralizing simply to follow somebody else's tracks only because of his greater Camino experience. Even if right now I feel sorry about it because he was nice and had meant well. But as an individual, sometimes one has to choose one's own direction even at the risk of falling flat on one's face – a very important insight in itself, especially for me as father of a twelve-year-old daughter.

I attached a couple of photographs and posted the entry. Then I went to bed. But should I really miss Rainhard and the others, I would only have to slow down my pace a bit over the next couple of days and I would soon be amongst the old crowd again - inside 'my' Camino compartment.

Chapter Twenty

Reliegos – León

After yesterday's marathon stretch, my aim for today was to cover only the twenty-four kilometres to León, the capital of the province. I was hoping to arrive there in the early afternoon so that I would have time for a visit to the cathedral and the city's historic old town. If I hadn't covered the whole distance between El Burgo Raneiro and Reliegos the day before, I would have had to walk a total of thirty-seven kilometres to León and would have arrived too late in the evening for feeling like a sightseeing stroll through the town. That's at least how I was easing my conscience, because walking off on someone had never been my style.

Feeling slightly melancholy I set out on the Camino amongst unfamiliar faces, already beginning to miss the close-knit community that had formed during the first half of the Way. I even got out my mobile phone, called pilgrim brother Rainhard and wished him well for his trek today and asked him about his destination. He said that he wouldn't reach León before tomorrow, and I almost felt rather disappointed about this. Oh my God! We had just behaved like an old married couple.

However, a new pilgrim community did also have its advantages.

I would get to know different people and at the same time have the freedom to make my own decisions.

The description of today's stretch of the route in my guidebook sounded rather sobering. There was mention of "a trail along the left-hand side of the busy N-601 main road" and of industrial and commercial areas. On top of that it had started raining again. I wanted to get this stretch over and done with as quickly as possible and 'switched on' my Santiago turbocharger. This meant a pace of around five kilometres per hour and according to my calculation I would arrive in León at around 1 p.m. The cars which were shooting past me the whole time on the main road would probably reach León within a quarter of an hour.

The stretch between Reliegos and León belonged without doubt to those which many a pilgrim skipped, preferring to use buses for covering the distance – pilgrims who weren't so stupidly stubborn as myself and strictly abided by the rules. Meanwhile I had figured out that my mind was adapting to the environment as a chameleon would to the colours of its surroundings. When hiking in sunshine through an idyllic landscape my thoughts were mostly cheerful. When slogging along through dreary suburbs and industrial areas, however, they darkened like the sky above León at the moment.

Today I just wasn't capable of developing any reasonable ideas. The word 'chameleon' also contained León – the town I was heading for. I'd gained far more significant insights along the Camino than that. But today it just wasn't possible. Instead I thought of the astonishing similarities to my twelfth stage of the St. James Way. It seemed like an eternity since I had set off only six days ago from Agés to the provincial capital of Burgos. With a distance of twenty-four kilometres the stretch had been just as long as today's, it had also rained like today and it felt as if I was walking along the same busy main road, through the same bleak suburbs and industrial and commercial areas. I remembered the cash dispenser that wouldn't spew out any cash, I remembered how I had surfed on a truck stop's computer through my distressing real life and had almost abandoned my pilgrimage. The twelfth stage of the Camino to Burgos had been the most difficult test so far - even if the test had only taken place in my head.

Today, conditions were just as precarious as my mind kept drifting off into the future. How was my life going to continue after the Camino? I had no idea whatsoever, but just one target in mind: Santiago de Compostela. Maybe afterwards I might also walk on to Cape Finisterre – the end of the world.

A totally and very unwelcome thought suddenly crept into my mind. I had been there before. After my wife had left me for another man I had packed my 'Easy Rider' motorcycle's saddlebags and had set off on an Iberian Peninsula road trip. A few days later I stood on the cliffs above Cape Finisterre and, for a moment, seriously thought of jumping. Ten years later I was again on my way to the end of the world.

I can well claim to have experienced quite a lot in my lifetime, more than many considerably older than myself. That after completing my pilgrimage all of my sins would, supposedly, be washed away in Santiago, didn't help the fact that as far as women were concerned I had as little success as with my job and business and my career as an author could quite probably be improved by a spectacular exit – the works of dead authors and artists being more in demand than of those still existing! Furthermore, I would be in the best of family company: my uncle threw himself in front of a train, ten years later my mother followed his example and my grandfather threw himself off the fourth floor of a building.

Such were the thoughts going through my head ten kilometres before reaching León. But I pushed them out of my mind with a loud: "No! Never!"

At this point I had to think of my beloved mother's funeral that had taken place in the church of my home town of Plainfeld near Salzburg. My mother had been a very popular woman in the local community and it seemed that all the town's inhabitants had attended the funeral service. Some of them even had to follow the service outside the church over loudspeakers because there wasn't enough room for everyone inside. Towards the end of the service I stood next to the coffin and addressed my last words to her:

Dear Mum, I'd like to say a few last words to you in my name and on behalf of the family. Words that, on this most devastating day of our lives, can neither easily be found nor spoken. There is still so much that could be said, but because of your sudden tragic death, your decision to leave us behind for good these words unfortunately come too late. But we want you to know that we could need you right now, just as you always needed us. That we admire you as you always admired us. That we love you as you always loved us. And that we are still as proud of you now as you were always proud of us.

You were the mother and the wife that anyone could have hoped for. We could never have wished for a better example than you were for us. You gave us the strength that could have come from no other source. You gave us a love that couldn't be felt more deeply. And you gave us an immense zest for life – which one cannot lose in a more devastating way. You helped us so much – and we couldn't help you.

We want to thank you one last time for everything you did for us in your devoted and loving way. And we ask you to forgive us for not having expressed our gratitude often enough to you during your lifetime. We hope that you can still hear us and all our prayers. We love you and may you rest in eternal peace.

Afterwards I sat down on the church pew where my father embraced me for the first time in my life.

I heard the congregation of mourners including the priest sniffling and swore by all that was holy to me that under no circumstances and no matter how hopeless a situation might seem, would I choose to take the emergency exit.

My thoughts continued to circle around my mother. Was she watching me from above right now and following my life's path?

Was she perhaps the guardian angel who had been accompanying me for so many years? Sadly I hadn't had any chance to say good-bye to her. Her death had come too sudden – at least for me.

I had learned about it whilst driving home. I had at long last just become the owner of one of those mobile phones that were rapidly spreading in popularity but not nearly as smart then as they are nowadays. So it was something special when my mobile rang. Furthermore it was my father who was calling me for the first time on this new number.

"Hello Dad! Good to hear from you. How are you? How's the weather in Austria?", I started chatting away. Silence at the other end of the phone, interrupted only by a sniffle.

"Everything OK, Dad?"

"I'm sorry, I've got some bad news for you", he said with a

monotonous voice. Before this call from my father, when I hadn't begun to jerk in fright at every ring tone which meant a call from my homeland, I would have imagined that it was about nothing in particular. I waved at a friend who happened to be passing, and asked my dad, "What's the matter?"

"Your mother … she's … this morning … she's dead."

"What do you mean – dead?"

"She threw herself in front of a train."

My mobile fell to the ground. I kept on driving along, groping for it, came off the road and – blinded by tears – rammed a dustbin. I would have loved to have smashed the bloody phone but it had obviously rolled underneath my seat. At a bus stop a bus was blocking my way so I raced along a parallel road instead. A car approached me. The driver was hooting and gesticulating, but he couldn't be blamed because I was driving in the wrong direction down a one-way street. I screamed, thumped the dashboard with my fist and drove on so that the guy immediately reversed out of the street and let the crazy idiot pass.

Somehow I made it home without an accident and fell, sobbing, into the arms of my girlfriend at the time. She comforted me and wisely poured everything alcoholic down the drain. But that was the last thing I was in the mood for. I had to function properly. I had to go home. My girlfriend drove me to a travel agency and the following morning we both flew to Salzburg. I was glad to have her support and company at this distressing time. We had been together for more than a year and had been planning to travel to Salzburg in a few weeks so that I could introduce her to my parents. My mother would certainly have liked her. Unfortunately it was too late for that now.

After our arrival in Salzburg I gradually learned the full background details. "Your mother had been suffering from severe depression for months and had even been treated as an in-patient in a mental hospital", one of my aunts told me. "Your mother had tried to take her life once before by taking an overdose of sleeping pills. She was found just in time", one of her friends added in passing.

I could hardly believe what I had heard and began to lose my temper at everyone. I, her eldest son, seemed to be the only one not to have been aware of her depression. No-one – not even my father or my brother or my mother's sister – had thought it necessary to keep me posted on the matter. And my mother herself hadn't done it either. Never had she mentioned anything about her illness in our telephone conversations – she'd probably have felt too embarrassed. I would most probably not have been able to prevent my mother's death, but had I heard of her illness and her first attempt at trying to commit suicide I would have flown to Austria straight away and at least tried to do so. This thought remains with me until the present day.

After the funeral we went to the "Kirchenwirt" inn in Plainfeld where all the mourners were invited to the traditional funeral feast. But after the upsetting final farewell to my mother, the last thing I felt like was socialising. In the overcrowded dining room I sat at a raised table together with the closest relatives, where everyone could stare at us full of pity and utter irrelevant words of consolation and comfort.

The father-in-law of one of my cousins had, mistakenly, also taken a seat at our table even though I had only met him once and he had hardly known my mother. The man drank quite a lot and kept entertaining us with a number of really stupid old man jokes. I mourned my mother and couldn't stand his gossip. I presumably didn't have the confidence then to stop him or I expected someone else to do it – my father or my aunt. But nothing of the sort happened. To this day I deeply regret not having strongly given him a piece of my mind and thrown him out for disrespect, even if I would have caused a scandal.

Three days after the funeral Simone and I met in the evening with some old pals of mine. I had to fly back to Spain the next day but Simone was going to take the train to Hamburg where she was studying medicine at the time. She usually spent her vacations in Spain and from time to time I visited her in Hamburg. She was of Croatian descent on her mother's side with long black hair and a voluptuous figure - a real eye-catcher according to some of my pals.

In the days following my mother's death I had discovered completely new sides to my girlfriend that triggered off hitherto unknown thoughts. An important part of my family had died. Perhaps it was now time to think about founding my own family? Just the way Simone had stood by me during these days, caring for me, comforting me, showing me that I could rely on her in difficult times, singled her out as a potential woman for life and made me seriously contemplate proposing to her some time soon.

Or were my spontaneous marriage intentions merely the desire to find a quick replacement for my mother? I decided first of all to think it over more closely before buying an expensive ring – but as things turned out that wasn't to be the case anyway.

The farewell night with my Austrian pals helped me to switch my thoughts to something completely different. But at the same time it was also a farewell between Simone and myself for a longer period. It wouldn't be until her summer vacation began in three months time that we would see each other again at my home in Andalusia – but fate was to determine that this wouldn't happen either.

Once back home in Spain, I listened to the messages on the answering machine in my diving school. The office had been closed in my absence and quite a few had accumulated. The first message came from a group of Spaniards who wanted to book an organized dive. The second message had been left by the sales representative of a diving equipment supplier who wanted to present the latest catalogue to me. And the third message utterly shocked me. Background noises, heavy breathing and then a quiet, woman's voice. "Eddy? Are you there? I … just wanted to say good… well, it's not important. Bye. And … take care, my son!"

That moment a client came into the diving school. In tears I asked him to leave as we had closed for the day. I listened to the message for a second time, a third and a fourth. For a short while I thought my mother was still alive. Had she been identified at all? And, if yes, by whom? I hadn't asked these questions back in Austria. Maybe the whole thing had been a mistaken identity? Because how else could mum have left me that message?

However, the time display on the device shattered my hopes. My mother had left me that short message the evening prior to her death. Quite obviously she had intended to say good-bye to me and hadn't reached me in the office at night. Why hadn't she tried to get me on my mobile phone? Why didn't she want to live any longer, why, why. Just *WHY*?

The remaining messages ran on but I was hardly listening. Only the last one caught my attention. A friend from Austria had called and asked me to call back immediately although we had only just met two days ago at my farewell party. What could have happened in the meantime that was so important? After I had halfway recovered from the message from beyond, I called him back.

"I've been thinking long and hard about whether I should tell you this or not", my friend started off. "And even now I'm not quite sure. But you're my pal and should know the truth – even though it might hurt you", he added. At long last he managed to speak out and told me that my girlfriend, Simone, had made very obvious advances to him while I had left the room to go and wash my hands and all the others had been engrossed in conversation. She had also slipped him her telephone number under the table, thereby allowing her fingers to stroke his inner thigh in an unmistakable manner, and had invited him to her apartment in Hamburg. He tried to reassure me that, of course, that would have been quite out of the question for him.

I sighed. "Listen, I'm not in the mood for jokes like that right now." I was sure that the story must have been a sick hoax. But he knew, like all of my other friends, what tales were below the belt and what not.

He insisted and assured me that it had happened that way. As proof, he gave me her correct phone number. How the hell would he have had her number if it hadn't come from her? I still didn't want to believe it. I cut the line and dialled Simone's number. She didn't even try to deny what had happened and admitted that she had simply found my friend "rather cute".

Never before had I been so wrong about anyone. And so now I had lost my mother and my girlfriend within the same week.

One year after my mother's death, by the way, my father found a new partner. He met Anneliese, also widowed, in fact by a similar tragic circumstance. She and her husband had been attending a family party. There it had come to an argument that had escalated.

In the end, the host had taken a shotgun out of an adjoining room and shot Anneliese's husband right in front of her eyes. He had wanted to kill her too, but he missed and she escaped.

I was happy for my father and Anneliese that fate had been kind to them – and in the meantime for many years now. Furthermore, through this liaison my close family circle has increased from Anneliese's side by three delightful half-brothers and sisters together with their own charming relatives. This book is in fact dedicated to the wonderful Pongratz family.

Wishing me a *"buen Camino"* a small grey-haired woman pilgrim overtook me. Whilst deep in thought about my family's history, I hadn't noticed that I had fallen back to a snail's pace over the past two kilometres. Originally I had wanted to concentrate only on positive thoughts on my way to León - despite the dreary countryside. On top of that I wanted to be smarter this time than on the stretch to Burgos. I still had a little over one hundred euros in my pocket, so there was no need to be afraid of the local cash dispenser and I would be careful not to enter an Internet café in León.

Since I couldn't think of anything positive I delved into my "time-travel database" and searched for memories – preferably St. James' Way 'scallop shells' that had had an impact on my journey through life. I decided to continue with my flashbacks where I had left off yesterday when I arrived at the hostel and began calling to mind some of the episodes of my first sailing trip, which I hoped would put me in a better mood.

As feared, my parents as well as my boss hadn't been exactly enthusiastic about my wanting to leave everything behind to sail around the world with someone I had only met in a pub the night before. Especially since I didn't have any money and my nautical knowledge was limited to surfboards and rubber dinghies on the picturesque lakes of the Austrian Salzkammergut near Salzburg. But the tour was a done deal and I had got so excited that I hardly slept through the following nights.

I acquired stacks of nautical literature and books about circumnavigating the world and, in the period before we set sail, dreamt of desert islands and lonely South Sea atolls. As we had agreed, Walter went ahead and sold his flat to his father, the proceeds of which formed our budget for purchasing our sailing boat. We combed through the classified ads in various water sports magazines as, although the Internet had already been invented, it would actually be years before either of us were to become acquainted with it. Thus the search turned out to be a time-consuming and costly process. One weekend we drove to Northern Italy in order to look for sailing yachts for sale around the local marinas, but all we could find were 'plastic bowls'. However, what we had in mind was a robust steel-hulled ship, an indestructible vessel in which we could defy violent storms, hazardous reefs, collisions, pirates and other perils. We discovered exactly such a boat a little later in a rather small advertisement.

She belonged to a German and was located close to Empuriabrava, a tourist town north of Barcelona. The yacht, with the name *Orion*, was twelve metres – or just over thirty-nine feet – long, and had two masts. The selling price was eighty thousand Deutschmarks. It was a bargain and just within the limits of our financial means. There was no further information on the boat other than in the four-lined advert. Not even a photograph. Nevertheless we set out for Northern Spain. We met the seller who presented his 'unsinkable sailing ship' to us. This attribute was pretty hard to check as the yacht sat in dry dock. She had a red hull, a white deck and black masts that were secured on deck with an unusually large number of strong wire ropes, the so-called shrouds and stays. The sails were dirty and frayed, but at least not porous. The ship's interior needed spring-cleaning, but, more importantly, the hull seemed to be in order – at any rate a hollow 'clonk' resounded as we hammered on to it with our fists from the outside.

It was love at first sight. The seller must have noticed this as he made no attempt to go down in price – not even one Deutschmark. An hour later we had signed the contract and made a down payment. As proud owners of a yacht we entered the first harbour pub we came across and celebrated the purchase of our *Orion*, with which we were going to sail and conquer the seven seas. Walter Daxer and Eduard Freundlinger would go down in the history of seafaring and their names added to those of Christopher Columbus, Ferdinand Magellan, Captain Cook and other discoverers – so much was sure.

Reality, however, looked somewhat different. Six weeks later, the preparations were completed. We had given the *Orion* a new coat of paint and lovingly got her into shape. We had said goodbye to our friends with a roaring farewell party, and now there was no turning back.

The first trip with our own sailing yacht took us to the neighbouring village of Rosas, where a crane was to lift the boat out of the water for a last and final repair to its hull. Two friends of ours, Roland and Manfred, were going to join us for a week. In addition we had Wolfgang on board, a charter guest, who had paid for the trip across the Atlantic. Together we raised a toast with a glass of *Cava* Spanish sparkling wine and then chugged by engine out of the port. Right in front of the harbour wall we turned to 'port', which on a ship means 'left', of course. I had at least already picked up that much theoretical seafaring knowledge. We had to struggle against a light current and low waves that rolled in from the direction we wanted to steer into.

Unfortunately we only made progress for roughly one nautical mile – and that was it! Could it be that our engine was too weak? According to the former owner it was an old but extremely robust tractor engine, but this part pounding away down in the ship's belly could not have much power if we didn't even manage to beat a light current. We had no choice but to reverse and manoeuvre back into the safe harbour.

As soon as we had turned around, we picked up speed again. What we hadn't known at the time was that the propulsion had only been driven by the current. The ship's propeller had long since come to a standstill as there was something defective in the gearbox. When we came around the bend of the harbour entrance, the drama began to unfold. The current pushed *Orion* towards the breakwaters at the harbour entrance. We were only a few metres short of our boat being smashed to pieces. I stood on the forecastle and turned to Walter at the helm. Hadn't he claimed to hold a sailing licence? Gesticulating frantically I pointed towards the harbour entrance, but the skipper just made a what-shall-I-do-gesture and steered us straight into doom.

I shall never forget the sound of the first impact. The *Orion* was hurled up by the waves on to a wall of stone blocks. The ship's masts were lashing out threatening to strike the people dead who were hurrying to our aid. As soon as one wave had receded, our sixteen-ton 'barge' slid down the breaker until it was hurled up by the next one. No ship could withstand such battering. One member of the crew jumped into the cabin to rescue our passports and money.

I clutched the mast and thought of the embarrassment that would await me back home. Our plan to circumnavigate the globe had been announced in three Salzburg local papers. Everybody was aware of our daredevil venture. And now the *Orion* was about to sink after not even half an hour. I could imagine the headlines: *Salzburg based adventurers Walter Daxer and Eduard Freundlinger capsize and drown during their circumnavigation – while exiting their first harbour!*

"Eddy! Come on! Give me a hand! Quick!" Roland ripped me out of my day's nightmare. He had some years of sailing experience and bellowed commands that got me out of my lethargy. Luckily he seemed to have a plan how to rescue our ship. At the bow the anchor was lowered into the water and a long rope was attached to the stern. Manfred and I rowed with the rope end in a dinghy towards the opposite side of the harbour entrance where a helpful German was already waiting with his camper van. Hectically we tied the rope to the trailer coupling and the man jumped into his camper.

It was, after all, quite a dangerous undertaking as our twisting and rolling ship was certainly four times as heavy as the camper van and could have pulled it over the pier into the harbour basin. But we were lucky this time. The camper accelerated gradually, tightening the rope and slowly pulling the *Orion*'s stern away from the breakers. Our ship was now stuck between the anchor at the bow and the rope at the stern and blocked the entire entrance of the port of Empuriabrava. At least the *Orion* was still afloat – which seemed a miracle after she had been hurled against the rough breakers for around twenty minutes.

In the afternoon our damaged craft was towed to the marina of Rosas by the Red Cross. There the seemingly competent junior manager of a shipyard, who had studied shipbuilding in Germany, came on board. Fortunately, the ship's hull was only dented and scratched in some places. Gosh, this boat can take quite something, I thought. A yacht made of synthetic material would certainly not have survived. We asked about the estimated costs of the hull repair. The junior manager replied that it wouldn't cost a lot. "Great!" we said. "Will it take long? We're planning a circumnavigation and have no time to lose." The expert's expression was difficult to interpret – either he found this bundled naivety pitiful or he was simply trying to refrain from laughing.

There was, however, a small problem, he eventually said. Problem? What kind of problem? With his index finger "Mr. Boatbuilder" traced a circle around an imaginary globe and said that in the state our so-called yacht was in we could forget our project. Then he drew a circle on the ground with his foot and told us that at best we could make a round trip of the harbour basin with the *Orion*. But even then he would, for safety reasons, prefer to leave the ship first.

Slowly but surely this guy became increasingly disagreeable. Walter repeated the orbital movement around the globe and asked "Mr. Shipbuilder", whose intention was undoubtedly to squeeze as much money out of us as possible, what needed to be done for us to be able to carry out our plans with the *Orion*.

Just a few things, the man said, and listed the following: for example, a new engine, new on-board electrical system, new batteries, a new autopilot and a few more important bits and pieces.

Walter and I looked at each other and swallowed hard.

"And what do you think would be the cost of all that?" we asked in unison. "Come to my office this afternoon", he said, already rubbing his hands together with glee in his mind.

When we arrived at his office some time later, we were already fearing the worst and were not disappointed. The junior manager pushed a multi-paged cost estimate over the table and assured us that the work was absolutely necessary – even vital if we were to cross the Atlantic. Anything else would be grossly negligent.

We nodded somewhat vaguely and ran through the quote to the last page. I stared at the total amount: 7,254,178.00 Pesetas. With trembling fingers I pulled the cut-throat's pocket calculator over to me and converted the amount into Austrian Shillings.

"What? But ... but ... that is more than we paid for the whole ship!" I blurted out.

"I'll bet it is", replied the shipyard upstart, who even spoke fluent German. "It's only the ship's hull that's any good, everything else is, please forgive the expression, scrap!"

With the quote in our hands we two prematurely shipwrecked sailors returned to the *Orion*. We had only just bought her and now our queen of the seas had to be completely overhauled. And this fact now raised a series of problems for us. Firstly, we didn't have enough money, secondly we had already taken a considerable number of reservations for charter trips in the Caribbean and had long since invested the respective advance payments in the ship. This meant that we *had* to sail to the Caribbean. And thirdly, we also had Wolfgang, the charter guest, on board who had paid a large amount of money for the passage across the Atlantic via Gibraltar and the Canary Islands. In spite of this fact he had so far helped us with all maintenance work and had even climbed the masts to paint them. Wolfgang was thirty years older than me and was a friend of my ex-boss. Now he wanted to know how we were going to carry on.

"Unfortunately, not at all! That is to say, we actually have a small problem", Walter said and explained the delicate situation to him. The *Orion* was not seaworthy and we didn't have the money to get her refitted.

Wolfgang stroked his grey beard and shook his head. "Then I guess there's no other option for me than to get off here, boys. When will I get my money back?"

"Well... hmm ...", Walter started.

"You've already spent it?" our charter guest concluded sharply.

Walter and I nodded sheepishly. "As I said, at the moment we are faced with a small problem", Walter said meekly.

"You call that a *small problem*? I'd call it *cheating*, my friend. I paid twenty thousand Austrian Shillings for this trip. For that I had to work on board like a galley slave and already during our first rather short trip we almost drowned. Now it turns out that you bought a rusty wreck, on which nothing works at all, the voyage is over before it has even started and you can't pay my money back. I must say, you've really got a nerve! Both of you!"

"Just a moment, please", I tried to turn on diplomacy and charm. "Of course we're terribly sorry, but we couldn't have known in advance. You seem to be a nice guy and we really don't want to disappoint you. Besides, the trip doesn't have to end before it has started. Maybe ... if you could ... put up the money ... well ... in advance ..."

"Then am *I* supposed to lend *you* the cash?", Wolfgang rasped, pounding his chest with the index finger.

"You'll get it back", I tried to assure him.

"I should think so. Including interest", Walter agreed.

Lost in memories, I had meanwhile reached the town walls of León. My 'pilgrim manager', Rainhard, seemed to have got lost and so I had to take care of my accommodation for the night myself. My clever little guidebook had an insider's tip at hand. In the catholic students' hall of residence 'Hermanas Trinitarias' single rooms were available at a "very favourable price/quality ratio".

Since the pilgrim community in large towns was scattered anyway, I decided to indulge in this luxury for once. The friendly nun at the reception quoted me a price of fifteen euros, breakfast included. Then she inspected me from top to toe through her horn-rimmed, pebble-lensed glasses and lowered the price to twelve euros. Without any bargaining. I must have looked a pitiful sight. Then she showed me the room. Eight square metres of sheer luxury. A single room with an *ensuite* bathroom. Compared with my previous lodgings, it looked like a "pilgrim's business upgrade" almost like a high-class hotel.

"Will you be staying for one or two nights?"

Good question. Once again I had to consult my inner demon first. But he was already jumping and dancing around with joy like a cheerleader at the Super Bowl. He stretched out his hand holding twenty-four euros to the nun and was just about to kiss her lips when I intervened.

"I'll think about it", I replied.

Are you completely insane?, my demon raged at me.

We've been hiking on our pilgrimage for five hundred kilometres now and urgently need a day's rest in the comfort of this room. Recharging batteries and licking our wounds. And besides, that pretty pilgrim sister, Johanna, from Bulgaria could catch up with you. If I'm not mistaken, during the last evening meal together she seemed to idolize you as if you were a direct descendant of the Apostle James himself.

"I'll think about it", I repeated, ignoring my demon. I applied some first-aid to my feet and rested for a while. Then I went out and drifted around the town. According to my travel guide the 'most beautiful cathedral in Spain' was worth looking at indeed, but the admission fee was expensive and on top of that it was so full of noisy tourists that no inner reflection was possible.

The historical town centre was interesting, but the crowds of people in front of rowdy pubs and the dense traffic were hindering me from making progress. I got jostled at, picked on and stared at and, dressed in my pilgrim's gear, felt like a foreign body amongst the chic, well-dressed passers-by and business people and one which the town wanted to spit out again as quickly as possible. Since on the Camino one hiked from one idyllic village with a couple of hundred inhabitants to the next, I was simply unable to cope with the noisy city. I couldn't even make it to dinner. In order to compensate for the higher costs of accommodation, I had to save on food. At a quarter past nine at night I went into a kebab kiosk and ordered a falafel menu with French fries and a Coca Cola for four euros ninety. In front of me, however, a group of young people had ordered the full kebab menu, so that at ten o'clock my falafel wasn't even in preparation. As the gates of my hostel closed at ten sharp, I had to leave with an empty stomach.

Back in the student's hall I explained to the nun that I could only stay for one night. My inner demon broke into a tirade of insults. I stuffed imaginary plugs into my ears and ignored him. Another day in León would only unnecessarily lead the very special flow of energy connecting body, mind and soul, which I was fortunate to experience on the Camino, against an obstacle, behind which turbulence was awaiting.

With the certainty of having made the right decision, I fell asleep.

Chapter Twenty-One

León - Villavante

At six o'clock in the morning I woke up and felt as fit as I hadn't felt in a long time. Breakfast was plentiful. There was bread and jam and even muesli. Before seven o'clock I was ready to tackle the thirty-one kilometres of the next long stage. In front of the hostel I clutched my hiking poles like a skiing ace did with his ski poles in the start hut before the notorious Kitzbühel "Hahnenkamm" downhill race. I almost ran out of León and didn't stop at all until after roughly nine kilometres. This was where a decision had to be made.

The main track lead straight ahead and, like yesterday, along a very busy main road for its entire length. My guidebook hit the nail on its head when it said: *this route is only recommended for masochists, hardcore car enthusiasts and people who want to atone for particularly great sins on the Way of St. James.*

To the left, on the other hand, a much nicer path led over the vast expanse of Castilian fields, over farmland, meadows, maize fields, autumnal forests and alongside an idyllic stream. More than ninety percent of the pilgrims walked along the roaring main road as, according to the guidebook, it was three point four kilometres shorter. I cast a quick glance at my inner demon, who would surely have followed the crowd, but because of yesterday he huddled sulkily in the farthest corner of my consciousness.

"Ah, kiss my ass", he was growling. "Ever since we started this crazy pilgrimage, you haven't been listening to me any more. What's more I was against it from the very beginning. There's no way you're going to find out anything here. In this goddamn wasteland? I could laugh my head off. Ever heard of Google and Amazon? *There* you can find everything!"

I ignored his idle chatter and set off on the longer but more appealing path in my best mood, because today I had achieved another important insight – and that at an early hour.

I had literally run away from pilgrim brother Rainhard because he had increasingly tried to determine my route. Yesterday and today, however, I had become aware that there was indeed another pilgrim brother, whose intention was also to show me the way. But I could never run away from this one, not even if I walked a hundred kilometres a day. He was with me all the time, had been even before the pilgrimage, and he would still be with me after it: my inner demon. It was only on the Camino that I became fully aware of his existence – perhaps because I had to fight against him several times a day, and he could be a real heavyweight champion indeed.

At home, unfortunately, I had all too often given up without a fight. "All right, if you say so", I had thought or: "OK, let's do it your way". I regretted much of what I had done for his sake, and regretted some of what I had *not* done because of him. Now I regretted having listened to him so many times. My demon had become so present during the past days that today I even gave him a name: Amancio Vázquez. That was the name of the villain in my third crime novel, *Im Schatten der Alhambra* (In the Shadow of the Alhambra). I thought this was particularly appropriate.

My demon villain, Amancio, had a thousand faces. Sometimes he would manifest himself as a public bus and whisper "Get on!" into my ears, at other times he took on the form of a cash dispenser in front of which he would ask me "Well, come on, draw out some large bills and treat yourself to something decent", or he appeared as a menu bearing the image of a juicy one-and-three-quarter-pound steak. And these were just his Camino faces.

However, he would have to come up with something quite new after my return, in order to dissuade me from taking the right path. After all, a car owner wouldn't be tempted by a public bus, and after my separation from Tatiana, a single room would become such a depressing reality that I would sooner rather than later be longing for a dozen snoring pilgrims.

"But I have got to know you well on this journey, Amigo Amancio Vázquez, and whatever form you are going to assume in the future, I shall recognize you", I said in a low voice. "Let one thing be clear to you: you might continue accompanying me all my life, but you'll no longer lead me and certainly not determine my life's path. From now on I'm the boss here, and you'll get a muzzle and in future will trot along on a short leash behind me, understood?"

If, on the previous day, walking between industrial districts and commercial zones, I had thought that it would suit the dramaturgy of my life if I were to throw myself off Cape Finisterre, today, in this fascinating expanse of land, I experienced a feeling of such elation that I would have liked to have screamed out with happiness. Was that normal? How would a psychologist diagnose my reaction? I couldn't care less.

Whatever, I would stay away from psychologists for the rest of my life anyway. The psychotherapist hadn't been able to help my mother, even at the time when she had needed help and support the most. To crown it all, after mother had taken her own life the good woman presented our mourning family with a horrendous bill for her services, which included fees for pre-arranged appointments that mother had been unable to attend as they had been made before her death. Thereupon I had sent an extremely angry letter of complaint to the practice.

Today I felt an enormous inner energy and an unshakeable self-confidence, just as I had felt during my years sailing on board the *Orion* when Walter and I were bursting with euphoria and testosterone because of our mutual adventures. Nothing could have harmed us. We felt invincible and regarded our ship as being unsinkable. In some situations, however, we had just had pure luck. For example with our charter guest, Wolfgang. He had in fact agreed to lend us the considerable amount of money we needed to bring the *Orion* technically up to date and to provide her with a new engine. After that, our adventure could finally begin.

Two years later we had paid off the loan including interest, and today Wolfgang is still one of the people I admire – even though we had quite a few quarrels whilst on board and often had very differing opinions.

Our interim destination at that time had been the Caribbean island of Grenada, where we had to arrive on a set day and time as the first charter guests would be ready and waiting for us there. So there was no time to waste. For the whole way along the Spanish coastline we were almost continually becalmed and so we had to head south using our new engine. The dangers, however, were awaiting us ashore. In a bar in Torrevieja, Skipper Walter fell desperately in love with a Swedish model, an affair which would subsequently result in dozens of love letters, expensive telephone calls and trips to Scandinavia. In the port of Marina del Este close to Almuñécar in southern Spain we had to wait for a long time for a spare part. This idyllic stretch of the coast appealed to us as it had not yet been affected by mass tourism. At that time we had no idea that four years later we would set up a diving school there.

The fact that we were still alive at all was thanks to Neptune, the god of the sea, who, during those days, had to put in a lot of overtime because of us – inexperienced goons. One example was in the Straits of Gibraltar: we had set sail early in the morning and had passed the straits by nightfall. We set course for Grand Canary. It was actually the first time since our departure from Rosas that we had set full sail and were so far away from land that all we could see around us was water.

Walter assigned the night watches. I was on from midnight until half past two in the morning, during which time my duty was to look out for other vessels crossing our course and keep an eye on the position of the sails. Aye, aye, Captain. In the meantime I was quite aware, of course, that a ship at night had a green navigation light on her starboard side and a red light on her port side, so that one could easily detect the course of other vessels and vice versa. So much for the theory.

In practice, however, during my watch heavy sea fog began to set in so that I could hardly detect the position lights on our own vessel. And the *Orion* was not equipped with a radar system. On the other hand there was this new autopilot that was steering the ship without any intervention from my side. While the *Orion* sailed on as if participating in the America's Cup, I began to get rather sleepy. In Gibraltar we had moored side by side with the luxury yacht of the McDonald's licence holder for the whole of Rome, on to which we had invited ourselves and celebrated well into the early hours.

A repeated, muffled tooting woke me up from my doze. What was that? Mesmerised I peered into the pea soup fog in front of our bow, but couldn't see anything. For safety reasons, I switched off the autopilot and took over control of the helm myself. Seconds later there was the sound again and this time seemed more penetrating and closer. Slowly but surely the situation was becoming too much for me. What was I supposed to do? Blow our horn in greeting in return? Wake up the skipper? Change course?

Just as I started seriously considering this last option, the decision became urgent. All of a sudden and out of nowhere a giant wall arose about fifty metres in front of the *Orion*. A tanker of such vast proportions that at first glance I couldn't detect which was bow and which was stern. Then I saw lights and a spotlight. The monster was crossing our course from starboard to port. As there is no brake pedal on a ship, I wrenched the rudder around all the way to starboard. The sails slammed to the other side and the ship's hull was now rolling parallel towards the monster vessel.

The *Orion* was hurled about by the metre-high waves that the tanker's wash was generating. We continued to drift towards the giant vessel, but at some point her stern rolled past the *Orion's* bow with a last angry blast of her horn and without any collision. Walter dashed up on deck. My whole body was trembling. Even our *Orion* would never have withstood a collision with a super tanker at full speed.

Walter took over my watch and sent me off to get some sleep.

But the night was not over yet. It had a much tougher test for us in store.

Still in shock I lay down in my bunk. Because of my nautical incompetence I felt lousy, after all I had just put my life – and Walter's and Wolfgang's at the same time – at risk. Before, while we were both on deck, the skipper had explained to me – unfortunately a little too late – what the first signal sent out by the tanker had meant: "We alert you to your obligation to give way and change course to starboard." Had I known this earlier we wouldn't have got into this precarious situation in the first place. Full of shame and distress I finally fell asleep.

It felt like only five minutes later that I was suddenly awoken by Walter shouting the alarming words: "Quick! All hands on deck! Our lives are in danger!"

Was I dreaming? Apparently not, particularly since I felt as if I was on the back of a bucking rodeo horse. As I followed Walter through the ship's cabin I kept stepping on crockery, books, clothes and other stuff scattered around on the floor. As a young boy I had once climbed into a water butt. My cousin had given it a kick and I had rolled down a hill in it, long before the guys from *Jackass* were born.

Right now I felt just as helpless. I fell down twice before I was able to climb on deck.

Walter had not exaggerated at all. Was this a hurricane? As far as I could make out in the moonlight, waves as high as the mizzen mast were towering up around our ship which suddenly seemed so tiny. Walter yelled commands at Wolfgang and myself which I could hardly understand because of the waves and the roaring wind. Luckily I had no time to get frightened. To have been washed overboard would have meant certain death. We buckled on our safety straps and struggled on to the forecastle. It was necessary to take in the full set of sails and to hoist a small storm sail. Meanwhile the waves rolling in from behind lifted the *Orion* as if she was made of paper. Then we surfed down from the crests into the trough causing a spine-chilling noise as we were exceeding the nominal hull speed. Somehow we had to slow the ship down and at the same time keep our course under all circumstances. By no means should we get alongside the waves, as this way we would be washed over by their first strike and topple over on to our side, the next wave would then push the masts under water and the third would have finished us off.

After a flash of genius from our skipper, we fished out two long ropes from the locker, fastened them to the cleats and tied two big pasta cooking pots to their ends before throwing them into the sea. The ropes and the pots actually slowed down the *Orion*, but the danger had not yet been averted.

The storm continued for four days during which we fought the elements for our lives and neither slept nor ate. For the first time the *Orion* had to prove her seaworthiness. The pressure on the rudder was immense. If the cable on the steering gear should rip, we would be completely and utterly at the mercy of the waves.

On the fifth day the storm abated somewhat and the day after we reached the port of Grand Canary. We had been scared to death, but we had made it. At least for the time being. After all, a twenty-five-day crossing from Grand Canary to the Caribbean lay ahead of us. During those stormy days and nights I had at any rate learned how to sail. I had felt like a learner driver who was participating in the Paris to Dakar rally. Those were the first nautical miles I had ever sailed, of which thousands more were to follow in the years to come – but I was never to experience such a storm again.

The port authorities allocated us a berth alongside the luxury yacht whose crew we had already got to know in Gibraltar. These guys had waited for the storm to pass and had then managed to race over to Grand Canary in only two days. They had been worried about us and so a big cheer went up from the crew while we were mooring our *Orion* next to them. And so instead of first taking a rest after four sleepless nights, that morning we climbed aboard the neighbouring ship for just a drink. Once on board we partied with our crew chums until the afternoon of the following day, before I finally fell into a sixteen-hour comatose sleep.

It was actually quite unbelievable what I had withstood at the time, I thought, as the church of the village of Villavante came into sight. My jump into the sailing deep end back then in the Atlantic Ocean had been quite indicative, if not typical for my life. No long drawn out test phases, hesitation or wavering – just go for it! Therefore in keeping with this philosophy I hadn't learned to sail in the calm of inland waters, but during a howling gale whilst crossing the Atlantic. I had successfully completed my diving teacher's certificate but instead of subsequently working for a diving school and gathering experience there, together with Walter, I just bought a diving school upon our return from the Caribbean. With regard to my real estate business and writing novels things had been more or less the same. Instead of first trying a short story, I had written a four-hundred-page novel. And for my first longer hike I hadn't planned just a weekend tour, but a whole month on the Way of St. James.

At three o'clock in the afternoon I checked into the hostel. Almost thirty-five kilometres lay behind me, and I didn't even feel tired. Slowly but steadily my body had grown accustomed to the daily foot march. After I had taken care of my 'work', consisting of laundry, writing a blog entry and bringing my diary up to date and had enjoyed a refreshing shower, Amancio Vázquez wanted his voice to be heard. He suggested that after such a long trek he felt like a chilled beer.

How nice to be able to see eye to eye with one's inner demon for once. *Vamos*, let's go, Amancio!

Chapter Twenty-Two

Villavante – Astorga

Today a stretch of twenty-five kilometres to Astorga lay ahead of me. According to my guidebook this town has been a significant stopover on the St. James Way since the Middle Ages being the intersection of the *Camino Francés* and the St. James Way track coming from Seville, the *Vía de la Plata*.

I got caught unawares by chill in the air outside the hostel. The sunrise was taking its time and my fingers started getting cold. As I had no gloves with me I put my second pair of socks over my hands and walked five kilometres on gravel tracks to the village of Hospital de Órbigo, where, over breakfast, I wanted to wait until it warmed up. To mark the occasion – I had meanwhile reached the last third of the Camino – I ordered three fried eggs on toast. I sat at a table overlooking the spectacular Roman bridge two hundred metres long. If one were to build this bridge today, it wouldn't need to be more than five metres long: the trickle of water now running beneath it wasn't any wider.

The trail now led through picturesque landscape. I took photos of trees with magnificent crowns of yellow and orange leaves, of cotton-wool clouds over the vastness of the Castillian countryside, and of a cross on a hill in front of which a grey bearded pilgrim knelt and prayed. I followed his example and was surprised that I still actually remembered the Lord's Prayer. Afterwards I just took in the wonderful view before walking off on the last few kilometres to Astorga, unaware, however, that there the emotional low point of the whole journey would be awaiting me but that at the same time a very important person would enter my life.

About an hour later I arrived at the municipal hostel, which was managed by German pilgrim friends who did not speak any Spanish. At the reception I had to translate for a group of Spaniards who afterwards complained that the Camino had obviously become so international that they could hardly get on in their mother tongue.

The hostel had a large communal kitchen and I planned to take advantage of it that evening as I was eager to be able to prepare food myself at last. In my room I met a guy from Lithuania whom I had already come across the week before. He could hardly walk any more. This tall man had walked over forty kilometres a day on each of the last stretches he had covered, in the course of which he had contracted a carpal tunnel syndrome on his left leg. Because of this inflammation he had already been stuck in the hostel for two days and hadn't even been able to do any sightseeing. He believed his pilgrimage was probably over. I felt sorry for him.

The friendly woman at the reception desk pointed out to me the way to a well-stocked supermarket and gave me a map of the town. I drifted through the streets and passed a shop specializing in pilgrimage equipment, where I had a look for a rain poncho and a pair of gloves. The poncho seemed to be of good quality, but cost fifty euros. No way! I would manage the last third of my pilgrimage without any waterproof covering. The cheapest gloves were fifteen euros a pair, but even that was too much for my budget. Over the next few days the route would lead me through mountains again, where temperatures could be around freezing early in the mornings, but my socks converted into gloves would have to suffice.

I strolled on further to the town hall square where the supermarket was also located. In front of an inn a billboard advertised a large beer for the price of three euros. I could abstain from a rain cover and gloves, but certainly not from a cold beer at the end of this long stretch. On the other hand two beers in this tavern would cost more than a night in the local hostel.

Luckily the supermarket had a display counter for refrigerated drinks. I bought two half-litre cans of beer for one Euro each, was quite pleased with having saved four euros and sat down with my purchase on a park bench next to the inn. A passer-by gave me a rather scornful look. I pulled my Camino scallop shell out of my pocket and hung it around my neck. Now everyone would recognise me as a pilgrim rather than a down-and-out – for which I could have easily been taken given my beard, my uncombed hair, slouch hat and the beer can in my hand.

I then got out my mobile phone and was pleased to be able to get hold of my father at last. At an earlier stage on the Camino I had asked him to walk the last hundred kilometres with me from Sarria to Santiago. Unfortunately I hadn't heard from him since then. My father played golf almost every day and was fitter than most of the other men on the St. James Way. A hike of a hundred kilometres would not have caused him any problems and being retired he could have easily made time for it. Unfortunately he turned me down, which I thought was a pity. I tried to understand his reasoning but was still disappointed and even sad. Then the conversation turned to me. My father asked me what I intended to do after the Camino.

"No idea", I responded truthfully. Obviously that was not the kind of answer a concerned father would wish to get from his son. Therefore he got straight to the point. My father spoke plainly and directly and addressed the problems which I was trying to run away from on my St. James Way pilgrimage. After half an hour the call was over. I wiped the tears from my face, drank my beer and bought two new cans in the supermarket.

I had to admit to myself that my father was right. I had arrived at the lowest point in my life and had absolutely no idea how to proceed. But not like this, anyway. Also the strain of the continual roller-coaster ride of emotions on the Camino was telling on me. Many a time I had had tears rolling down my cheeks whilst hiking the Way, as had been the case just a couple of minutes ago for everyone to see. At the end of our conversation my father had told me that because of my hopeless situation with no prospect of improvement he would have many sleepless nights in future. Quite obviously I had disappointed him so much and I felt very ashamed. I drank half the fourth can of beer and threw it into the waste bin.

In Astorga there was an impressive cathedral to visit as well as the Episcopal Palace built by Gaudí in neo-Gothic style which also housed a museum, dedicated to the Camino. Maybe some culture would set my mind at rest. Feeling somewhat tipsy after four beers, I entered the cathedral and strolled down its central nave, lit a candle without throwing the required Euro into the slot and took a photo. A young priest approached me. Quickly I put away my mobile phone. Maybe it was not permitted to take photographs? Or had he observed my candle theft? But the clergyman just wanted to talk. After I had told him about my journey so far, he described the cathedral's history. Even though at the time of its construction Astorga had had only two thousand inhabitants, it had taken three hundred years to build this monumental church. I became so overwhelmed with emotion, that tears welled up in my eyes again. The priest noticed it and I mumbled something about 'problemas personales'. He said a few comforting words and embraced me, which made me cry even more bitterly.

Ashamed of myself, I stumbled out of the cathedral and almost bumped into pilgrim brother Rainhard. Where had he come from all of a sudden? It didn't matter. In fact, although I had run away from him only three days ago, I was now immensely happy to see him. He was eager to know whether I had already visited the Bishop's Palace and once again immediately took over his role as my personal Camino guide. Together we visited the bishop's residence that, according to Rainhard, had actually never been one. The reason being that upon first entering the palace, the new bishop at the time had instantly taken dislike to the elaborate architecture and fled the building.

During the sightseeing tour I made some calculations about distances. Even though I was still a little woozy, I always came to the same conclusion: under normal circumstances Rainhard could never have been able to catch up with me by the time I reached Astorga. The last stretches I had covered had been far too long −

unless the good man had been longing for my companionship so much that he had cheated a little and taken the bus for twenty kilometres or so. However, I was rather pleased with our reunion, even more so as he paid for the beer after our cultural programme. Another beer?

"*Buena idea, amigo!*"

It felt good to pour my heart out to Rainhard. As it turned out, not only did he have good advice for the Way of St. James, but also for other situations in life. Naturally just one beer hadn't been enough to celebrate our reunion, so it was nightfall before I staggered back to my lodging feeling as if I had spent the entire day at the Munich Oktoberfest. Rainhard was staying overnight in a different hostel, but we agreed to meet the following day at our destination, the village of Foncebadón.

I unpacked the contents of my supermarket bag in the kitchen. Inside were a family pack of pasta, two different pasta sauces, three bars of chocolate, and two bottles of wine. Out of sheer frustration, I had decided to scoff off all of it tonight. Inside the kitchen as well as in the common room it was rush hour and I had to wait for a free saucepan. When one finally became available, I prepared my spaghetti in double quick time. Ludovica, a bespectacled, brunette Italian girl standing in front of the neighbouring pan, stared at my ready-made sauce and with a shake of her head uttered, "*mamma mia!*" As there were no other pots free in which I could have heated up both my sauces, I had just mixed part of the hot pasta with cold green pesto and the other half with cold tomato sauce. In the end everything in the small pot got mixed up anyway and so I also stirred the grated Parmesan into the mishmash. Ludovica imagined herself to be part of a candid camera broadcast and tried to explain to me that under no circumstances should the sauces be mixed and that the Parmesan cheese had to be sprinkled over the pasta just before eating.

I assured her that at home I could conjure up much better pasta given more space, more pots, spices, ingredients, more time and inclination and, last but not least, in a sober condition. She would be welcome at my place at any time to prove it. But she declined my generous offer with a forceful shake of her head.

As I couldn't find a plate that was big enough for my pasta portion there was no other option but to hijack the cooking pot and munch my supper straight out of it.

Unable to believe her eyes Ludovica looked at me. "Please don't tell me, you're going to eat all that alone?"

Even a person of twice my size might well have had a problem dealing with this mountain of pasta. But I was hungry, frustrated and drunk.

"Would you like some?", I asked her, but she also turned this offer down. Instead she asked me where I came from.

"Austria", I said and probably didn't do my home country any favour.

The common room was absolutely packed and the atmosphere high-spirited. It was only myself who didn't feel like being in a good mood today. I wanted to be alone and to wallow in self-pity. A staircase led to a roof terrace, which was normally used for hanging out the laundry. A rather taciturn Finnish guy was perched all alone at a table. I sat next to him holding my pasta pot and a bottle of wine and downed more than half of my generous helping.

Little by little other pilgrims joined us: Txema, a bearded Spaniard, Ludovica, who surely wanted to see whether the greedy Austrian had burst in the meantime, Rosa, a pretty Mexican girl, who didn't look quite like I imagined a Mexican woman should and I wasn't quite certain whether I would still find her pretty after I had sobered up. And then there was Sandy, a red haired German girl from Dresden. She sat at the other end of the table but I didn't pay much attention to her as even after another bottle of wine she didn't seem my type. However, here it must be said that in the twilight of a five-watt light bulb my eyesight was no longer at its best.

It should have been a lovely evening, but I couldn't get the phone call with my father out of my mind. I shared wine and chocolate bars with my fellow pilgrims and then retired to my bunk bed.

All that night I could hardly sleep. At two o'clock in the morning I woke up. My pillow was wet – either from sweat or from my tears. I must have wept in my sleep and still did so now. I thought of the conversation with my father. I thought of my problems at home. I thought of the cliffs at Cape Finisterre. I was finally at my emotional low point.

In such a situation it was certainly not a good idea to share feelings with thousands of Facebook users — but I did so anyway. At four o'clock in the morning I posted an entry that I regretted immediately afterwards. I had revealed myself in front of the entire world as a complete failure:

Yesterday someone held the mirror of reality up to me. It wasn't one of my pilgrim brothers, it wasn't a demon, it was my father. He spoke frankly about what I have been trying to push to the back of my mind whilst on the Camino and what I would be glad to run away from: I can't live off writing books and my one-man real estate business is running badly — since this 'one man' prefers to put all his energy into walking the St. James Way or, like last year, invests his money in sailing trips in the Caribbean. I'm forty-five years old, have no money, no capital, no stocks or shares, no pension plan and no property of my own. I don't own anything, except for an old car, in which I could sleep if necessary. I'm a nothing, a loser. My father hadn't put it quite like that, of course, but that was my shocking insight of yesterday when I looked into that mirror of reality. He's right, of course, and I have let him down. My father is more concerned about me than I am about myself. I'm really sorry. As my father will be reading this here, too — so sorry, Dad.

On the plus side of my life's balance sheet up to now, there are a few 'irrelevant' things like a wonderful daughter, travels to more than fifty countries, three books published by Piper, quite a number of good friends and the good fortune to have so far led a great, stress-free life. On the other hand, however, one cannot live off 'assets' such as these so they probably don't count much.

I'll be off on my way again in a couple of hours — the physically most strenuous stage of the journey leading straight into the mountains is ahead of me. I'm going to tackle it even after having seriously thought of abandoning my whole trip tonight. Just as I intend to get my life back on track after completing the St. James Way pilgrimage to Santiago. Today I'm going to reflect on disappointments. After all, I'm disappointed in myself because I disappointed my father. And being disappointed can be compared with a small stone in a hiking boot. Let's see how I can get this stone out of my boot.

Chapter Twenty-Three

Astorga – Foncebadón

O vertired, hung-over and emotionally shaken, next day I walked for twenty-six kilometres up to the second highest point of the entire route. In spite of everything, I made good progress. However, every few hundred metres I wished I had deleted my nocturnal blog entry as my general intention had been to report on positive developments and valuable insights rather than to burden my Facebook community with my everyday worries. But by now it was too late for that. The entry had already triggered off dozens of comments. Most of them were encouraging, others of a philosophical nature, some expressed concern and one of them advised me to quit the Way of St. James immediately as the venture had quite obviously become mentally too demanding for me. Here, this person was not mistaken. I found myself in a state of emotional emergency. During a break I read some touching comments, amongst which was one from Peggy, a dear friend of my mother's:

Your mom up in heaven would say 'Eddy, I love you so much and I'm so proud of you just the way you are … your adventures have made you what you are today … My wonderful son, you're on the right path! I can feel it!'

Whilst reading it I was having tea together with Txema, Rosa and Ludovica. Afterwards I had to make an urgent visit to the men's room and this time it was my tear duct and not my bladder that kept me there for a while.

The track today led uphill through barren heathland. Ludovica had obviously overcome her pasta trauma and asked whether I wanted to join the group. This time I gratefully declined the offer. I had to think, and more urgently than ever before. Meanwhile I had recognized my father's scolding as being an important sign for me at the right time.

The sun came out, and slowly my mood improved. I thought about the term 'disappointment'. One could be disappointed in oneself for not achieving a certain goal, such as losing ten kilos of weight, for example, or one could be disappointed by a friend when he or she hadn't got in touch for a long time. Disappointments can have as many different faces as my inner demon, Amancio Vázquez.

I myself had already experienced several disappointments in my lifetime, bigger and smaller ones. I was more interested in what I had to change in order to be able to cope with disappointments in a better way.

Disappointments arose from unfulfilled expectations. A tried and tested home remedy would be just to scale down expectations. Perhaps the set target to lose ten kilos in weight might have been just too ambitious. If, instead, one could settle on a reasonable five kilos, then disappointment could be avoided altogether.

But that couldn't be the whole truth of the matter. After all, one should set oneself ambitious targets and not strive for mediocrity. Downscaling the expectations of oneself and others could only be one third of the way to avoid disappointment.

What did expectation actually mean? The noun 'expectation' also contains part of the verb 'to expect'. Haven't we often been disappointed because we've been waiting for something that hasn't (yet) materialized? Maybe the friend who had promised to call would get in touch next week and then everything would be fine. Instead of being disappointed shouldn't one allow oneself and others simply a little more time or a second chance?

I realized that even this was not the ideal solution for fighting disappointment, but at least the next third of the way to achieving it. Many of my disappointments would have ceased to exist had I only had sufficient patience and been able to wait.

But some things would never happen no matter how long one waited. For example, the job one had applied for and hadn't got. Also the marriage to my ex-fiancée Tatiana would never take place. Shouldn't one simply have faith in being able to find a better job or a woman who suited one better? I wanted to believe that, in retrospect, even painful failures and the ensuing disappointments would make sense in the end.

If I were to lower my expectations slightly, be able to wait and see for some things and even recognize positive signs in failures, wouldn't disappointments become as unnecessary as the small stone in my hiking boot? Even though this was a rather simple pilgrim's philosophy, a better one hadn't yet occurred to me today. As far as my own disappointment was concerned, I had been able to get rid of the little stone. For whoever had the discipline to walk eight hours a day for a month towards a target, would surely also have the discipline to solve his own problems at home! Or not...? Anyway, I couldn't wait to get started.

Once again I had managed to pull myself out of the depths of a psychic pit without help – the deepest pit I had ever been in so far on the Camino. In Rabanal del Camino tasty rice with vegetables was served for lunch. Meanwhile I had read all the reactions to my blog entry. It was amazing how far the Internet community opened itself up if one did so oneself. Along with dozens of public comments I also received a variety of private messages in which users I hardly knew poured out their hearts to me and openly described their feelings and problems, just as I had done.

Foncebadón was a mountain village that consisted of only a few stone houses. In the Middle Ages, however, the place had been so significant that according to my travel guide even a council of churches had taken place there. The houses had lain in ruins until the turn of millennium. It wasn't until later that the place had been rebuilt step-by-step.

As I approached the hostel, my pilgrim brother Rainhard was waving at me. He was already sitting on the terrace and had a beer in his hand. Rainhard had also booked a bed for me. Today I was actually grateful for that as there were more pilgrims than usual on their way and the number of hostel rooms was limited. The natural stone building with a slated roof looked as if Asterix & Obelix were about to rush out of it on their way to hunt wild boars.

In the evening, vegetarian Paella and lentil soup were on the pilgrim's menu. Rainhard and Martin, an IT technician from Germany who didn't talk a lot, and a Korean woman, who didn't understand any other language but her mother tongue and with whom I was nevertheless joking, joined me at the table. And then there was also Sandy from Dresden again, who first of all had to remind me that we had already met last night in Astorga. Sandy was doing the Camino in three stages and had returned to the route only just before Astorga in order to walk her last third and final stretch of the St. James Way to Santiago. She was twelve years younger than me, was completing an apprenticeship as a nursery school teacher and worked in a trendy pub in Dresden. According to her own explanation, she had collected the clothing she wore from hostels' lost & found boxes. Equally unconventional as her clothing were her manner as well as her questions – where we had something in common.

She asked whether I had ever cried whilst hiking along the Camino. A cool guy like me – crying? Stupid question. "Of course not!", I would have answered if a different woman had asked the same question.

"Yes, sure. Yesterday and today. Actually several times", I admitted. And then I told her why. And as if to prove that my confession was true, tears came into my eyes again.

Chapter Twenty-Four

Foncebadón – Ponferrada

W hat I hadn't considered during my rather hectic preparation for the Camino down in hot Andalusia, was the cold weather in the north of Spain in October. For a few days now early morning temperatures had been around freezing. Today I started off on the twenty-seven kilometres to Ponferrada in shorts with socks as replacement gloves. The sunrise was absolutely spectacular and symbolic for me. Something new was about to dawn.

I took several photographs of the stone houses that seemed aflame in the red glow of the sunrise. Only a loudly jabbering American broke the peace of this perfect idyll. I tried to get away from his audible frequency, but each time I stopped to take another photo the guy was back into my earshot. So I began to dawdle and let myself fall behind, but then he stopped, too, and loudly admired the panorama. The American and his two female companions continued chasing me until I reached the top of the pass forty minutes later.

There one of the most highly symbolic spots of the Way of St. James was located – the Cruz de Ferro. It was a huge pile of stones, on top of which stood an oak tree trunk bearing an iron cross. For over a thousand years pilgrims had been symbolically laying down stones representing their worries and burdens in order to get rid of them. Some of the pilgrims had brought their own neatly inscribed stones with them from overseas hoping to be able to live a carefree life from then on. Good idea, I thought. Unfortunately I had only learned about this opportunity from Rainhard the previous evening. In vain, I searched on the edge of the forest for a suitable stone. So I decided to pick up a few stones from around the Cruz de Ferro and read the inscriptions.

After careful thought, I decided on the one of an Argentinian woman. Her worries roughly resembled mine, except for the unwanted pregnancy of her seventeen-year-old daughter. I scribbled a couple of my own problems on the back of the stone, which didn't work too well with my biro, and solemnly left the stone by the Cruz de Ferro.

During the descent, my thoughts were revolving around letting go. The words *"From this point I leave behind people and things that no longer serve me"*, were written on a board next to the Cruz de Ferro. What a marvellous idea. But who whispered into one's ear which things and people were better to be left behind? And which standards should be applied?

An anchor gives a ship support and safety in calm waters.

But should you get shipwrecked in stormy seas and are threatened with drowning, it would be better not to cling on to an iron anchor. Therefore one should probably focus on things and people who offer advice and support even during difficult times. Or is there a choice to be made at all in this respect as some turn their backs on you in bad times anyway? Could this possibly apply to places, too? Sunny Spain had been a safe haven to me, at least in good times – but what would it be like now? Was I possibly deceiving myself and my ship had long since been wrecked? Was I just desperately trying and keep my head above water by clinging to the anchor instead of letting it go? Was the Camino about to advise me to go back to Austria, because only there would I stand better chances of success? I hoped not.

I didn't get any further with my train of thoughts on this morning. After two upsetting days it was now time anyway to give my head a breather. Furthermore the picturesque, sparsely forested mountain landscape offered majestic panoramic views.

Today I was trekking most of the time in the company of Rainhard, Martin and Sandy. Both men seemed to be more in a hurry than Sandy and myself, so the red-haired girl from Dresden and I hiked together for some kilometres. I had never had such a pleasant conversation with anyone along the Camino so far. It turned out that we had quite a lot in common. We had travelled the same countries, we laughed about the same things and neither of us took ourselves too seriously.

Unfortunately it was clear from the beginning that I was not really her type and vice versa. Between the two of us there was as much sexual attraction as between Angela Merkel and Donald Trump. And, furthermore, I had already accepted my fate that in the long run it wasn't going to work between women and myself in this life. Nevertheless, I genuinely enjoyed walking side-by-side and chatting away with her.

In Molinaseca we caught up with Rainhard and Martin. They were sitting at a restaurant table in the middle of a field with a view towards a Roman stone bridge and the river. The village radiated such a sense of calm that we decided to enjoy a two-hour break there. Afterwards I didn't feel at all like hiking on. However, we somehow managed to cover the remaining seven kilometres, each one of us at his own pace. Rainhard hurried on ahead, Martin followed a few hundred metres behind, then I came and Sandy brought up the rear. Our target in Ponferrada was the catholic hostel offering one hundred and eighty-four beds. There was a kitchen located right at the entrance to the hostel which had already been requisitioned by a horde of Koreans. I would have loved to have prepared a meal for myself but due to this crowd I decided to take a stroll around Ponferrada.

Although it would have been well worth taking a look at the beautiful Knights Templar castle from the twelfth century, I didn't particularly feel like going there. Instead I wandered through the old town and visited the cathedral. In a supermarket I grabbed a packet of seafood paella suitable for heating up in the microwave as I wanted to have an easy job in the crowded kitchen.

The set of rules for pilgrims allows the following: one is allowed either to walk the Way of St. James, use a bicycle or ride a horse. In order to finally receive the '*Compostela*' certificate of verification that one has abided by the rules, the pilgrimage must begin at least one hundred kilometres away from Santiago. This is why many Spaniards make a weekend trip out of their

St. James Way pilgrimage and walk for three days with their iPods the minimum distance required distance towards Santiago. If one started in León, there would be just half the Camino left to be hiked, a distance which could be managed within two vacation weeks. However, the most intense experience is to be had by setting out in Saint-Jean-Pied-de-Port in the Pyrenees, the official starting point. Although that is not entirely correct either. There are St. James Way routes to Santiago leading virtually through the whole of Europe, hence one could extend the total distance by quite a bit. However, such pilgrim freaks were as rare as a five-hundred-Euro bill in my wallet – but they did actually exist.

Since leaving León one couple had caught my eye several times. I generally overtook them during the day and met them again in the evening in the hostel. He was tall and slender and gave the impression of being Indian or Pakistani – she, in contrast, was small, pale and obviously well-nourished – probably an Englishwoman. To look at, they were as similar a match as a tall stout Austrian guy and a small fine-boned Russian girl. They held hands at all times and walked very slowly. I met them near Astorga at a pedestrian traffic light. At green they stepped on to the zebra crossing and if it hadn't been for me regulating the traffic with my hiking poles, the two of them would have been run over. Nonetheless at the end of the day they had managed the same distance as I had – which might have been due to the fact that the two lovebirds hadn't stopped at every second 'pilgrim's diesel' filling station!

The social centre of a hostel is the communal kitchen. There I came across the two slowcoaches after my stroll through Ponferrada. His backpack seemed to be stuffed half full with exotic spices and he was preparing a tasty meal for himself and his wife – in fact in such enormous quantities that the two couldn't possibly eat it all alone. I was hoping that they would share it with other pilgrims in need like myself. I sat opposite them with my microwave paella that probably contained as many fruits of the sea as a municipal thermal spa and began to try and butter them up by starting an 'intellectually stimulating' conversation in English:

"And where did you start?", I asked him, although I already anticipated the answer. After all, I had only seen them on the St. James Way since León.

"In Rome", the man said. Funny. They didn't look like Italians.

"Ah. Va bene. I'm Austrian. Well, what I meant was, from where did you actually start hiking on your pilgrimage towards Santiago?" I broached the subject again peering hard at the pan full of delicious food. His wife was just getting the plates. I was hoping for three …

"In Rome."

"You mean León?"

"No, Rome."

"But Rome is located in Italy and not in Spain!"

"I know."

"Well, but... are you saying that you began your pilgrimage in *Rome? On foot?*"

In order to avoid any linguistic misunderstandings I 'walked' with my index and middle fingers towards the rice pan.

"Yes." He was a lousy rhetorician, but probably a great cook. The food smelled terrific.

"No kidding? At this...er..." I was just about to say 'snail's pace' but fortunately the English term didn't cross my mind on that evening. As I then found out they had got married in May and afterwards had set out from Rome to Santiago on foot.

"And why are you doing it?"

"If we manage this path together as far as Santiago, then we shall be able to cope with any other challenges thereafter", he said. That was a really good point and, in fact, one that I wanted to believe.

I couldn't get the two of them out of my mind for a long time afterwards. I hoped that they would be right. Unfortunately relationships tend to separate in good times rather than in bad. That had anyway been the case between myself and the mother of my daughter – and also with a number of couples in my circle of friends. Therefore I wished them both that they would always remember this insight from the Camino for many years to come.

Chapter Twenty-Five

Ponferrada – Trabadelo

I f this hadn't been the French Way route – or *Camino Frances* – of
the St. James Way but the Tour de France, yesterday and today's
stretches would have been called the "King of the Mountains"
stage. I had conquered the first stretch without any doping, apart
from some pilgrim's diesel. The route I had planned to tackle this
day was, according to my calculations, thirty-six kilometres long and
in some parts led steeply uphill. For this it was important to carry
along enough provisions. In a supermarket I bought a baguette,
about half a metre long, cheese, tomatoes and a bottle of wine,
which I poured into my '*bota*'. Well equipped I set off alone for the
second longest stage of the Camino. I would probably meet up with
Rainhard later on and maybe also Sandy, with whom I had chatted
last night for quite a while about this and that, long after lights out
in the hostel.

The first twenty-four kilometres of the track led through undulating countryside and a wine-growing region. The latter somewhat
reminded me of the Tuscany. I nibbled a lot of red grapes and felt
like being in pilgrim's heaven. After I had walked through Navarra,
Rioja, Burgos, Palencia as well as Castile and León, I was now

approaching the autonomous region of Galicia, where Santiago de Compostela is also located.

At one o'clock in the afternoon I arrived at Villafranca del Bierzo. Lunch break. I sat down on a park bench and prepared my outsize cheese sandwich. Two women pilgrims, who were poking at their salads in a restaurant across the road, obviously found my picnic so appealing that they took photos of it. One by one familiar faces began arriving. Rainhard and Martin for example, whom I had actually overtaken with my speedy pace. Both of them were looking for a lodging for the night and had called it a day.

I had intended to walk on to Trabelado, but on account of my full stomach, plus having consumed half a bottle of wine, all of a sudden the thought of continuing cost me quite an effort. The more so as Villafranca del Bierzo was a beautiful place offering quite a large selection of quaint lodgings. It was also known as the "small Compostela" since in the Middle Ages pilgrims could apparently have their sins forgiven here if they had fallen ill along the Camino and were thus unable to continue their hike to Santiago. Did the single blister on my left heel also qualify for that treatment?

As I sat on the park bench, a man joined me and introduced himself as Markus. I offered him a swig of wine after which he soon became quite chatty. He was fifty years old and held a manager's position with BMW in Munich. A short while ago he had had a vasectomy. Although he had discussed it with his wife before, who also didn't want children, both of them were now at odds with the decision. Slowly but surely I seemed to be turning into the shrink of the St. James Way because of my straightforward questions. After all, Markus wasn't the first one to talk to me about very personal issues after only a few minutes' acquaintance.

So everyone has a burden to carry along the Camino, I thought, buckled up my backpack – and my burdens – and shook hands with Markus. It was already two-thirty in the afternoon, and my inner demon, Amancio Vázquez, couldn't of course find one reason for me to hike a single step more today.

It actually didn't make any difference whether I stayed in Villafranca del Bierzo or walked on to Trabadelo, where nobody would be waiting for me. Markus seemed a nice guy. He and the others would be staying here. So it looked like it would be a pleasant and sociable evening.

In spite of this, I pulled myself together to continue to Trabadelo. Markus asked me for my mobile number when saying good-bye so we could stay in touch along the Camino. I fished one of my very important-looking business cards with the lettering "Freundlinger & Partners – International Real Estate Consultants" out of my wallet and scribbled on to the back of the card, "Our new feature: sperm donations! Top Credentials. Good quality at fair prices."

Luckily the Bavarian seemed to have a sense of humour.

At the end of the village I noticed a cash machine. A hasty check of my finances added up to seventeen euros and thirty cents in my wallet. I inserted my card into the slot and, as always, feared for the worst. Thankfully, this time the cash dispenser spat out one hundred euros without further ado making me jump for joy.

Once outside Villafranca del Bierzo my guidebook presented me with two options: either to walk along a very busy motorway approach road in the valley towards Trabadelo – or to take a much more beautiful turn-off over a hill. In my travel guide as well as in the vernacular it was called ‘*Camino Duro*’ – which meant ‘the hard track’. This alternative was about three kilometres longer and at the beginning led up over steep slopes. Gasping for breath, before I could get annoyed with myself for my wrong choice, however, I was rewarded with a fantastic view.

I walked at a leisurely pace through chestnut woods in a blaze of autumnal colours. Sometimes I looked down into the valley, where a dozen or so pilgrims were marching along the arterial road. Were they really only interested in reaching their destination? Along the *Camino Duro* at any rate I didn't encounter any other pilgrim during the three-hour hike. Just a few local people were busy harvesting chestnuts.

Nevertheless, I was facing a problem. My water supply had been exhausted long ago, the sun was blazing down from clear blue skies, and there were no wells. I drank up the wine and ate some raw chestnuts that I had picked up from the ground. Both simply increased my thirst even more. Again I thought of the incident on

Blanquilla Island off the coast of Venezuela where I had almost died of thirst. Fortunately today it was not as bad as then, and according to my clever travel guide I couldn't be that far away from the village of Pradela, were there was supposed to be a tavern.

Dried out like a prune in an oven, I arrived one and a half hours later. For quite a while I had been imagining how I would 'inhale' two pints of shandy – one right after the other – as soon as I had reached the bar. The village consisted of a farm and a few houses. A dog was roaming the street and an old woman looked suspiciously at me out of a window. The rest of the inhabitants seemed to be at the chestnut harvest in the woods. I asked the elderly lady the way to the village inn. It was closed, she said. I cursed so loudly that the woman locked all her shutters. Nevertheless, I set off in search of the bar as I just couldn't believe that it was really shut down. Surely this village elder must have been suffering from dementia, had misunderstood me, or had simply been wrong about the day of the week.

Two street corners further on I stood in front of the closed bar. In rage I kicked against the door. Without getting anything to drink I couldn't possibly carry on down into the valley.

I roamed around the ghost town and managed to get into the farm courtyard. Here, too, there was no-one to be seen except for some cackling chickens. I was hoping to find a well and I actually did. However, it was not one with clean spring water, but rather a cattle trough with a swarm of water fleas dancing Samba on its surface. In one corner yellowish foam was floating, and at the bottom of the wooden trough lay a drowned mouse. Thirst was greater than disgust, and so I plunged my head in and guzzled like a hippopotamus after a period of drought.

I arrived at Trabadelo just before dark. I had had an eleven-hour march behind me and just wanted to shower, prepare some food and go to sleep. Fortunately I found a grocer's shop, even though it wasn't much larger than the deep freezer in the meat section of my supermarket back home. There I met Ludovica from Milan once again, who I had come across a number of times along the track already. She obviously remembered my frustration-spaghetti-revelry in Astorga and now saw me once again with a jumbo pack of pasta in my arms. However, she seemed to sympathize with me and told me that she had met a group of Italian women at her hostel and that this evening she was going to cook risotto for everyone. She asked me whether I would like to share the meal.

Of course I wanted to! Since I hadn't managed to get any of the curried rice dish yesterday because the loving couple had packed the remaining food away for the following day, a tasty risotto came at just the right time. I accepted the invitation with thanks, put my pasta back on to the shelf and promised Ludovica to contribute the wine. Splashing out, I even bought two bottles of red wine for two and a half euros each.

Back at the hostel I immediately started preparing for my blind date with half a dozen Italian ladies. I imagined them to be like the ones I had often watched in TV advertisements: Ramazotti, Giotto, Segafredo – or maybe even something to do with lingerie. My tiredness had long since faded away. I shaved off my pilgrim's beard, had a shower using the liquid hand soap from the dispenser in the ladies' bathroom as I had left my shower gel behind in the last hostel, slipped on the less dirty of my two t-shirts and styled my hair for the first time in three weeks. With my fingers, mind you. Using a comb would have been too painful.

Dressed up to the nines, I made my way to the communal kitchen. There, Ludovica was standing at the stove stirring a pot of delicious smelling risotto. Next to it was a pan of chestnuts. What was that for? Were we going to have chestnut risotto? Well, it didn't really matter. The table had been beautifully set and even a burning candle stood in the middle. However, there was no sign of the Italian ladies. Instead an Italian guy sat at the romantic-looking table reading a book. The man was so outrageously good looking that just for this reason I could have had a go at him with the spaghetti tongs. It was perfectly clear who was going to make the hearts of all the Italian pilgrim sisters melt – and it wasn't going to be me!

My rival simply ignored me and continued to read in his thick tome. How daft did one have to be to lug such a weighty volume all along the Way of St. James? He was smiling all the time, obviously confident of victory! But a very special aura seemed to surround him and one thing was already clear to me: someone who had such a relaxed smile on the face, could have neither worries nor problems. He must certainly have wealthy parents and lead an exciting life in the lap of luxury, I thought to myself. He just wanted a break from it all knowing very well that it would only be for a short while. Perhaps he was a descendant of the Fiat dynasty? Or from a banker's family? Or was the guy sitting opposite me an offspring of a Mafia clan? Of course! That was it. A member of the Mafia on the Camino? What a disgrace. Fortunately tomorrow's weather forecast predicted bad weather. Then lightning was sure to strike him!

The Italian ladies finally arrived in the kitchen. As a matter of fact they all really did look like the women on TV. However, more like the ones in adverts for denture adhesive.

A Spanish couple joined us as well. Then the risotto was served. The pan full of chestnuts was still sitting on the stove. I was just about to wolf down my share of risotto, when the son of the Mafia godfather drew our attention. He asked us to take each other by the hand. Then he said a prayer. Meanwhile he had put away his book. It was a bible. I was stunned.

It turned out that the man's name was Luca. And Luca also spoke Spanish. My curiosity was aroused. Had I been wrong about him? I had to know. While all the Italian 'Dentagard' ladies were waffling on, I asked Luca a lot of questions. In doing so I found out that he came from a small village on Sardinia, where there was hardly any work. His family was poor and he also had no money. He had set out on the Way of St. James for religious reasons.

He was in fact the first pilgrim of his kind whom I had come across along the Camino. Now the Spaniards also got interested. They asked the Italian where he was going to stay overnight. He replied that he would be sleeping in a tent as he had no money with him. Meanwhile I was deeply ashamed of my prejudices, of which, fortunately, I hadn't uttered a single word out loud.

"And no credit cards either?" This ridiculous additional question came, I'm sorry to admit, from my side. No, Luca didn't have a single cent on him and also no credit cards – ever since he had disembarked from the ferry from Sardinia. He had hitch-hiked to

Saint-Jean-Pied-de-Port, from where I had also started my journey, and had since hiked the track without a cent in his pocket. I was completely fascinated by him.

"But how do you manage with food?" I wanted to know.

"God provides me with what I need", he said and pointed towards a bag of chestnuts.

At least for today that was true. Although Luca must have had enough to eat after two plates of risotto, the caring Italian ladies continued to stuff him with chocolate and biscuits. In doing so he hadn't even touched the food he had planned to eat in the first place – the chestnuts in the pan he had picked up along the way during the day. I had also walked over thousands of chestnuts on today's stretch, but I had only been hoping to find a supermarket where I could buy pasta. I asked him, whether he ever worried that there might be days when he wouldn't find chestnuts or any other food.

"No", he said. "God has let me experience so much charity and warmth along this path that I don't have to worry about it."

Chapter Twenty-Six

Trabadelo – O Cebreiro

I had breakfast in the hostel's cafeteria. The gum-chewing waitress, who had already seemed quite fed up when I arrived, was grumpy again and without saying a word slammed down some bread and jam from the day before on my table. Then Luca came in, obviously rather chilled through from the night in his tent.

"For heaven's sake! Why didn't you say anything? The waitress scolded him. "We'd have found a bed for you for sure. Are you hungry? Would you like some eggs?"

A short while later, not only did he have three fried eggs with bread in front of him, but also enough provisions for the rest of the day.

During today's leg of the route towards the mountain village of O Cebreiro I thought a lot about Luca. He had taught me that prejudices were uncalled for because, as a rule, people were different from what you had originally thought. He had given me the chestnut principle to take along with me: *God provides me with what I need.* That evidently didn't only work with chestnuts, I thought, but also with helpful people along the Way.

I would have liked to have asked him if God would also pay my mortgage, my car insurance and the child support for my daughter. Probably not. Or maybe..?

I looked back at the past years. I had organized charter trips on the *Orion* in the Caribbean, owned a diving school, a company dealing in solar energy and a real estate brokerage. I had imported open fireplaces from Germany and I had written books. Some of these enterprises had gone well, some badly, some not at all. I had had to cope with many crises, but somehow things had always carried on. Then all of a sudden I had found a 'chestnut' at exactly the right spot. It was Luca who had made me realize that it had been 'raining chestnuts' for me, too, over the past twenty years, and that it was therefore superfluous to worry too much about the future – because this would stay much the same for the next twenty years. This was definitely one of the Camino's particularly meaningful insights.

One and a half decades ago I had found myself in a similar situation. For personal reasons I had said good-bye to my company Solartex, Daxer & Freundlinger S.L. and had transferred my shares without any financial compensation to Walter, with whom I had founded the enterprise two years before. All that I was left with was a 39-foot yacht that I sometimes sailed on behalf of its English owner to prevent the moving parts from rusting. Out of necessity, I organized day trips for tourists with it and earned a few extra Pesetas, until the owner decided to sell the ship a couple of months later.

After that I had no further income and also no money. I was left with nothing. No, not quite: Virginia, my girlfriend at the time, was pregnant. A joyful circumstance on the one hand, but on the other it was the cause of many sleepless nights. If one got into difficulties in Spain, one had to manage without any State support. There were no unemployment benefits or family and child benefits whatsoever. And lo and behold – during this time I had met Thomas by chance. He came up with the idea of founding a real estate company with me – which we actually did and with quite some success.

Unfortunately, fifteen years later this once well-functioning business relationship became history. However, in retrospect it proved to me that the chestnut principle had worked perfectly for a long time without my being aware of it. Now I was curious to find out which groundbreaking 'chestnut' would be awaiting me on my journey through life in the near future.

But first I had to settle for cow pats underfoot. The Camino now led me across the border from Castile and León to Galicia, the last autonomous region of the St. James Way, which generated in me a short burst of endorphin. There were still some hundred metres difference in altitude to

O Cebreiro to overcome, but fortunately there were no really steep sections. Scenically I felt as if I was back in my childhood, when sometimes on Sundays I was allowed to walk with my parents up to an alpine pasture in the beautiful region around Salzburg – or, according to my feelings at the time, *had* to walk with them.

In Galicia I was welcomed by green meadows, woodlands and fields, fog-shrouded hilltops, the smell of cow manure and the rattling of tractor engines – only the mountain huts were missing in this area. Instead I found a pilgrim's inn a few kilometres before O Cebreiro. It was just about noon and I had plenty of time left. I ate an outstanding rice dish, which, for a change, didn't have the consistency of filler compound from a DIY shop. A little later Ludovica and Txema, the bearded Spaniard who had been unsuccessfully trying to chat up the Italian girl for a couple of days, arrived. Also with them was Rosa from Mexico, whom I should have perhaps also tried to win over for that matter, if I hadn't given up the subjects of women and love in the same way as I had career and success. Only eating and drinking still seemed to be functioning excellently. I ordered a second plate of rice and another large beer before tackling the last part of the day's stretch.

By the time I set out it had started raining, but in the meantime I had become so used to the erratic and unpredictable weather that it didn't bother me. At three in the afternoon I arrived at

O Cebreiro. The village was situated at an altitude of fifteen hundred metres and reminded me of Asterix' home town in Gaul. No wonder, as the partly well-preserved stone houses with thatched roofs dated back to a two thousand five hundred year-old Celtic building tradition.

According to my guidebook a miracle had apparently taken place in O Cebreiro, which didn't surprise me in the least in such mystical, fog-shrouded surroundings. Legend has it that, despite a storm, a pious peasant was the only one who had come up the mountain to attend the Holy Mass celebrated by a monk who doubted the existence of God and secretly made fun of the stupid devout peasant. However, during Mass the bread and wine were transformed into the flesh and blood of Christ – and the monk was cured of his disbelief. He was buried in the eighth century church of Santa Maria, which also happens to be the oldest church along the St. James Way. A visit seemed worthwhile to me, but, as so many churches on the Camino, its doors were unfortunately locked.

In the hostel I was allocated bed number twenty-nine. Apart from myself there was as yet no-one else in the dormitory, which had capacity for fifty-six people. I inspected the nearer surroundings and wasn't very impressed. Still in dripping wet clothes, I asked the hostel warden to allocate me either bed number seventeen or bed number forty-seven. The resolute lady, whom I easily could have imagined to be a prison officer, sized me up disapprovingly but eventually met my request and allotted me bed number seventeen. The beds were all the same, but numbers seventeen and forty-seven were the only ones which had sockets nearby for re-charging my mobile phone, as well as a window. Furthermore, in such a large dormitory for accommodating a correspondingly large number of guests, a location near a fresh air supply seemed an optimal choice.

In the town I handed my dirty laundry to a lady with a grey plait and hung out for the rest of the afternoon at the hostel. As I was occupied in preparing my blog entry, the dormitory began filling up with pilgrims. Most of them were noisy Spaniards, who chatted about where and what to eat. Food and beverages were the dominant issues for this type of pilgrim.

Soon my fellow German-speaking pilgrim brothers and sisters arrived, and so together with Rainhard, Sandy, Martin, Markus and Heinz, a sixty-year-old man from Dresden, whom I hadn't yet met on the Camino, I went to have dinner. Needless to say tonight it had to be the local speciality 'pulpo a la gallega', Galician octopus, slowly simmered until tender and seasoned with smoked paprika.

The restaurant couldn't have been quainter. From the beams of the low wooden ceiling hung huge medieval pots, garlic braids and dried peppers. The stone walls were decorated with ceramic plates, ancient photographs and copper pans. In one corner an open fire was burning and in front of it a table for six was free. Apostle James meant well for us today.

Sandy sat down next to me. In the light of the open fire I noticed a subtle change in her appearance: her green woollen cap was missing and her long red hair fell playfully around her décolleté, which without the usual thick pullover had all of a sudden taken an interesting shape. She even wore some modest makeup.

The delicious *pulpo a la gallega* was accompanied by a fine white wine served in shallow ceramic bowls.

We held pilgrim's talk, until Heinz and Markus started discussing business, politics and share prices. This irritated me so much after one hour that I asked Heinz whether he wasn't even able to switch off from business talk and relax on the Way of St. James. As a result of this Sandy and I were left alone at the table a quarter of an hour later as the others suddenly didn't know what to talk about any more.

But it still didn't develop into a date because according to my reasoning, at least one of the two should have desired more than just enjoying the moment. That wasn't the case with us. We drank one rum and coke after another and forgot the time altogether and it wasn't until after ten o'clock that we ran, laughing, back to the hostel which fortunately had not yet locked its doors. The dormitory was packed to the last bed. It smelled of damp clothing and body odours of fifty-six pilgrims in a very confined space. I stuffed plugs into my ears and was so able to shut out the sounds of creaking beds, rustling sleeping bags, murmuring and snoring until I was only aware of the resonance inside my own head. It resembled the eerie end-of-transmission tone on television channels decades ago.

Sandy's bed was less than three metres away from mine. I surprised myself with my last thoughts before falling asleep: what if the two of us had been in a double room of a hotel instead?

Chapter Twenty-Seven

O Cebreiro – Triacastela

The next morning was simply dreadful. Pilgrims wearing high-tech rain gear and headlamps left the hostel at an early hour. I owned neither one nor the other and therefore hadn't the slightest desire to step outside into the dark in the pouring rain, fog and cold. And as a result of the five rum and cokes last night I would have had a fair chance at a casting for a lead role in *The Hangover 5*.

I sneaked off into the common room and brought my diary up to date until at ten o'clock the merciless cleaning crew ladies kicked me out of the hostel. Sandy had given me a rain poncho that she had found in a lost and found box. She had already left at eight o'clock. She hadn't known how far she wanted to walk today any more than I did. Yesterday I had probably spent my nicest evening so far on the Camino with her, and yet it was not certain whether our paths would ever cross again. We hadn't exchanged mobile numbers and I couldn't find her on Facebook either as I didn't know her surname. But that, too, was the St. James Way: a kind of life in fast motion. People accompanied me for a while and then I never saw them again – only it happened much faster than in real life.

It rained all day long. Sandy's rain poncho was as thin as a plastic rubbish bag and soon got torn in several places. At the first opportunity I threw it away into a dustbin – I was already soaked to my underpants anyway. Through the rain there was hardly anything to be seen of the landscape and similarly I had about as many insights as I could see landmarks. At least most of the time the track led downhill. As I had been the very last one to have left the hostel that morning, I was the only pilgrim far and wide. If I had only left at eight o'clock together with Sandy, I said to myself. Did I really miss her? Could this fact be a hint that I actually had a bit of a crush on her...Or was I just looking for a charming companion to distract me from this boring stretch of the Way?

I thought about it for a while and came to the conclusion that it couldn't be anything serious if I had to think about it at all. On the other hand, Tatiana was hardly in my thoughts any more, even though we had been engaged until two weeks ago. It seemed to me now as if that had been in another life.

As much as I had learned to love the Way of Saint James, I was very much looking forward to arriving in Santiago. To finally reach my target in order to be able to set myself new goals afterwards. But what were they? My mind was as foggy as the landscape I was trudging through, but I still wanted to deal with these thoughts today. Earlier on I had usually only set myself ambitious aims around New Year's Eve and then most of the time quickly given them up as they had seemed unachievable – or the price to pay for fulfilling them too high. At some stage I had thus decided to not set myself such goals any more, especially since I could never be sure whether I would be happier after reaching a target or fulfilling a dream than before. Just now on the Camino I had learned that happiness has to be searched for along the way and not at the destination – because there the journey is over.

One goal in life that I had achieved was the dream of writing books one day. It was the target that I had most persevered in pursuing. As I was walking through the Galician mountain scenery, soaking wet and freezing cold, I wondered whether the effort had been worth it. Especially as the price to pay had been damn high. The divorce from the mother of my daughter, the resulting loss of my house with swimming pool and ocean view as well as the closure of my import company probably came indirectly at the cost of my uncompromising realization of this life's dream.

At the age of twenty I had decided to become an author one day. I had made that decision on the beach of the island of Margarita in Venezuela. However, not because I had discovered a particularly great talent for writing in myself, but because I had associated ultimate freedom with this supposedly dream job. After all, I only needed a typewriter and paper and I could work wherever and whenever I wanted, even under palm trees on that Caribbean beach – I thought then.

What I couldn't have known at the time was that I would be writing this manuscript twenty-five years later at a shaky desk on an office chair with a missing wheel. And of course I had not taken into account in my high-flown plans that with the replacement of the typewriter by a computer the situation on the book market would turn to the author's disadvantage. Free books, ninety-nine-cent eBooks, social media and other virtual distractions have meanwhile thinned out the readership. On top of it all, the average stressed citizen hardly finds time to read a book and is confronted with a flood of one hundred thousand new publications per year. I really hadn't been aware of all this when I chose my career. Otherwise I might have been interested in the job of an astronaut. This profession might not have turned out much more difficult.

It was now twenty years since making the decision to become a famous bestselling author one day and the actual implementation of this absurd project. During all this time I had kept the dream alive and had thought about it almost every day – without even having put a single line on paper. Instead, I had tried my hand at many other fields or work, which had only increased my frustration year by year. Until an opportunity arose in the course of a crisis.

For the misjudged "best side" of a crisis is its role as a forerunner for new opportunities and perspectives. Albert Einstein already knew this, from whom the following originates:

We can't assume that things will change if we keep doing the same. A crisis can be a real blessing to any person or nation. For all crises bring progress. Creativity is born from anguish, just as the day is born from the darkness of night. It is in times of crisis that innovation and ingenuity are found and strategies developed. Whoever survives a crisis, overcomes himself without being defeated. Those who attribute their failures to the crisis, violate their own creative potential and spend more time searching for problems instead of solutions. The real crisis is the crisis of incompetence. The difficulty for persons and countries is finding the right solutions to their problems. Without crises there are no challenges, without challenges life remains a routine and stays stuck in monotony. Without crisis there is no merit, for it is in times of difficulty that the strengths of each and every one emerge.

In 2008 the Spanish real estate market started to drop fast coinciding with the global financial crisis of 2007-08 and the speculative property bubble burst. I was bored stiff sitting in my office without a single customer for days and weeks. But instead of hanging around in bars like many others in my situation and scolding the government, I began searching for a way out of the slump. One night I had a confused nightmare. I dreamt that my brother had paid me a visit in Spain and had been found dead in his hotel room the next morning. In his early thirties and perfectly healthy, there were no signs of external violence and the police assumed suicide. However, there was no way I could believe that and started investigating the case myself, together with the receptionist who had checked-in my brother. Shortly afterwards her mother disappeared without a trace. She had worked as a cleaning lady in the hotel. Everything seemed to be linked together somehow. We soon had our suspicion but I never found out how our investigations continued as the dream came to an end right at this point when my alarm clock went off.

As I was sitting in my office some time later I recalled this utterly vivid dream and asked myself what more might have happened if I hadn't woken up. So I began to continue the story further as a day dream, wondering how it could have ended. The story took some surprising turns by itself until I hit my forehead with my flat hand. That was it! I had a story! The main reason I had hesitated for almost twenty years before finally tackling my rising career as an author was namely quite trivial: I hadn't known *what* to write about. And now I finally had an idea for a crime novel.

Over the next three months I wrote the first hundred pages of the thriller quite haphazardly and unstructured. However, I considered the preliminary result as being ingenious. Even a title had sprung to mind: *Pata Negra*. That suited the debut novel of the latest shooting star of German-language crime literature perfectly, I thought. In the meantime I had set up an author homepage as well as a Facebook account showing forty-two Freundlinger followers. In my wallet there were now business cards bearing the words *"Eduard Freundlinger – Author"*, which I generously distributed. After all, I had to be well prepared for success as by now it was quite obvious, to myself at least, that my new glamorous author existence would be taking me very far. To the top of the *Spiegel* magazine bestseller list at least. My book would be translated into two dozen languages and, of course, it would be made into a film. Needless to say, not produced by the 'Bavaria Film Studios' in Munich, but in Hollywood. After all, both Brad Pitt and Penelope Cruz looked very much like my two protagonists.

Reality, however, was rather different. I exchanged views on the Internet in a forum of people sharing the same interests – that is to say with other, equally megalomaniac and unpublished authors. The forum gave the opportunity to upload one's texts and have them evaluated by other members. On the one hand I was afraid that somebody less talented might have the idea of stealing my brilliant text, on the other hand after a creative period of three months in the silence and loneliness of my little workroom my ego was desperate for feedback. I thus uploaded the data file and waited for comments.

Unfortunately the results were sobering. Instead of the expected euphoria and hymns of praise, there was a barrage of criticism. I felt like a talent show candidate who had just been told by a member of the jury that he should rather keep his mouth shut than continue getting on other peoples nerves. At least a few critics had endeavoured to outline for me *why* my words had caused them chronic itching. Unfortunately they were right. Even though I had learned to write at school, this was obviously not enough to enable me to 'compose' a novel.

So, what now? Give up? No way! I began to look at writing as being a craft that one had to learn to master first. Fortunately there were plenty of books available on creative writing. I got hold of all the relevant handbooks I could find in German and English and in the months that followed worked through a kind of study course in writing. I learned how to develop an interesting plot, what a golden thread is, how to create authentic characters, how to build up suspense and maintain it, how to write dialogues, how to present the settings as concretely and vividly as in real life and what constituted a successful writing style altogether. To future authors – and I have met many of them over the years – I gave and would still give only the one piece of advice: do it the same way – first of all learn the craft before you start writing!

Afterwards I read through my initial text, that – given my newly acquired knowledge and expertise – could now best be compared to a bumpy Andalusian goat track, and I had to admit to myself that the critics of the first hour had been absolutely right. But on the other hand "a fault confessed is half redressed". Highly motivated I started on the revision. I rewrote many passages, reworked all the characters and gave them more depth, deleted all superfluous filler words, streamlined the story and pepped it up with a touch of Andalusian flair instead, as after all, the thriller was set in my adoptive Spanish homeland. Two years after I had started writing I completed the book. The data file consisted of four hundred and twenty pages and I was more than proud of myself. However, that wasn't all there was to it. Now the book had to be published.

Meanwhile a few friends and acquaintances had read my manuscript, and all of them had come to the same conclusion: my detective story had been remarkably well written and was so exciting that they could hardly put it down. Well, there you go, I thought. My self-confidence had returned. I – the new star author – would be showered by offers from publishers. I sent exposés of *Pata Negra* to the twenty largest publishing houses in Germany. The result was almost suicidal. Six publishers didn't respond at all and of the other fourteen I received a standard rejection letter. Each refusal brought me down to earth until I was on the verge of mouse-clicking the result of two years' work into the virtual Nirvana.

Fortunately, some remaining optimism averted this. I must not give up! Never ever! So I kept on fighting. I wrote to ten literary agents and received nine rejections. However, one literary agency from Berlin considered *Pata Negra* had potential and signed me on. That at least meant some success for my battered ego. Eduard Freundlinger, the literary newcomer, represented by an agent!

The following year my agent offered my manuscript to a number of publishers. At first she, too, unfortunately also only received letters of refusal. Until one day she reported with joy that the Munich publishing house of Piper had shown interest in my work. Piper? Incredible! I began cheering and leaping for joy around my house, so much so that my cat Lola jumped up in fright, disappeared and didn't show up again for three days. Piper was renowned for having landed some major coups with quite a number of bestsellers – most recently with the book by the German enter-tainer, Hape Kerkeling, about his experiences on the Way of St. James entitled *Ich bin dann mal weg* (I'm Off Then). I browsed through the publisher's home page and soon was certain that at long last fate now meant well for me. Piper would be the ideal home for *Pata Negra*. Every week I checked with my agent to see if there had been any news from Piper. Unfortunately not.

It took a further three months before my agent informed me that Piper had decided, after careful consideration, to refrain from publishing my book. And so my last hopes had been dashed and the cooperation with my agent ended. For three years I had invested all my energy in fulfilling my greatest dream. Now I was on the brink of collapse.

The same applied to my private life: my wife, Virginia, had meanwhile met someone else, who obviously gave her more atten-tion than her husband, the would-be author. She packed her bags and moved in with her new boyfriend taking our five-year old daughter, Paula, with her.

My business ventures weren't going well either, of course, as I had devoted all my energy to my writing career. The import company dealing in ethanol fireplaces had to be closed, and my real estate brokerage made such losses that soon I could no longer bear the overhead costs of my house.

On dull winter days I sometimes sat all alone in the living room admitting to myself that I had put all my eggs into one basket and it had turned out to be a major flop. Occasionally my mobile phone rang, but I hardly ever answered it. Could it be that I would soon be facing another problem? According to some research I had done into psychiatric disorders after my mother's death, a strong symptom of an incipient depression was to ignore the doorbell and/or the telephone. Was this the sign of the beginning of depression?

I slipped and almost fell on the wet leaves covering the steep sunken path. This brought me back to the present, which actually didn't look much better. Still hungover, drenched and half frozen, I felt no inclination whatever to take even one more step although there were only five kilometres left to the next village – and these seemed never-ending.

Around two o'clock in the afternoon I eventually arrived at Triacastela. I threw all my clothes into the hostel's tumble drier and subsequently had a two-hour siesta. At night I strolled through the village and looked in vain for any familiar faces. O Cebreiro was a sort of mandatory stop on the St. James Way. From there pilgrims normally hiked further than the mere eighteen kilometres to Triacastela. Rainhard, Sandy & Co. must have been over all Galician hills and far away by now – a fact which, in Sandy's case, I felt was rather a pity. When I wasn't reminiscing about my clumsy first steps as an author, my muddled thoughts got entangled in the long red hair of this extroverted girl from Dresden.

As I scoffed off the pilgrim's menu all alone in a restaurant, I flipped through my guidebook and caught myself figuring out in what village Sandy would probably be staying overnight the following day. I guessed it would be Ferreiro. However, that was thirty-six kilometres further on from Triacastela. Twice the distance of today's stretch. Back at the hostel I asked myself whether I was about to start running after a woman, who wasn't even my type.

Had I perhaps fallen in love? I hoped not. I had already suffered enough and had other worries to deal with. And anyway … red hair? That was asking for trouble! Added to that she had a complexion like a marble statue in the Vatican and had more freckles on her face than I had hair on my head. Besides, I believed more that the Virgin Mary would appear to me in front of Santiago town gates than that I could ever fall in love again.

With the insight that Sandy would never mean more to me than a nice acquaintance on the Camino, I fell asleep. My subconscious obviously seemed to have different ideas. As if my day hadn't been lousy enough, I had to dream of her in quite a vivid way. However, in my dream Sandy was not lying next to me in a soft four-poster bed, but in the arms of the two-metres-tall Hungarian Peter. Even though the professional pilgrim Casanova had already grabbed Julia, the sweet girl from Duesseldorf, now he had started working on Sandy as well?

I watched them whispering sweet nothings to each other for a while, before I woke up drenched in sweat. A new day was about to dawn on the Camino. This one could only be better than the last.

Chapter Twenty-Eight

Triacastela – Ferreiros

The following day started promisingly. I even had three good reasons to be cheerful. To begin with the sun was shining again after yesterday's downpour. My negative thoughts had evaporated like the rain clouds in the sky. It was not a coincidence that I had chosen the Costa Tropical in Spain, with an average of only ten rainy days per year, as my adopted home region. This rather short stretch of the southern Spanish coastline is quite correctly advertised as having a perfect sub-tropical climate with warm winters and long hot summers. Neither in rainy Ireland nor in the sombre Norwegian winter nor in the misty regions of Austria would I be able to live a happy life in the long run. Depression would then be my permanent companion.

The second reason for rejoicing was a stone at the roadside on which an inscription announced that it was now only one hundred kilometres more to Santiago. Light footed I wandered through Galician villages, autumnal chestnut forests, green fields, over country roads with hardly any traffic and covered in cow pats, along ancient Roman paths and over bridges. As the Camino had already given me more insights for my further life than I had ever dreamt of, I didn't want to spend any more time brooding over things on my last days. I tried to meditate whilst walking and enjoyed the scenery as well as the sun after the heavy rain. In short, I did what 'permanent pilgrim' Marcelino had impressed upon me to do whilst we were leaving the village of Logroño:

Listen to the silence of the Way.

Now, the third reason for my good spirits was some news in my email inbox. It came from a member of the Piper Publishing Company staff, who euphorically informed me that the latest in my series of crime novels, *Im Schatten der Alhambra* (In the Shadow of the Alhambra), had been mentioned in 'Bunte' magazine – by far the most important German women's magazine. This was, of course, exactly my target group. The question was, whether it would actually change anything in terms of sales?

Hardly. After all, *Im Schatten der Alhambra* had not actually enjoyed exploding sales figures after it had been mentioned in the weeks following publication in 'Bild', 'Focus' and a dozen other daily German newspapers and magazines. The write-up in 'Bunte' essentially consisted of two phrases: "The discovery of an ancient find has murderous consequences. Ideal holiday reading." Not a particularly informative 'book review'. Nevertheless, I was proud to have managed a mention in this magazine at all. When I come to think of it, it had long been unclear whether I would ever get one of my books published at all.

Since at the time all major German publishing houses had decided against *Pata Negra*, I had decided to try the second row and contacted some smaller publishers. And, look what happened: it appealed to the small publishing house of Allitera based in Munich. At the time Allitera had only five employees, one trainee and one student apprentice and was located in the private house of the publisher himself, Dr. Goebel. I sensed that there wouldn't be a sizeable advance payment here. But money was the last of my motivations for getting my book published.

But after some promising telephone conversations with Dr. Goebel there had sadly followed a refusal. Regrettably Allitera could not take the significant financial risk of publishing a book by an unknown author. The next hit below the belt.

Inspired by the positive assessment of my test readers, I had no choice but to fight on. I made an appointment with the publisher and his managing director and flew to Munich. Wearing my most stylish suit, I shook hands with both of them showing the self-confidence of a nouveau-riche Russian oligarch and asked them what the problem was. If it was money, then that shouldn't hinder a deal as I had enough of that, I assured them, claiming to be the big Spanish real estate tycoon, which, of course, I was not. Nevertheless, my strategy of taking on the financial risk seemed to work. An hour later, we had a deal. I agreed to advance the printing costs covering the first edition of three thousand copies. Because I didn't have so much ready money, as I had just tried to make Dr. Goebel believe, we agreed that I would financially guarantee a sales revenue on one thousand copies, to put them in a position to pay for the printing costs. Thus, if the worst case were to happen and no-one was interested in my book, I would in effect have to buy the one thousand copies of my own publication – and would be financially ruined. This clause was placed at the top of our contract, which I then signed with a very uneasy feeling.

For the hopeless venture of selling one thousand copies of a not-yet-printed book by an unknown author at a price of sixteen euros and ninety cents each, I had three months. During this time the term 'friendship' assumed a completely new relevance for me. Before then I had known that I had a lot of friends with whom I could have a beer and a chat every now and then. Afterwards, I knew that I had a lot of friends I could really rely on when it mattered. Many of my friends and relatives bought twenty, thirty, forty, fifty copies in advance – two of them even one hundred – in order to give them away as gifts in their circle of acquaintances after printing.

For my part I started using Facebook in a big way and tried to persuade users into buying my books. I got cautioned three times regarding Spam and my account was blocked every now and then – at the end of the three month-period, when I really overdid things, this was for even two weeks. However, by then all book stores, libraries, bloggers and users with names like 'Bücherwurm' (bookworm), 'Leseratte'(avid reader) and 'Krimimaus' (crime novel mouse) knew, that a certain Mr. Freundlinger existed, whose debut novel was called *Pata Negra*.

Through self-marketing and the support of numerous friends nine hundred copies of my thriller were ordered in advance. Only the remaining one hundred copies I had to buy myself. Three years after I had commenced writing, my detective story finally got into print. Three years full of highs and lows, deprivations and disappointments.

Three long years, during which I could have also invested my energy into more lucrative occupations.

On 2 March 2011, I held a bound copy of *Pata Negra* in my hands for the very first time. It was almost as intense an experience as the birth of my daughter eight years previously. However, now things really had to get going. Of the three thousand first-edition copies, two thousand were still in the warehouse of a wholesaler. And I really didn't want to blame myself afterwards for not having given my utmost in pushing the sales of my books.

Unfortunately, this initially involved substantial investments on my part. I agreed with my publisher that we would share a stand at the Leipzig Book Fair in 2011. I covered fifty percent of the costs and therefore half of the stand was to be covered in my books. As a marketing gag I got an eight-kilo '*pata negra*' Iberian cured ham and some bottles of Spanish red wine.

As soon as the fair had opened, I didn't let anyone pass our stand without first having taken a look at my thriller. In the first half hour I managed to sell five books, which I proudly announced to my publisher when he arrived at the stand a little later. Instead of rejoicing for me, he seemed to get an acute asthma attack. By the time he had calmed down, he told me that it was strictly prohibited to sell books at the stand. We could even lose our stand permit. There was a separate special fair bookshop in Hall 2. There three copies of *Pata Negra* were on sale. I caught my breath - had I heard correctly? Only *three* copies? Asthma actually seemed contagious.

I hurried towards Hall 2 and straight into the huge fair bookshop. The current bestsellers had been artfully stacked to form enormous towers. In between there were tables on which books written by well-known authors were piled up. On the wall at the very back, lined up on a shelf fifteen metres long, were works by authors in alphabetical order, in whom nobody showed much interest. It took me a while to discover the spines of the three copies of my book under the letter 'F'. That was quite different from what I had imagined. The chance that amongst all these thousands of titles somebody would come across my book by sheer accident was equal to winning the lottery.

However, I was so motivated that there was no holding me back. Together with a combination of cafè latte all round and Austrian charm I bribed the team of the fair bookshop to allow me to build a tower of one hundred copies of my novel. And for doing so I picked a prime location: right at the entrance and next to the equally high stack of the bestseller at the time by Dan Brown. Beside my mountain of books I placed a chair and a table on which I presented the Iberian ham. Subsequently I advertised autograph sessions and a tasting of *'pata negra'* cured ham. I made good use of my 'gift of the gab' as well as my sales experience and counted on the human being's herd instinct. Whenever there were just three people standing in front of my 'autograph session' table, actually more interesting in scoffing off my expensive ham than my book, automatically others queued up assuming that the chap there had to be a renowned author as otherwise no fair visitor would queue up for an autograph.

It worked perfectly, only the exhibition shop owner looked at me with increasing scepticism while I brandished a long sharp knife like Zorro in his book store in order to cut slices of ham off the joint. In this way, I was hardly able to keep up with signing my books for four whole days. The German courier service, DHL, even had to bring another load of books by express delivery.

At the end of the last day of the Book Fair, the manager of the store congratulated me on my success. According to his calculations *Pata Negra* had become the best selling book of his fair store with a total of over five hundred copies sold. Even better than Dan Brown's and all other bestsellers.

But the other authors hadn't been on the spot taking care of signing their books and handing out slices of expensive Spanish ham. If I hadn't offered my thriller in the same way as a market trader shouting out his wares, it would undoubtedly have remained unsung amongst the multitude of books presented. After all, nobody had ever heard of me. Any further success in sales was thus going to depend very much on me.

So much had I learned in Leipzig.

In the meantime *Pata Negra* had also been listed with Amazon and was climbing up the bestseller list there. For quite a while it was number one in the sector of crime novels set in Spain and ranked under the top 100 of all crime thrillers for more than a year. These first successes boosted my morale. In order to be able to take even better care of the sales of my novel, I relocated to Munich for a period of three months. I visited all book stores in the surroundings and tried to convince them to include my thriller in their stock. In addition I approached all bookshops in Germany, Austria and Switzerland or wrote emails to them for days on end. Within one month I had gathered about three thousand contacts.

Some of the branches of the Hugendubel chain of prestige bookshops in and around Munich became convinced of the potential of *Pata Negra* and subsequently integrated my thriller into their range. Unfortunately there was considerable competition amongst crime fiction and the potential customers who stood around the presentation table, which was roughly the same size as my bedroom, were browsing through all kinds of crime stories – all except *Pata Negra*.

Holding a copy in my hand and with a smile on my face I started chatting up some of the unsuspecting customers.

"A very good day to you. I can thoroughly recommend this thriller. The story takes place in Spain and it's very exciting – I know this particularly well as I'm the author!" (short chuckle ...). "Normally I live in Spain, but right now I happen to be here in Munich for a short stay and if you should decide on the spur of the moment to buy a copy of my book I'd be delighted to sign it for you with a personal dedication. Such an opportunity doesn't come along every day, does it? And if the thriller isn't quite your taste, it would always make a very nice gift for someone – even for Christmas – it's not that far away and time flies."

This sales pitch didn't work with everyone, of course, but at least with every second or third potential customer. Some of them even wanted to have several copies autographed. In only a quarter of an hour I managed to sell the five or six copies that had been on display on the table. Then I turned to the head of the crime fiction department, pointed out to her that my novels were selling like hot cakes and asked her to urgently place an order for more copies. Then I walked on to the next branch store and repeated my guerrilla marketing tactics.

In the months following the first publication of *Pata Negra* I was rewarded for the many efforts and struggles I had undergone beforehand. My motto never ever to give up slowly paid off. The first edition of three thousand copies was sold out after two months, and six further editions followed suit. *Pata Negra* became by far the best selling title in the publishing house's history. Also thanks to the proceeds from the sales of my book, Allitera relocated from the publisher's private house to it's own, more elegant offices. The Internet reviews showed around eighty percent positive results – which was far better than I had hoped for in the beginning. I even received fan mail, and readers touring Andalusia came to visit me in Spain in order to have their copy signed by me.

And all of a sudden things started to work out, even with a well-known publishing house. The sales success of *Pata Negra* ensured that I was offered a contract for a second thriller by the renowned publishing house of *Piper* in Munich, who had initially turned down *Pata Negra*.

I signed a contract and began work on my follow-up title *Die Schwarze Finca* (The Black Finca). From now on the surge of my literary success was not to be stopped. At least that's what I thought. My assumption was theoretically based on a simple calculation, even though at school my prowess in mathematics had been comparable to a Sumo wrestler trying his hand at pole vaulting. But this very calculation was ridiculously simple: if I had sold ten thousand books with the first publisher who only employed five people, sales through a publishing house with one hundred times the number of staff should also amount to one hundred times as many copies of my second thriller. All-in-all sales of one million titles. Unfortunately, as it turned out later, I had once again made a terrible mathematical miscalculation!

In the town of Sarria I got distracted by an illustrated menu billboard in front of a restaurant and my reminiscences were interrupted. It was around two o'clock in the afternoon and I had managed twenty kilometres. Actually I could have left it at that, but my travel guide advised me against doing so as at this point. Mass pilgrim tourism was rearing its ugly head. So I decided just to get something to eat here and then carry on walking towards Ferreiros. Maybe I would catch up with the others there. The menu was quite tempting, but prices were astronomical for pilgrims.

"Hi, pilgrim brother Eduard!"

Grinning I turned around. "Hello, pilgrim sister!" I gave Sandy, as well as her backpack, a hefty squeeze. As I had been hiking today's stretch alone so far, I was looking forward to companionship. For the rest of the day we strolled along together towards Ferreiros, which we didn't reach before late in the evening. In the course of this rather slow hike we exchanged stories of our lives – openly and without glossing over anything. I told her about my worries and problems, the calling off of my planned wedding and I even admitted most of my character defects and weak spots to her. In the end it seemed that we could make each other laugh and that we also had quite a lot in common. In a very short period of time Sandy had developed into a kind of soul mate. And what is more, I got to know some quite interesting 'facts' from her – namely, that the Burning Man Festival which took place in the Nevada desert, was "mega cool", that bananas had to "crunch" and that 'Calimocho' is a blend of Coca Cola and red wine – of which we had had abundant quantities that day – and was supposed to be the best energy drink ever. Sandy had contributed to a social project in Peru, had beaten her way for weeks through the wildernesses of Brazil and crossed the Alps on foot from Munich. And she had many more dreams still to be fulfilled in her lifetime and these were not so unlike my own.

Right on time for sunset we arrived at Ferreiros. Rainhard,

Martin and the others had obviously trekked on because we didn't see any familiar faces in the hostel. We kept to ourselves for dinner and ordered a bottle of red wine with the bill, which we then emptied together in the hostel's kitchen, wrapped up in blankets and nestling next to each other while the other pilgrims had long since gone off to bed. Without actually talking about it, it had become clear to us that as from now on we would be hiking together on our pilgrimage to Santiago.

When I crawled into my sleeping bag long after midnight, I thought of the irony of fate. If I had met Sandy earlier on the Camino, I would definitely have tried everything to avoid walking more than three kilometres at her side. After all, I still had so much to ponder on at the time. But now I was actually looking forward to hiking the remaining stretches together. The last leg of the Camino could be accomplished in three days, but we intended not to be so ambitious and take four days for it.

And there was something else I had to think about whilst slowly falling asleep: so far I hadn't had a real female friend, someone who was not a partner in a relationship but rather a platonic female 'buddy'. Sooner or later, however, it was usually doomed to failure as one or the other of the two wanted more than just a platonic friendship.

Now this seemed different between Sandy and myself. Even though we hadn't specifically touched on the issue, considering what I already knew – or thought I knew – about the other gender's body language, this told me that she would not be inclined to anything further than pure friendship. It was exactly the same with me – at least that's what I thought I felt at the time. In any case, we were planning to visit each other after the Camino in both Spain and Dresden. There was even talk of going on a longer hike together. Maybe even an alpine crossing. I could imagine many joint undertakings with her. After all, she was on the way to becoming my first platonic female chum ever. And no more.

Or maybe...?

Chapter Twenty-Nine

Ferreiros – Ventas de Narón

This "or maybe...?" gave me a sleepless night. I tossed and turned while she was lying beneath me – albeit underneath me in her lower part of our bunk bed, a situation which cost me even more of my sleep. During dinner, as had already happened in O Cebreiro, after my third glass of wine something seemed to have struck me about the appearance of my new *amiga*. Of course, women pilgrims didn't hike along the Camino sumptuously dressed up to the nines in short skirts and high heels. Therefore guys like myself who were inclined to have a rather superficial perception where young women were concerned, very easily failed to recognize the graceful femininity of many a female companion beneath their unkempt and sweaty pilgrim outfits. And this had also been the case with Sandy up to now. Earlier this evening, however, she had dressed up for our pilgrim's menu supper with all the appropriate items that her small backpack could offer as if we were about to dine in a gourmet restaurant. That the high heels and short skirt were missing didn't really matter - my fantasy took care of that, and it wasn't long before this fantasy had caused an evident stirring in a certain part of my masculine anatomy.

Unfortunately – or thank goodness – this condition didn't last long. Although I was as familiar with female thought patterns as I was with nanotechnology, even I realized that a shave and some hair gel wouldn't be enough to turn myself into Sandy's Prince Charming. I was sure that I was too overweight for her and with an age difference of twelve years, also too old. On top of that I had plausibly assured her during the last stretch we had walked together, that I was an absolute loser whom one should definitely steer clear of. At the time I hadn't regarded Sandy as a young and pretty woman, to whom I should present myself from my very best side in order that my courtship behaviour should have a chance of success. I had rather seen in her a psychotherapist in worn-out trainers, to whom I could complain about my misery, my fiascos and my inadequacies free of charge and uncensored. And I had done just that with ruthless candour and had even wept now and again. No, I was definitely not Sandy's type I told myself and clutched my damp pillow. The broken engagement, the marriage called off as well as my financial problems had severely battered my self-esteem and didn't leave me with any other way of thinking.

Sandy earned her money as a bartender in a trendy location in Dresden. There it was certainly brimming with successful young guys of Sandy's age with well-trained bodies, substantial incomes, chic clothing and expensive watches, who would court her with pricey iconic cocktails. If I were Sandy, I would choose one of them – rather than an unsuccessful author who carried too much weight and too many problems around with him, whose best years were obviously behind him and whose depressive disposition was more in need of sessions with a shrink than a new love affair. Furthermore I lived in Spain and she far away in Eastern Germany. Even if all other parameters and a horoscope, in which she believed, were favourable, this detail alone would make any prospect of a continued relationship off the St. James Way practically impossible.

And in three days' time the Camino would be history.

Around five o'clock in the morning I gave up trying to sleep any longer. As Sandy's omnipresence yesterday had preoccupied me so much, I hadn't had the time to look at the latest comments on my last Facebook posts on my smart phone and so I read them now. There were dozens. I was very moved. Once again I realized that hundreds of users were waiting for my daily entry. I felt deep gratitude for the attention I received and typed the following sentimental text into my mobile with fingers more like those of a forest worker than of an author:

My journey of a lifetime is slowly coming to an end, but despite all the exertion, hardship, aches and pains, I am indeed rather melancholy that it will soon be over – because there were also so very many positive experiences, wonderful encounters and acquaintances. The Way of St. James has changed my life. So what are a few blisters on my feet in comparison? Although my journey, and thus my travel blog, is not yet finished, I would like to write an acknowledgement now, as is usual at the end of a book. This time it's not a thankyou to a publishing house, to a publishing editor or to an agent, but to YOU all! Before setting out on the journey I had regarded Facebook as being a superficial medium, on which countless photos of cats can be admired or annoying Candy-Crush invitations received – and, of course, as a marketing instrument for my crime stories.

The truth is that up to now I had been too superficial in my own attitude towards Facebook. Once on the Camino, however, I wanted to change this. So now, instead of issuing a regular boring travel blog, I have been revealing my deepest feelings to you all, relentlessly and shamelessly. The result has been amazing: many of you have been doing exactly the same and have confided in me in private messages, for which I am very grateful. I have greatly enjoyed this exchange with you, and even more as it has helped me to deepen the knowledge and the findings I have gathered. Firstly, as I had to put my thoughts into words and therefore saw things more clearly and, secondly, because I have learnt a great deal from the many comments, private messages and emails I have received. There were moments in which I was almost at an end – mentally as well as physically – with hundreds of kilometres still ahead of me before reaching my goal. But just knowing that there were a lot of 'amigos' on the sidelines to spur me on, to encourage me with their comments, give me moral support whenever necessary and who simply believed in me, made it clear that giving up would never be an option. You made me surpass myself. Through your support you have contributed more to the success of my journey than you probably realize. For that

I would like to thank you from my heart. Muchas gracias for having accompanied me on the Way. With the warmest greetings from the Camino, Your pilgrim brother Eduard.

Sandy had the remarkable talent to change from one subject to another without any transition whatsoever. As I wasn't used to such an eloquent conversation partner any more, there was often the risk of some misinterpretations. For example, she had been telling me about a hike across a Brazilian plateau for days on end which she undertook accompanied by a young Russian. Then she listed the animals she had seen there including a giant snake, but in the next breath added that "...nothing happened between the two of us".

"Well, that was lucky", I replied. "Just imagine the snake had bitten you or strangled you to death."

"No, you idiot, what I meant was that nothing happened between me and the Russian guy! And the pyramids weren't built by the Egyptians. According to some YouTube videos that would have been totally impossible", changing subjects once again. Just as I was about to follow her in a mental speed of light to the Valley of Kings, the next quantum leap followed:

"Can you kiss at all?"

"I beg your pardon?" The shock almost made me step into a cow pat. We had been hiking through some wonderful autumnal landscape for about three hours by now and had been fooling around most of the time. The sun was shining, everything was fine. Until that question just now.

"Well, I asked you whether you kiss well?"

What on earth could one reply to that? Men more courageous than myself would probably have put an arm around the source of the question's neck, the other one around her waist, and without further ado would have provided convincing evidence of their talent in this respect. A slightly more spontaneous fellow would have subsequently taken her behind the next tree trunk and gone much further with her until it rained chestnuts. Sadly, however, I numbered among the rather shy guys. Besides, behind the next tree there was a toothless old woman busy harvesting chestnuts. Furthermore, Sandy didn't give me the impression that she had had that kind of development of the situation in mind when she posed that rather thoughtless question.

"I th-th-think so", I stammered. "If not, you could always teach me", I offered.

Wrong answer. Totally wrong answer.

"Oh, man, that's simply the crassest turn off ever! At the age of forty-five you must at least know how to kiss a woman!", she reprimanded me, and a split second afterwards was back on the subject of pyramids again and that they couldn't possibly have been constructed by the ancient Egyptians.

Two hours and many conspiracy theories later I noticed a forest clearing a little way off the path. Framed by trees bearing autumnal coloured foliage, there was a field of flowers the size of a soccer pitch. I led Sandy to its 'kick-off spot' in the centre, where we then lay shoulder-to-shoulder in the grass looking up into the cloudless sky. Our hands were touching at hip level. But no hand reached for the other. Without speaking we lay there for a while enjoying the bond with nature. How long had it been since I had last lain in a meadow simply relaxing and leaving all my cares behind?

But suddenly I was seized by an inner restlessness. It began to grow and sent my pulse rising. If I hadn't known the background any better, I would have been afraid of suffering a heart attack. I hesitated for a moment, then I made a decision. I leaned on my elbow and turned to the side – to Sandy's side. I reached over her with my left hand, supported myself beside her shoulder and just hoped that the bee on the dandelion next to her wouldn't sabotage my plan by stinging my finger. Then I looked deep into Sandy's eyes as I slowly bent down towards her closing my own eyelids a little. Her eyes, however, widened. My mouth gently opened. She pressed her lips together so tightly that all the colour vanished from them. Her mouth was only a nose length away.

Then she turned away and stared at the bee. I knew all along, that this stupid stinging creature would screw up my intentions.

"Would you like something to eat? I still have a banana in my backpack", I tried to save the situation as best I could.

"No, thanks. Let's move on!"

I knew it. I just wasn't her type I told myself during the next few kilometres. On the other hand she had asked me out of the blue pilgrim's sky whether I could kiss well and indirectly encouraged me to this daring amorous approach, for which I would now feel ashamed for the rest of the Way of St. James.

As said before, it was probably easier to get the hang of nanotechnology than of women's thought patterns.

During the rest of the day's stretch we chatted about more 'innocent' topics. Sandy had obviously decided not to make any further comments on the subject of the wild flower meadow and I crossed off any possible upgrade of our pilgrim-brother-pilgrim-sister relationship once and for all. In the afternoon we arrived at the village of Ventas de Narón that comprised of two pilgrim hostels and a farmstead. I did my laundry, compiled my Facebook blog and had a shower. The culinary offer in the hostel was not particularly varied, in fact just cold sandwiches, so we strolled over to the second hostel whose small dining area was almost packed to capacity. Only in one corner an elderly Dutchman sat alone at the table, so we joined him.

As soon as he had introduced himself to us, he told us about Toni. Toni was a frog, the first frog to hike along the Camino. Of course, Toni only existed in his fantasy, which seemed rather close to that of J.K. Rowling as during the course of the following hour he told us about a series of adventures that the brave frog Toni had had to survive on the Camino. If I had been his five-year-old grandchild listening to a bed-time story, I would have found it quite interesting. We did without our dessert and returned to our hostel.

There, the next extraordinary species of pilgrim was already waiting for us. Before dinner there had only been two Swedish women in our dormitory as well as ourselves. Now also Paco from Granada had joined us, a native of the same Spanish province in which I had been living for years. For this reason alone I automatically advanced to the status of his best friend.

Paco had spread the contents of his backpack on the dormitory's floor, which now resembled a Mount Everest base camp: high tech outdoor clothing, hiking boots worth around three hundred euros, survival provisions and a medical kit which could have belonged to an entire "Doctors Without Borders" team. As he was sorting his equipment, hectically and noisily, he bragged about his intention to walk the Camino from Sarria to Santiago in only three days. He had accomplished thirty-eight kilometres that day, tomorrow it would be thirty-six and on the final day he would manage thirty-nine kilometres.

I pretended to be impressed and stifled the obvious question of what he was hoping for by racing ahead. Instead I told him that we wanted to take more time for the last kilometres.

No problem, Paco said. In that case he would reach Santiago before us and by the time we arrived he would already know where to get the tastiest tapas and the best wine. I should definitely call him there, and he ceremoniously presented me with his mobile phone number. Sandy got as a gift from him a Saint James scallop shell, of which he had at least a dozen more in his backpack, as well as an ointment for joint pains.

I zipped up my sleeping bag and just hoped not to dream about either Toni, the Dutch frog, or Paco, the Spanish one-hundred-kilometre pilgrim.

Chapter Thirty

Ventas de Narón – Melide

From Ventas de Narón it was still seventy-five kilometres to Santiago. Unlike Paco, who roused us from sleep at six in the morning by packing his backpack with as much hullabaloo as possible, our intention was to take three days for the last leg of the route by hiking around twenty-five kilometres each day.

So much for our plan.

Having said this, we made only very slow progress and had to take breaks more often. Pilgrim sister Sandy said that her "hoof" was "mega sore", so that she couldn't walk any faster. As she was lying by the wayside like a lame nag and I was standing rather helplessly next to her, a Canadian passed by and asked whether he could help. He claimed to be familiar with such matters – as this was his job, he said.

"Yes, please!", I replied and once again started to believe a little more in the presence of the 'dear Lord'.

The man, who, on top of everything was a lookalike of the famous German sports physician and national football team 'Doc', Hans-Wilhelm Müller-Wohlfahrt, diagnosed an acute inflammation of the shin bone, kneeled down beside Sandy and started a reiki treatment. In the process he moved the palms of his hands to and fro a couple of centimetres above Sandy's bruised leg to get "the pain out of her body". I doubted whether this would actually work without even touching the leg, but the Canadian faith healer seemed to know what he was doing. At last he put some balm onto her lower leg and bandaged it using tape from his backpack.

"Your wife will be better soon" the doc assured me at the end of his open-air consultation. My wife? Quite obviously the man had a deficit in clairvoyance.

Sandy was amused by his remark. "Let's move on, my dear husband", she said.

"Wait a moment!" I turned to the Reiki expert and asked him whether he would be able to stroke away a few superfluous kilos from my paunch with his magical hands.

Unfortunately, his skills wouldn't go that far, he admitted, smiling, and walked on.

I lent my hiking poles to Sandy, helped her with difficult sections of the trail and suffered with her as if my own shin bone was hurting. After just a few kilometres, for which we needed two hours, we took a break in a rather idyllically located hostel. Next to the entrance stood a table and some chairs. I dragged all of it, which had been intended for smokers, out of the shade over to the other side of the road where there was sun, and got hold of some ice cubes wrapped in a cloth from the bar to cool Sandy's lower leg. As an anaesthetic I served her her favourable drink – Calimocho.

Some of the pilgrims who were passing by joined us for a chat. Most of them probably thought of us as a couple – after all we gave a happy, maybe even amorous impression to our fellow pilgrims. And that certainly applied to me. I had actually fallen in love with Sandy. Not, however, in the classic way. Through my new soulmate I had begun to experience a completely different form of love that was very satisfying. Maybe the term "brotherly love" was the most appropriate. Never before had I felt this intense kind of affection. And that had happened after a mere five days on the Camino, of which we had only encountered each other sporadically during the first three days.

Although during this time we hadn't come closer to each other physically, we had developed an intimacy on a mental and spiritual level. We had been philosophizing a lot about life in general, our journeys, society, literature, our dreams and expectations of ourselves as well as others. In doing so we had discovered an almost startling consensus in our views.

In addition Sandy had taught me a third kind of love: self-love. Although whilst on the Camino I had lost the classic sort of love in the form of my ex-fiancée Tatiana, I had experienced authentic brotherly love and charity from Sandy and many other pilgrims instead. Since then I had indeed started to love myself more than I had ever done before setting out on my pilgrimage.

The most striking words on self-love do not originate, however, from the pens of Sartre, Kant or Voltaire – but from the author Kim McMillan in her book *When I Loved Myself Enough*. For years, the following poem has been accredited to Charlie Chaplin – and the dispute over its origins whether from Chaplin or McMillan continues today. But whatever, Chaplin made it popular by reciting it in his speech on the occasion of his seventieth birthday and Kim McMillan's book must certainly have been an inspiration for it. The poem says:

As I began to love myself I found that anguish and emotional suffering are only warning signs that I was living against my own truth.
Today, I know, this is "AUTHENTICITY".

As I began to love myself I understood how much it can offend somebody if I try to force my desires on this person, even though I knew the time was not right and the person was not ready for it, and even though this person was me.
Today I call it "RESPECT".

As I began to love myself I stopped craving for a different life, and I could see that everything that surrounded me was inviting me to grow.
Today I call it "MATURITY".

. . .

As I began to love myself I understood that at any circumstance, I am in the right place at the right time, and everything happens at the exactly right moment. So I could be calm.
Today I call it "SELF-CONFIDENCE".

As I began to love myself I quit stealing my own time, and I stopped designing huge projects for the future. Today, I only do what brings me joy and happiness, things I love to do and that make my heart cheer, and I do them in my own way and in my own rhythm.
Today I call it "SIMPLICITY".

As I began to love myself I freed myself of anything that is no good for my health – food, people, things, situations, and everything that drew me down and away from myself. At first I called this attitude a healthy egoism.
Today I know it is "LOVE OF ONESELF".

As I began to love myself I quit trying to always be right, and ever since I was wrong less of the time.
Today I discovered that is "MODESTY".

As I began to love myself I refused to go on living in the past and worrying about the future. Now, I only live for the moment, where everything is happening.
Today I live each day, day by day, and I call it "FULFILLMENT".

As I began to love myself I recognized that my mind can disturb me and it can make me sick. But as I connected it to my heart, my mind became a valuable ally.
Today I call this connection "WISDOM OF THE HEART".

We no longer need to fear arguments, confrontations or any kind of problems with

ourselves or others. Even stars collide, and out of their crashing new worlds are born.
Today I know "THAT IS LIFE"!

After a two-hour break we wandered on. Meanwhile it was late afternoon and there were still ten kilometres to walk to Melide.

I honestly thought we would never make it, but Sandy held out bravely and limped towards our destination, which we finally reached around nine o'clock in the evening. Our lodging that night was a former hotel offering many smaller dormitories to accommodate from four to six people. We were lucky and got one room just for ourselves.

On our way through Melide we had passed a restaurant advertising the best Galician *pulpo a la gallega*. We wanted to have dinner there. Whilst taking a shower I asked myself how the evening would develop. After all, for the first time we would be dining in an elegant restaurant without mixing in with the other pilgrims. Could this now qualify as a date?

Sandy obviously had similar thoughts in her mind. She seemed unusually inhibited and reticent. There was a candle burning on the table, and in my heart feelings began to flare up like the flame. I tried to ignore these as much as possible as it was a sure thing that this delicate flame would, if at all, only continue flickering until Santiago, where it would then be blown out like candles on a birthday cake.

Back in our room I wanted to give Sandy a spontaneous hug before turning in, without any ulterior motives, just to let her know that she was a great pilgrim sister. But she probably thought that I only wanted to take advantage of the situation and resisted my advances. She murmured that we could hug each other when we got to Santiago.

Our pilgrim relationship didn't seem to be running completely without misunderstandings I sensed, but was too tired to try and discuss it that night. I lay down in the bed next to hers and immediately fell asleep.

· · ·

Like so many times before I woke up only two hours later and lay awake until the early hours of the morning. Sandy was sleeping just a metre away from me as I was tossing and turning in bed thinking of love.

Years ago, as a young man, I had still believed in true love, but after so many failed relationships this had long since changed. Now, at the age of forty-five, half of my life lay behind me. Would I ever experience real love again? And would any woman ever get the chance of it with me? Once bitten, twice shy! And afterwards even patting another dog would be a challenge for anyone! On the other hand, at times my love had been nothing more than sheer gratefulness for conveniences and comforts provided. From numerous man-to-man conversations I had learned that this was a widespread phenomenon amongst my fellow males.

There is no notion with more diverse interpretations than 'love'. A particularly auspicious one originates from the late Marcel Reich-Ranicki, a Polish-German author and publicist. In his autobiography he writes: "*What we call love is every extreme feeling which leads from affection to passion and from passion to dependency; it transforms the individual into a state of intoxication that temporarily restricts the sanity of the person involved or even the person affected: it is a joy that spreads pain, and a pain that gives people joy.*"

And sometimes, I had to admit, it wasn't my mind that was longing for love, but my desire that was demanding fulfillment. These kinds of relationships had, in general, a durability comparable to the shelf life of an open bottle of milk in the sun. Nevertheless, during my lifetime I had quite often been fortunate enough to experience the feeling of being in love. Some of my very strong emotions, however, had often led straight into a dead-end, as, for example, the affair involving Alejandra from Peru – a love tragedy that couldn't have been staged more tragically even in a Puccini opera.

I had met Alejandra in the Peruvian village of Cusco. While I was backpacking through South America, together with a few friends, I wanted to hike the classic Inca Trail that starts from Cusco. Alejandra was squatting on the steps of the cathedral and looked so adorable that, contrary to my usual nature, I just had to chat her up – taking into account a more than ninety percent chance of a rebuff. Although it must be noted here that at the time my dark hair had been bleached by the sun, my face was deeply tanned making my eyes sparkle like sapphires and even my body mass index was still within acceptable limits. In any case she seemed to be attracted to this Austrian globetrotter.

Alejandra came from Lima and was spending her vacation with a girlfriend in Cusco. For three days I courted this Latin American beauty more or less in vain. On the fourth day, however, an arduous foot march lasting several days across some of the Andean peaks towards the ancient Inca ruins of Machu Picchu had been planned. At the time I was travelling with a group of backpackers. We had only met en route: Arnie from Australia, Joe from New Zealand, Heiko, a German, Jamie from Canada as well as a Swedish guy whose name I can't quite recall. If I didn't want to lose sight of my new friends, I would have to join them on the trek to Machu Picchu. So there was just this one night left for an attempt at getting really closer to this Peruvian beauty for the first time. I explained my dilemma to Alejandra and she seemed to understand.

I met my beloved one in a quiet little bar. She had dressed up and looked so beautiful that I was afraid I was dreaming and soon my alarm clock back in Austria would go off and send me off to work. After just one drink we were strolling towards our love nest.

Beforehand, however, we had to deal with a small logistical problem. I was sharing my hotel room with Arnie and Alejandra hers, which was located three hundred metres down the road, with her girlfriend. So I had approached Arnie and asked if he would move in with Joe for the one night so I could stay 'undisturbed' with Alejandra. Of course he did me the favour, but, the chaotic jerk that he was, he had left all his belongings scattered around everywhere in our room.

The night of love was indeed a dream come true. At least the night was ... We didn't manage to detach ourselves from each other until the early hours of the morning. Alejandra then wanted to return to her hotel in order to preserve some sense of propriety in the face of her friend. I accompanied her to the hotel lobby and said good-bye to her there. This parting was only going to be for a week, as she had already given me her address in Lima. After the Inca Trail I intended to visit her in the capital and stay with her for a month. I could hardly wait as I had madly fallen in love with the Peruvian girl – unconditionally and without contemplating any potential future complications.

I returned to my hotel at an easy pace and went back to bed as a happy man. Just as I was about to switch off the bedside lamp it suddenly struck me that something was missing. Later on I would ask myself over and over again how anyone could have been so unbelievably stupid, but the fatal conclusion I had come to at this particular moment seemed to be the only possible one.

"No! No, please!", I murmured, and searched the room in vain for the missing item. Beside myself with rage and disappointment tears came to my eyes. How could she do this to me? That rotten, sneaky … well, just you wait!

I pulled on my jeans, ran down the stairs and along the street almost kicking the door down when the night porter didn't want to open up. When he finally let me in I stormed into her room and found Alejandra and her friend sitting cross-legged on their beds chatting. Without doubt about the naïve stranger whom she had just ripped-off.

"Where is it?" I snarled at Alejandra.

"I beg your pardon? What are you doing here?"

"Shut up and give me the wallet!"

She was playing the innocent. I opened up the wardrobe and ransacked it to find the stolen item. Once Alejandra had recovered from the shock of my furious performance, she started crying. But I wasn't going to fall for this sob story. Nevertheless I explained the matter to her in a somewhat calmer manner.

"Arnie's wallet was lying on the bedside table the whole night, on your side of the bed. And after you had left earlier, all of a sudden it had disappeared. Don't you think that's an odd coincidence? There was nobody else in the room except for the two of us, and as I certainly don't have it, it must be you who has stolen it. Now give it back, you miserable thief! I had really thought that I meant something to you. You should become an actress …"

"Are you talking about this one?" Alejandra asked, pulling a brown purse out of her handbag.

I nodded and stretched out my hand for it. "I won't report you to the police, even though I should do. But I just don't get it, why you ..."

"It's mine!" she interrupted me, screeching loudly.

"Um ... eh... w-what ... y-yours?"

Then she explained to me what had happened. When we had entered the room, first of all I had been very angry because of the way Arnie had left all his belongings scattered everywhere. While I had been clearing up some of the mess she had taken off her coat and had put her handbag as well as her purse on to the bedside table. The purse looked so much like Arnie's wallet that I had assumed he had forgotten it in our room. Later on I had noticed it was missing on the bedside table and had drawn the wrong conclusions.

As proof, Alejandra whipped a piece of paper out of the purse, onto which I had scribbled my telephone number and my address in Austria an hour ago in the hotel room.

I had quite often put my foot in it during my lifetime, but not as deeply and despicably as now. I babbled an excuse, but Alejandra just threw me out of her room. You dumb asshole, I thought to myself. To call Alejandra, who was about to become the love of my life, a thief, completely out of thin air, could only happen to me. Heart-stricken I dragged my feet back to my hotel.

Later that morning I told my friends about my blackout with such serious consequence. They burst out laughing so loudly that they could probably even have been heard in Argentina. Only the Swedish guy showed some pity and recommended that I should give it another try by sending Alejandra some flowers. I bought all the roses that were available in Cusco and compiled a very sentimental letter, in which I apologised a thousand times. After I had deposited both the flowers and the letter at the reception of her hotel, I set out on the march towards Machu Picchu together with my gloating companions. I was sure I would never ever see Alejandra again, which was such a terrible pity.

But I was to be mistaken. Puccini had not yet finished his drama in which Alejandra from Peru and a lovesick, blithering idiot from Salzburg played the tragic leading roles. It was going to get even worse.

Of the strenuous four-day trek across the mountains to the Inca ruins of Machu Picchu, all that remained in my memory later on was my desperate love sickness and the 'robbery' that had taken place in our camp at night. On the second night we, and a few other adventurers, had been squatting down around the campfire and enjoying the spectacular Andean panorama as well as life in general, which, as far as we were concerned at the time, still lay endlessly before us. There were also some local porters with us who carried the luggage for those members of the group who were in a financially sounder position. Obviously my pals and I did not number among these. These *"silleros"* took delight in scaring us by telling us horror stories. In and around the camp one should be especially alert, one of them told us, as there were sinister characters hanging around in the area. Right here there had often been attacks at night on unsuspecting tourists, he claimed.

This certainly caused some uncertainty among us, but on the other hand I was sharing a tent with Arnie and Joe and each one of us was probably a head taller than the customary Peruvian robber. To be on the safe side, we stowed our backpacks away into the tents, with the result that we ended up lying next to each other like sardines in a tin. We even fixed a tiny padlock on to the tent flap, although we realized that only a sharp knife was needed to slit open the rather thin canvas. But we also had knives ready at hand: the Australian Arnie a Crocodile-Dundee make and Joe his Swiss Army knife. When Arnie switched off his torch it was pitch dark. Feeling uneasy I wished everyone good night.

"Hopefully!", Joe replied.

That night each one of us was preoccupied with their respective amorous demons: I was mourning over Alejandra, Joe was in deep thought about the unrequited love of a fellow countrywoman sleeping in the adjacent tent, whilst Arnie had had to relinquish his girlfriend of many years to an American for the duration of his world trip. Added to this was the influence of alcohol as well as the latent fear of muggings at night. This was the only way I could explain afterwards the disastrous chain of events that took place later that night.

Arnie, who was lying on the far right side, turned over on to his other side and in doing so hit Joe, who was lying in the middle, straight on his nose. Joe sprang up with a yell thinking that his nightmare had come true and there were intruders in our tent. Half-asleep Joe lashed out on both sides. Arnie and I were rudely awakened by the din and thought the same as Joe: sinister figures were about to mug us. No one of us could see anything and therefore everyone was throwing punches on all sides. It felt as if a whole gang of robbers was in our three-man tent. Fortunately none of us had the idea of trying to find a knife in the heat of the moment. Eventually Arnie found his torch and switched it on, just as Joe gave me a punch on the chin. I'm quite sure that the story of the three 'gringos' who were beating each other up for fear of the evil man, will make the rounds amongst the local people for a long time to come.

After my return to Cusco from Machu Picchu the hotel porter had handed me a note with some happy news. Alejandra had forgiven me and asked me to visit her in Lima. I danced a tango for joy with the porter and said good-bye to my friends for about a month and planned to meet them again in Colombia. Then I paid a visit to a hairdresser's and subsequently took the bus to the Peruvian capital.

Alejandra worked in a travel agency and had her own small apartment, in which we spent a wonderful time. The Cusco incident only arose every now and then as an amusing episode. Alejandra had an unusually fair complexion for a Peruvian, which she had inherited – like her almond-shaped eyes – from her grandmother of Asian descent. She was the first woman I had met during my travels, with whom I could have even imagined continuing a relationship after my return to Austria. I simply didn't know how.

Alejandra also seemed to be developing plans in the same direction. Two nights a week she had been attending a German language course. However, it wasn't until the day before we had to say goodbye that, in tears, she came out with the entire truth. Some months ago she had met a man from Cologne during work at the travel agency. This guy was a policeman with the German border control and after accompanying a deported Peruvian to his home country had stayed on for a couple of days in Lima. He had dated Alejandra every night and had raved to her about the great carefree life back in Germany. On the day of his departure he had proposed to her and she had accepted.

However, she now assured me that she was only in love with me, but would have to marry the German, for whom she no longer had any real feelings but as she had been planning to leave Peru for a long time, the marriage would give her the perfect opportunity.

That was the end. Any more heartache just wasn't possible, I thought and once again misjudged the situation. Puccini had reserved the 'finale furioso' for the third act of his drama.

A couple of weeks after my return from South America, Alejandra called me in Salzburg and invited me to her new home in Cologne. Her fiancé had been sent away to the East to control the border between West and East Germany which was still in existence at the time. I could sleep at her place – we'd just have to be careful that the neighbour opposite didn't notice anything as he was a friend of her future husband.

I hesitated for a long time. On the one hand, as a single, there was the prospect of sex again after a spell of abstinence, on the other hand I had just managed to stop licking my wounds when Alejandra's call came. But eventually my hormones sent me off to the railway station. The chance of being able to get one over on this border policeman gave me an additional special kick.

Alejandra and I were not supposed to be seen together in the neighbourhood, so we stayed at her home most of the time. Every-where there were photos of the soon-to-be newly-weds – not a particularly nice sight. The guy was about twenty years older than her and looked like Stan from 'Laurel & Hardy'. Alejandra wasn't smiling on any of the photos. I was twenty-one years old at the time and terms like engagement, marriage and offspring were abstract foreign words to me. Nevertheless, during that week I seriously thought about asking Alejandra to marry me instead. She would then just get an Austrian passport instead of a German one.

On the day before my return trip a decision had to be made. I was strolling along the streets of Cologne and passed a jeweller's, where I let them show me engagements rings for "around one hundred Deutschmarks", maybe "with one small diamond". The shopkeeper looked at me like a doorman on whose shoes someone had just vomited and said that unfortunately there was no way he could serve me. Well, he was probably right. The ring Alejandra was already wearing must have cost the border policeman three times his monthly income or even a violation of the Anti-Corruption Act.

Next I entered Cologne Cathedral and asked for an inspiration from above, but in vain. Apart from the emotional confusion I was in at the time, I still didn't really feel up to the responsibility of being a husband. I explained this to Alejandra the night before we said good-bye. She cried on the platform and I wept in the carriage as the train slowly pulled away. I was sure I'd never see her again.

Weeks later Alejandra called again. She said that she would now be marrying her fiancé the Saturday after next and she would like to invite me to her wedding. Moreover she would really like me to be her witness at the marriage. No, that was really too much, I explained to her, and turned the invitation down. But she pleaded with me that she didn't have anyone else. Her family from Peru couldn't attend because of lack of money for the trip and the only friend she had in Cologne was a Japanese woman from her language course. "Please, please don't let me go through this all alone", she kept on imploring me.

I finally gave in and bought a black suit, as if I were going to attend a funeral. The day before the wedding I boarded the train for Cologne to act as a witness to the marriage of the woman I loved. It was about to become the most surreal weekend of my life.

Alejandra and Bernd were waiting for me at Cologne's main railway station. She gave me a kiss on the cheek and introduced me to her future husband as being an 'old friend'. I thought this was quite a suspicious statement especially to a policeman. First of all I wasn't old, and secondly I couldn't possibly be Alejandra's friend from school. Actually I had thought she had booked a hotel room for me, but Bernd invited me as a 'guest of honour' into his home, which was just around the corner and had a guest room, as he explained to me. If this guy had only known that I had long since been acquainted with every single spring of his mattress and had used his aftershave, he would probably have drawn his service pistol and shot me dead.

In the evening things got very lively. Bernd's stag party was due to take place. A dozen of his police colleagues came round and were drinking half the night with the groom. Shouldn't he be fit the next day? But he was apparently well trained. Alejandra told me later in the kitchen that her fiancé was an alcoholic. Oh my god, that too, I thought. When I had to go to the toilet or went to my room for a while because I felt the situation to be unbearable, she followed me and assured me how much she had missed me and that she loved only me. Bernd, on the contrary, she loathed. "In that case you can't possibly marry him tomorrow", I scolded, almost too loud. "It's too late for that now", she said and kissed me.

The wedding ceremony took place the next day in a Cologne restaurant. The local registrar had taken care of all formalities, rings were exchanged and toasts were proposed to the newly-weds. Everything pointed to a boring, but normal wedding party. But then Bernd and his police colleagues started a heavy drinking orgy. That in turn resulted in the bride and groom quarrelling more and more fiercely during the course of their party. Foul language was used, attacks lead to counter attacks, and the party turned more or less into a farce until Alejandra launched a last devastating attack and in front of all the wedding guests revealed her true relationship to her witness.

I immediately became the object of hostile glances. Bernd, who could hardly stand up straight, at least managed to smash all the wine glasses on his table against the wall. In any case, I had been exposed and had to run. My luggage as well as my passport were still in their apartment, to which Alejandra handed me the keys. I just wanted to grab my things and then look for a small hotel or guest house, but she asked me to stay where I was and wait for her. I did her the favour, watched TV for a while, almost fell asleep and went to bed in the guest room. Unfortunately there was no way to lock the door of my room, but that wouldn't have held back a furious lynch mob anyway.

Around midnight something made me jump. Now they had

come to beat me up, I thought, but it was only Alejandra crying on the edge of my bed. His colleagues had had to drag the completely sloshed Bernd back to the apartment, she told me. Now he was lying unconscious and snoring in the nuptial bed. This was certainly not how she had imagined her wedding night, she wailed.

I tried to comfort her and took her in my arms. At that she crawled under my duvet. And so it happened that the bride committed adultery with her marriage witness on the wedding night. Probably not an everyday occurrence. Never before had we made love to each other so intensely, as we both knew that it would be for the last time. This night was our final farewell.

I never saw Alejandra again.

Many years later as I lay in the bed next to my pilgrim sister Sandy in a hostel in the Northern Spanish village of Melide, I asked myself what might have happened to Alejandra. I didn't have the faintest idea but some bad misgivings.

Then I asked myself whether there was a chance that something could develop between Sandy and myself. Twice she had already rejected my careful approaches. The first time on the flower meadow and the second time last night, when I just wanted to give her a quick hug. Maybe it was better this way and it saved me the next romantic drama.

With these thoughts I finally fell asleep.

Chapter Thirty-One

Melide – Taberna Vella

During breakfast, pilgrim sister Sandy and I had chosen Santa Irene as our destination target for the day, a distance of some twenty-five kilometres. If we made it, we could be in Santiago de Compostela by the next afternoon.

The thought of this aroused ambivalent emotions in me, however. On the one hand, after one month's trekking I wanted to reach my destination at last, but on the other the last few days hiking with Sandy through Galicia had been the most enjoyable part of the entire St. James Way. A part of me kept dreaming that this wonderful time should never come to an end.

Antonio from Málaga had actually made this kind of dream come true. We met him at a disused bus stop. In his mid-thirties, Antonio had given up his job as a night porter in a hotel on the Costa del Sol. That had been seventeen years ago. Ever since then he had been hiking up and down all the existing routes of the St. James Way. His tame wolf, Lobo, always accompanied him.

While dozens of pilgrims were hurrying past us, we stayed for about an hour talking to Antonio. I wanted to know more about him, while Sandy romped around with his wolf as if it were a cuddly toy. Antonio lived off small jobs he was given along the wayside and sold self-made souvenirs. I supported him by buying a dreamcatcher. His heavy backpack weighing around fifty kilos contained a tent, a cooker, pots and pans and further household items. With this kind of weight on his back he only managed around ten kilometres a day.

He assured me again and again that the life concept 'pilgrim' made him happy. He philosophized with me about freedom, self-determination as well as the possibility of always being able to go wherever one chose. If this freedom were to be taken away from him, as had once happened in his old job, he would start looking for someone else to blame, such as the hotel director, the personnel manager, the hotel guests, his landlord, the State and even the entire system, in which he himself and everybody else had to function properly in order to avoid total collapse. He also assured me that he would continue making pilgrimages on the network of St. James Way routes as long as his feet would carry him. Up to now he had completed all the Spanish Caminos – the French one even sixteen times, there and back! Soon he was going to embark on his greatest project: to complete an international pilgrimage starting from Santiago, then via Lourdes and the Vatican City to Jerusalem. And back! He estimated that this undertaking would take him around eight years.

After we had said good-bye to Antonio and Lobo, Sandy and I carried on discussing this encounter for a while. If one had only cast a quick glance at the bearded Antonio in passing, one might have assumed him to be a pitiful homeless person, someone whom life had treated badly and who was living a sorry existence on the fringe of society. But if one looked into his eyes and took the time to listen to him, his story of being the happy long-term pilgrim was easy to believe.

Especially at the beginning of my hike on the Camino I had often thought a lot about the term 'happiness' and gained some important perceptions about its meaning. Freedom, independence, and the chance to go one's own way – those were the significant happiness factors along the Camino, for me also. Should I therefore follow Antonio's example and henceforth walk all the pilgrim trails of our globe? Would that be the simple and lasting formula for happiness? I doubted it.

I knew from experience, that 'change' also ranked amongst the top ten on my happiness chart. The appeal of the new and unknown carried more weight for me than holding on to familiar habits and procedures. The happiness parameters varied individually, of course. What might make some people happy could well cause misery for others.

Change was imminent for me as well. It wouldn't turn out as radically as Antonio's, but would still be reasonably drastic. Inspired by the permanent pilgrim philosophy, I already had a vague concept in mind. The prospect of it filled me with eager anticipation.

In order to make up ground for the hour spent with Antonio, Sandy and I walked on faster. Her shin bone inflammation had luckily disappeared, but now I had a problem which had somewhat worsened over the past ten kilometres. My right lower leg had suddenly begun to ache with every movement. A sign of strain.

The previous day we had made slow progress because of Sandy's shin bone and had been on our feet for a full ten hours. I had lent her my hiking poles so that she could relieve the weight on her legs while walking downhill. Furthermore, I had hardly drunk any water recently, which, according to the experienced pilgrims, was the primary cause of inflammation. I was now paying the price for all this. Every step hurt like hell and suddenly the remaining forty kilometres to Santiago seemed unreachable for me.

Just as I had taken care of Sandy yesterday, she was now taking care of me. She massaged my lower leg, put ice cubes on it and taped my calves as well as my shin bone. Unfortunately, her efforts were of little help. Supported on my sticks, I limped along the Camino. This way I couldn't manage more than two kilometres per hour. I was ashamed because I was holding Sandy up and told her to go ahead as I would be able to cope alone. But she wouldn't even think of it.

During one of the many breaks I had to take, I glanced at my guidebook. We would never make it to Santa Irene this way. Quite generally, I began to doubt whether I could walk all the way to

218

Santiago at all. I had never experienced such an inflammation before and had no idea what to expect next.

My booklet told us about an insider tip five kilometres further ahead, where a pilgrim friend named Heidi had a house with an annex in which she sometimes put up pilgrims. Although it was not a designated pilgrim's hostel, one could certainly try one's luck there, the editor of the guide recommended. A telephone number was also given. I punched it into my mobile phone and had a very friendly chat with a woman who happened to come from Austria. Even though she and her husband were on Majorca right now, we could still stay at their hostel, she said. A man called Simon would take care of everything – including food. That sounded fine. I tried to ignore the pain in my right leg and struggled on.

Two hours later we crossed a stream. From there it was only five hundred metres to a garden gate on which we were supposed to knock. Simon had been informed of our arrival, let us in and showed us around. The garden was truly magnificent. There were hammocks and deck chairs and a fantastic view over the Galician countryside. The accommodation comprised one room with eight beds and a bathroom with two modern showers. Everything seemed new, clean and hardly used.

There was no doubt that we had found 'pilgrim's paradise'! Although we had only managed to cover twelve kilometres due to the pain in my leg, it was still only two o'clock in the afternoon. Our arrival in Santiago would be delayed by twenty-four hours, but instead we now had half a day of pilgrim's vacation. We decided to enjoy it in full, particularly as we were the only guests.

We chilled out in the garden until Simon came and served us with coffee and home-made cake. I asked him to join us and tell us a bit about himself. I had the feeling that his story would be just as interesting as Antonio's. Simon was fifty-five, British and a former soldier of the Royal Marines, who had taken early retirement. From his appearance he could easily have passed for Bruce Willis' brother. At the same time he radiated a gentleness, kindness and inner peace that one hardly found in today's hectic, performance-oriented society any more. As a Royal Marine he had been stationed in almost every crisis area around the globe, constantly surrounded by war, suffering and devastation, although as a paramedic he had not fought on the front lines.

Paramedic? Immediately I thought of my injured leg, but didn't want to interrupt Simon.

At some point everything had become too much for him. A military psychologist had diagnosed him with burnout and sent him into retirement a year ago. Simon had then been discharged from the Royal Marines at his base in Gibraltar. After that, he hadn't known what to do with his life. He was divorced and had a daughter who lived in Singapore, a country he was not allowed to enter as an ex-military from a special forces unit for the next five years due to a political treaty. Many of his former comrades had stayed in Gibraltar or the nearby Costa del Sol and liberally indulged in alcohol – even before lunch. But that had never been his thing, our Brit said.

So he had grabbed his backpack and decided to make a pilgrimage to Santiago. There was no official Camino route from Gibraltar to Santiago, but being well-trained he had set off with his tent and a compass across Spain to Santiago. Two months later he had entered the cathedral there as a new person. Within only eight weeks he had overcome his traumatic past and had cured his psychological problems.

He had met very few people on his Way of St. James. One of them being Heidi. They had walked a stretch together for one day before their paths parted. One month later Simon had been hiking the French Camino and had passed by Heidi's house by sheer coincidence. The joy at seeing each other again had been great. He had helped her renovate the house and after three days Heidi and her husband had invited him to stay with them for good. A marvellous friendship had developed between the three. As the owners often had to travel to Majorca on business, in their absence Simon took care of the house, the animals and any pilgrims, for whom he liked to cook. Heidi had allocated him an area of land on the property on which he wanted to build himself a small modest house next year – but first he planned to walk the Portuguese Way of St. James.

Simon had found his peace of mind in this remote area of Galicia and I was truly happy for him.

Unfortunately, later that afternoon, our cosy twosome was over. Heike and Simone from some remote part of Germany had obviously been using the same travel guide as myself and had also discovered the insider tip. Simon welcomed them as warmly as he had done with Sandy and myself.

Secretly I was annoyed, as I was still nurturing hope that something might happen between Sandy and myself on our last but one night. The beautiful empty dormitory would have been the perfect setting for it. Now this was unthinkable after the arrival of the two pilgrim sisters.

Heike and Simone worked for the administrative council of their home town back in Germany. They had set out on the Way of St. James at Sarria, just about one hundred kilometres before Santiago, and had taken a week's vacation to do so. Until now they had only been staying in hotels. This was their first "real" pilgrim's lodging, they proudly announced. Sandy made an effort at some small talk with them. I didn't feel like it, got into a hammock and dozed until dinner was ready.

Simon served a courgette cream soup and afterwards a mountain of pasta. The two "administrative council spinsters", as they were secretly named by Sandy, spoke hardly any English, so we had to translate questions to Simon such as "Does it always rain that much here?", "What brought you to this place?", or "What does one actually do all day long here? There's … uh … nothing here …". Thankfully they were soon overcome by tiredness and smilingly headed for the dormitory wishing us "*a guads Naechtle*" – or 'goodnight' in their local South-West German dialect.

When they were finally gone, I remembered Simon telling us about his function as a paramedic with the Royal Marines. I explained to him the problem with my leg and that the pain had not improved despite Sandy's loving care. Simon felt my leg and also came to the conclusion that it was an inflammation. He applied some infernally burning ointment to my leg and bandaged it up anew.

About an hour later we also drank up our last drops of wine and, with a hug, said good night to Simon. I wished Sandy good night and climbed into my single bed. Heike and Simone seemed to be asleep already. I was just falling asleep when I suddenly got a shock. Something had sneaked into my bed. Or, more precisely, someone.

"Sandy?"

"Shh!" she whispered.

Chapter Thirty-Two

Taberna Vella – Lavacolla

Heidi's house was located near kilometre stone thirty-two. Normally it wouldn't have been a problem to reach Santiago that night – after all, my longest stretch had been forty-three kilometres. But that was out of the question. My leg hurt far worse than the day before, so once again we hardly made any progress.

Limping through the next village an elderly lady of at least ninety years old overtook me with her rollator walker. I was almost tempted to grab the thing from granny and run, but in the end let it be as the running away wouldn't have worked. When we passed a pharmacy Sandy, the Reiki fan, tried her best to stop me from buying painkillers, but I got my own way and in a pub toilet secretly stuffed pills into my mouth like popcorn in the cinema. After that things went a little better. My insight of the day: a healthy person has many wishes. A sick guy only one.

Despite worrying about my leg, I was in good spirits. This was also due to the – in its own way – unforgettable night at Heidi's hostel. Just the two terms 'tonsils' or 'deeper' had to be mentioned, and we couldn't stop doubling up with laughter.

Of course, I had been more than startled when Sandy had come sneaking into bed with me. She had snuggled up to me and fondled my chest, shoulders, belly, knees and butt. So far I hadn't had the faintest idea that erogenous zones existed in these places. But anyway it felt extremely good and the one or the other contented sigh must have escaped me, because from Heike and Simone's corner came unmistakable murmuring and coughing. So they hadn't been asleep after all. Damn it. But we hadn't been that noisy.

"Well, *you* certainly were! You were moaning like a tennis player in the Wimbledon finals", Sandy told me the following day.

Of course we hadn't let the prudish pilgrim ladies stop us and had carried on fumbling around with each other.

"Can't you go outside and get on with it?", the "administrative council spinsters" complained not even a minute later.

"Free love!", Sandy demanded loudly.

"Don't you have any earplugs?", I added.

"What cheek!", raged Heike and Simone, apparently imagining themselves to be in Sodom and Gomorrah.

Alas, that was the end of it. Sandy and I hugged and tried to go to sleep. However, there was one thing I still wanted done.

"Um … what do you think you are doing?", Sandy asked softly.

"I'm kissing you. Shouldn't I?"

"Well, yes … but not like that!"

"Well, then how?"

"You've got to go deeper!"

"Should I polish your tonsils, or what?"

At that there was no holding us back. For minutes we were screaming with laughter. Heike and Simone found it less funny and protested furiously. Sandy couldn't care less. She explained to me that by "going deeper" when I had kissed her she had meant "just let yourself go and relax". Even though I was now no wiser than before, I just let the matter rest.

Sandy showed no sign of leaving my single bed, so I moved to one right next to Heike and Simone – and snored even more loudly than usual out of revenge over the thwarted night of love. At breakfast they both ignored us completely. Obviously we had ruined their night.

It had been just the same for us, I thought, while I was limping along the track the next day. And now we only had one night left. That was why we wanted to pool our money and stay over in a guest house that night. We had already discovered quite a tempting advertisement along the wayside: "double room twenty-five euros, three-bed-room thirty euros". To get there it was still a ten kilometres' walk. The thought of finally being alone with Sandy spurred me on – a little, at least. I tried to suppress the rest of the thoughts that were going round in my head. Today you are going to spend a marvellous night together. Tomorrow you'll be on your way back to Andalusia and she'll be winging her way home to Dresden … and then what?

Not to worry, I'd just rely on fate, as I had so often done along the Camino over the past weeks. And 'fate' didn't take long to appear on the scene. Two kilometres before reaching the hostel it gave a clear signal – in the shape of an elderly man named Lau, who came from Manchuria. We saw him sitting at a bus stop, without water, without food and without any energy. He had set off on the Camino in northern France and had covered about two thousand kilometres on foot within three months. Since the morning he'd walked forty kilometres and now he simply couldn't go a step further, he told us in pretty awful English and almost started crying. That was why he was sitting there, he whispered, waiting for a bus to take him the twelve kilometres to Santiago.

Of course we talked him out of it. We gave him water and food and persuaded him to walk the two kilometres with us to Lavacolla, where there was a guest house. He gratefully agreed. I was glad that we had done a good deed, but on the other hand I feared the worst – namely that the double room could now become a triple room.

Meanwhile twilight had set in. Sandy and I had needed eleven hours for twenty kilometres, which, under normal circumstances, I would have covered in four or five. Despite all the pain and potential health risks, I *had* to get to Santiago somehow – even if it meant crawling into the cathedral.

The 'pension' in Lavacolla turned out to be the private home of an obese lady who rented out two rooms on her ground floor. One of which happened to be a double room, the other containing a double as well as a single bed. The question of which room Sandy and I would take and which one our Far Eastern friend would occupy unfortunately didn't arise because the double room had already been taken. Lau, who had meanwhile regained his strength, thought about whether to continue on to Santiago – after all, there were only ten kilometres to hike from here.

"That is a splendid idea indeed, my friend", I encouraged him. "And then you'll have reached your final destination by the end of today", I added, as if that – after a three-month hike – would be of any importance.

"Nonsense!" Sandy intervened to my irritation. "You're going to stay overnight with us in our room, and tomorrow we'll walk together to Santiago recovered and refreshed."

If I had been only slightly ready to resort to violence, I just might have strangled her. Lau kept us in suspense and took his time to decide. Finally he accepted Sandy's suggestion and the three of us moved in. Sandy and I eyed our narrow double bed, at the end of which was a folding bed onto which Lau from Manchuria had just put his backpack. I cursed to myself as extensively as possible in three languages and without the hint of a guilty conscience – after all as of tomorrow all my sins would be forgiven anyway.

We were allowed to use a small kitchen on the ground floor and there was a corner shop in the village, which we visited together with Lau after showering. Sandy wanted to prepare a tasty pasta dish and filled a bag with the necessary ingredients. I bought alcohol: wine, Cava – Spanish sparkling wine – a small bottle of rum and some coke to mix with it. If there wasn't going to be any sex that night, at least I could enjoy getting drunk.

We invited Lau to eat with us, but he gratefully declined. He had bought a pack of rice and a bag of peanuts for which he had paid two euros and fifty Cents. I asked him whether he had the rest with him in his backpack.

"Which rest?" he asked.

"Well, salmon or tuna, chicken, vegetables, tofu or whatever you normally have with rice", I explained.

Lau shook his head.

Most probably he simply hadn't understood what I had meant.

About an hour later Sandy had finished cooking. She had

prepared an *insalata caprese* with mozzarella cheese, tomatoes and basil, followed by pasta with a delicious tomato *sugo*. We had also bought something sweet for dessert. I opened a bottle of Cava for Sandy and a bottle of red wine for myself. Lau also sat at our table, eating a bowl of boiled rice on which he had sprinkled a handful of peanuts. With it he drank a glass of tap water.

I felt sorry for him. The man had been on the road for three months, and as a retired calligrapher in Manchuria probably didn't have a particularly generous pilgrimage budget at his disposal.

"Please, Lau … have some food from us as well. There's plenty for everyone", I repeatedly offered, but the stubborn old Manchurian wouldn't have it.

"No, thank you. I don't need more than this", he replied and pointed at his bowl of rice. And that after forty kilometres? No wonder this guy weighed just half as much as I did. He also refused to drink our wine. He never touched alcohol, only water and tea, he explained. Was this really the way to survive the Way of St. James? Again I looked at him pityingly while I stuffed myself with pasta and 'inhaled' the wine.

Then, however, the enlightening moment followed in which we kept eye contact for several seconds. Only then did I begin to understand the message he was sending out. And *that* definitely made me think. Because Lau was looking at *me* with pity. He was satisfied with his bowl of rice, the few peanuts and the lukewarm tap water. He just didn't need anything more. I remembered my backpack, out of which I had removed everything superfluous at the beginning of the Camino. Lau restricted his diet to the bare essentials. In his eyes I probably resembled a pilgrim carrying a thirty-kilogram backpack. A pitiful being!

After Lau had eaten his rice and had gone to our room, Sandy and I stayed in the kitchen for a while. I couldn't have slept anyway. I actually felt quite sick from all that food. I also began to suspect what my final insight from the Way of St. James was going to be. We were drinking rum and coke and making big plans. Over dinner Lau had told us that he had already made a pilgrimage in Japan and had covered the eighty-eight-temple hike, which led over one thousand and three hundred kilometres around the fourth largest

Japanese island. Sandy and I had decided to follow suit. We were also ready to cross the Alps, to establish a pilgrim hostel on the Camino and walk the Pacific Crest Trail – the American long-distance hike, which runs four thousand kilometres through the USA from the Mexican to the Canadian border.

By the time we finally went to bed, we had made loads of plans which I unfortunately knew would already be forgotten the day after tomorrow on our respective ways home.

To begin with Sandy and I wished each other a well-behaved "good night", but of course we couldn't leave it at that. Since Sandy had not been particularly impressed with my smooching technique, I decided to go about it tactically better this time and quite boldly pursue another activity with my tongue!

Apparently my efforts succeeded to her full satisfaction, judging by the strange grunting sounds I could hear, which even continued when I came up for a 'breather'. I then realized that the curious noises hadn't been coming from Sandy's mouth but from our haggard old Asian fellow who was grunting in his sleep like a sumo wrestler in a peep show. It didn't really matter. At least the coast was clear now and the playing field was ready for kick-off, so I was prepared to go the whole way. Unfortunately, our bed was sonically not designed for such activities.

Lau awoke from the creaking, and as soon as Sandy became aware of it, she pushed me off. Frustrated, I rolled aside while Sandy turned her back on me. Sleep was now out of the question. I tossed and turned in bed and several times had to turn over my pillow, wet with perspiration. I felt rather guilty. A few days previously Sandy had confided an unpleasant experience of her youth to me. With that knowledge at the back of my mind, I should have approached things with much more sensitivity and less haste.

I reconsidered the whole situation and came to a conclusion. Tomorrow we would be going our separate ways anyway. So why not keep the good-byes short and painless? Sandy and Lau seemed to be asleep anyway.

I dressed as quietly as possible, packed my backpack, took a last look at Sandy's silhouette in bed and left the room. By the time she reached Santiago around noon, I would have already departed. We had exchanged neither mail addresses nor mobile phone numbers. I would never see Sandy again. Happy endings only seemed to take place in love stories.

I had always been denied them.

At two o'clock in the morning I stepped out into the night and started to tackle the last ten kilometres of the Way of St. James.

Chapter Thirty-Three

Lavacolla – Santiago de Compostela

I hadn't slept a wink last night, in the dark I could hardly recognize anything along the track, my shin inflammation hadn't got any better and for the first time on the Camino I felt lonely and depressed. This was really not how I had imagined the finish would be. In my fantasy I had pictured to myself completing the last stage amidst a group of dear pilgrim friends, with whom I would later on celebrate. While I had cut myself off with Sandy from the others over the past few days and had hardly been able to make any progress due to my leg problems, most of my Camino acquaintances had probably long since arrived at Santiago or had even continued from there to the Cape Finisterre. I had also intended to tackle the additional eighty kilometres to the "end of the world", but with my bad leg this was now out of the question. I simply couldn't manage more than two kilometres an hour. I had been pushing my untrained, overweight body to its limits for the last four weeks, and I was now paying the price.

While I was passing through an industrial district and afterwards dragging myself along a main road towards the much-photographed town sign reading "Santiago de Compostela", I kept thinking of pilgrim sister Sandy. She had been the highlight of my Way of St. James. And yet I had just sneaked away. What would she think of me when she woke up in a few hours time and discovered I was gone?

I should at least have left her a message. But telling her what? I didn't even have an explanation for myself for why I had left. After all she had done nothing wrong and we hadn't had any argument. The real reason for running away probably had to do with my being afraid of once again suffering disappointment and hurt in matters of love.

Since I did not want to sink into self pity all the way to the cathedral, I rather began reviewing what had happened during my pilgrimage on the Way of St. James. I looked back on my experiences, insights, encounters, conversations, moments of happiness, highs and lows which I had so far had the privilege to undergo along the Camino. So much had happened that it felt as if I had been on the road for a whole year. And yet it had only been a month. How quickly, however, this time would have passed in everyday life.

But all the flashbacks I had been experiencing recently had been triggered off by one and the same thing, over and over again: Sandy. I hadn't even known her for more than a week and nor had I even had proper sex with her, if one ignored the twelve erotic seconds last night. My ex-fiancée Tatiana, with whom I had spent the past five years of my life, was long forgotten.

Next to the town sign of Santiago I unbuckled my backpack and sat down on a traffic island right in the middle of the main road. I stared at the sign and contemplated my feelings. It was the same potpourri of emotions that had arisen when I had finished writing a crime novel after a one and a half years of work: relief, pride and the joy of having achieved something great. In addition, however, there was fatigue, despondency as well as the fear of how things might continue once the goal had been reached.

I shot a selfie in front of the town sign and limped on.

The last two kilometres obviously led through the pub district of Santiago. It was five o'clock on Sunday morning and last night's revellers were pouring out of the city's bars and clubs. Not a particularly pretty sight. A young lady in a mini skirt and high heels vomited next to a street lamp, a couple were arguing heatedly and a flock of young lads staggered towards me babbling with slurred speech something unintelligible. The alleyways were sticky with spilled drinks and covered in broken glass. With my backpack, hiking poles and floppy hat I felt quite out of place.

I had imagined the end of my Way of St. James to be more contemplative. But perhaps this environment was the best place to reflect on my last insight.

Lau from Manchuria had made quite an impression on me. While I needed around thirty euros per day on average, five of which were mostly spent on accommodation and twenty-five for food and drink, this man easily managed on ten euros a day. After all, he didn't drink any alcohol and only ate rice. At first I had felt sorry for Lau because of his meagre food – and then I had envied him for his frugality.

Conversely, he had seemed to pity me for over-eating and drinking. Both were vices which had not exactly improved while I was on the Camino – on the contrary, I had thought that my body needed masses of calories and carbohydrates to cope with the long hours of hiking each day and thus I had eaten even more than usual. I would probably become the first pilgrim to go down in the history of the Camino de Santiago who, instead of losing weight, had in fact even gained it.

Now, however, at dawn on my last day, surrounded by drunken young people, I vowed to become more frugal in the future as far as food and alcohol consumption were concerned. Since the negative effects thereof were vividly being demonstrated to me by Santiago's youth at that moment, I made a point there and then of promising the Apostle James, my supreme moral authority on the Camino, not to touch a single drop of alcohol for the next few months.

After all, I still had half a life in front of me and was now convinced that I wanted to stay fit
for it.

In the city centre I was welcomed by a banner sponsored by Opel bearing the headline "one thousand metres to go". This rather surprised me but I followed the sign which I naturally assumed referred to the last kilometre of the Way of St. James. The route led through the city in zigzag. There were no scallop shells to be seen and helpers in yellow signal jackets were putting up barricades. One of them blocked my way and told me that I was not allowed to walk any further. I beg your pardon? I had hiked eight hundred kilometres and now just before reaching the cathedral I was supposed to turn back? This had to be a very bad joke, I thought, and wanted to push past the man.

Only when he explained to me that I was not on the St. James Way, but at the finishing line of today's fun run, I turned and limped back towards the banner. I detected a scallop shell sign on the opposite side of the square and followed it down a narrow alley.

Chapter Thirty-Four

Santiago de Compostela

A t six o'clock in the morning I entered the cathedral through a side entrance. I sat down on one of the front pews and looked at the statue of Saint James above the altar. Apart from myself there were only two widows dressed in black in the cathedral at this hour. So, this was it at last. If I had been sitting in my car, a rather pleasant female voice would have announced: "You have reached your destination".

And what now? First of all I was overcome with emotion and tears rolled down my cheeks. At the beginning of the St. James Way to Santiago I had considered my chances of completing its full length to be next to nothing. Now I had conquered the Camino despite all the physical and psychological stresses and strains. I closed my eyes, muttered the Lord's Prayer but fell asleep before the passage "… and lead us not into temptation …".

I must have slept for quite some time as, meanwhile, it was 7 a.m. Was Sandy already awake? Had she noticed that I was gone? I suppressed this painful thought.

Now all that remained was to complete the formalities and set out for the return journey. Behind the altar area a staircase led up to the statue of the Apostle James. Next to the staircase was a sign showing a crossed-out camera. I climbed the stairs and took photos of the statue from all sides. Then I put my arms around it and kissed the ornamented coat collar. According to my guidebook my pilgrimage was now officially over. I took a last selfie for my Facebook blog and left the cathedral.

In a cafeteria I met a Belgian woman who had finished her Camino the day before and was now waiting for the pilgrim office around the corner to open for the day. She had set out for her hike in front of her doorstep at home in Belgium and had now been on her way for three months. Although I found this quite impressive, I just wanted to get my Saint James certificate and then leave for home. In the pilgrim office I had to present my 'credencial' – or pilgrim's accreditation – bearing the hostel stamps as proof I had accomplished at least the last 100 kilometres of the Way on foot and then answer the question whether I had made the pilgrimage on the Camino for religious or for sportive reasons. In order not to mess things up at the last moment, I decided to tick off answer A and received my *'Compostela'* certificate.

The text of the Compostela is actually written in Latin and can be translated as follows:

"The Chapter of this Holy Apostolic Metropolitan Cathedral of Saint James, custodian of the seal of Saint James' Altar, to all faithful and pilgrims who come from everywhere over the world as an act of devotion, under vow or promise to the Apostle's Tomb, our Patron and Protector of Spain, witnesses in the sight of all who read this document, that: Mr/Mrs/Ms ... has visited devoutly this Sacred Church in a religious sense (pietatis causa).

Witness whereof I hand this document over to him/her, authenticated by the seal of this Sacred Church.

Given in Saint James of Compostela on this (day) ... (month) ... Anno Domini ..."

And so with this document in my hands the fascinating journey to find myself had now also come to its official end.

I limped the one and a half kilometres towards the bus station. I swore to myself that once home I would give my legs a long rest and use my car even for the shortest distances. The man at the counter explained to me that my bus wouldn't be leaving before five o'clock in the afternoon. The next morning I would have to change buses in La Coruna and in the afternoon also in Pamplona, before arriving at Saint-Jean-Pied-de-Port the following evening, where one month ago I had begun to tackle my Way of St. James and where my car should still be parked – hopefully unscathed – in a public car park.

Darn it! All I wanted now was to get back home to see my daughter whom I was longing for. Now I would be stuck in the waiting hall of the bus station for eight hours, after which I would have to sit on buses for twenty-six hours before a subsequent four-teen-hour drive to Andalusia. After not getting any sleep the night before, I now had another forty-eight hours of sleeplessness in front of me.

Pilgrim brother Rainhard had mentioned some time ago that on Sundays, around noon, a pilgrims mass worth visiting took place in the cathedral, during which the *botafumeiro*, a giant incense burner, was swung through the central nave. On the one hand this would be appealing, on the other hand I had now discarded my pilgrim status and had no desire to walk to the city centre and back on my aching leg.

So I decided against it, put my feet up on to my backpack and closed my eyes. In my mind Sandy appeared vividly to me. She was wearing her usual colour-coordinated pilgrim's outfit consisting of blue leggings, a red sweater, a brown cape – which she called a "snot blanket" –worn-out white sneakers and green woollen socks. She also wore her giant vintage sunglasses, had twisted her long red hair into a plait and had put on her green knitted cap with the orange spots. In her hand was the obligatory water bottle, from which she nipped every one hundred metres, and the beige backpack on her back, which was hardly bigger than my daughter's school bag. She was actually smiling at me, although she really ought to have been mad at me after what had happened. I hugged her and was happy to see her. After all, I still had so much to tell her.

An announcement woke me up from my doze and the lovely

vision faded away. The joy of having reached Santiago was over-shadowed by the loss of a good friend. And yet destiny had been kind to us: we had kept on meeting by chance along the Camino. Since I had become sensitized to signals and signs off the main route, in retrospect I shouldn't like to think that this had been a coincidence.

I left my backpack with someone at the counter and decided to give fate one last chance.

The pilgrim's mass began punctually at 12 noon. The cathedral was packed to its last seat. I just managed to grab one of the last places in a back row of pews and let my gaze wander over hundreds of believers. But there was no-one wearing a green knitted cap under which a red plait was dangling out. The chorus sang a beautiful cantata and the organ music was so deeply moving that it gave me goosebumps. Whereas I'd hardly felt anything when receiving my Compostela at the pilgrim's office, I now got carried away by a wave of emotion. Just at the moment when the *botafumeiro* was being swung through the cathedral nave by half a dozen priests and the scent of incense filled the air, somebody patted me on the shoulder from behind.

"Hi, pilgrim brother Eduard", a familiar voice said.

"Hello, pilgrim sister Sandy...!

Chapter Thirty-Five

Eduard's Way

During the two-day return journey by bus and afterwards in my car I decided to integrate everything I had learned on the Camino into my everyday life and to continue to lead my life in the pilgrim's modus – only without a backpack, miles and miles of long hikes and snoring Frenchmen. I decided to stay a pilgrim on my own 'Way', Eduard's Way.

In the meantime it had become quite to clear to me that my life definitely needed a radical change. Only when I embarked on something very intensely, was I able to put my heart and soul into it. Everything else didn't really attract my full attention. So when thinking of change, it wasn't buying a new mobile phone that I had in mind.

Out of every crisis new opportunities arise.

Anything else but a complete realignment of my life would not have been possible considering the devastating starting position I had before I had set off to walk the Camino. I had to leave my current path of life in order not to fall by the wayside. From a business point of view there were merely two alternatives to choose from: one was to carry on working even harder for longer hours, to borrow money from somewhere and invest it in my company to keep it afloat in Spain. The other option was to go back to Austria, where there were indeed plenty of work opportunities, but due to the higher costs of living the overall situation would hardly change for the better for me.

Was there really no third choice available? I didn't want to believe it. Luckily the Way of St. James had taught me to throw unnecessary ballast overboard if the backpack had become too heavy. With that in mind I started to act the day after my return.

Until now I had been living in a house which would accommodate fifteen people – in a sort of pilgrim's lodging just off the Camino, so to speak, with a beautiful garden and a swimming pool. Actually a dream, if it hadn't been for the incredibly high mortgage rate. In order to be able to pay it off, I would have to let the house to holiday guests for days or even weeks and at the same time rent an apartment for myself. Basically a nightmare.

After my return I gave up my house and moved into a flat. I took a similar approach with regard to my real estate company. It had generated extremely high costs, while the income had remained modest and unsteady. The highest cost factor had been online marketing. Through the Internet portals I had received numerous enquiries on a daily basis. I invested a vast part of my working time in answering them in detail, although most of the time the sender couldn't recall the "great interest" he or she had expressed as the enquiry had been one of dozens sent out more or less just for fun. The remainder of my time had been used up by unsuccessful property viewings and taking care of the online portals. I had wasted my time with senseless correspondence and had even spent a lot of money on it. Nightmare number two. I subsequently closed down the company two days after returning, thus reducing my running costs by approximately eighty percent within just three days.

I banished everything from my 'backpack' that burdened me, that didn't do me any good or even harmed my health. After the encounter with Lau I didn't drink any alcohol for three months and later on only to a limited extent. Furthermore I started eating less and became more conscious of my diet and subsequently lost weight.

The free time I now had at my disposal I used for writing – but also for travelling in order to develop my mind further and to become a little wiser. I discovered interesting new books on the subjects of Buddhism or Philosophy and read biographies about interesting people. What a luxury. After merely a few days on my very personal Eduard's Way my life had changed for the better. The little money that I still needed to cover my basic costs of living would be made available to me by life itself purely because I was now walking my new path more attentively, more balanced, more light-heartedly and much happier than before – of that I was dead sure. Now I was also able to define the term 'happiness' in a new way – namely as the composure to know without doubt that one is on the right path.

I only had smaller worries left and thankfully took them as a stepping stone to my own spiritual growth. I felt great, even though some people in my circle of friends and acquaintances found it hard to believe and tried to cajole me into accepting money loans so that I could re-burden myself with unnecessary things. I firmly rejected their offers, of course. Never ever had I thought that the Camino would change my life in this way.

Thinking back, there is a life for me before the Camino and one thereafter. I have become more relaxed, calmer, more thankful, more modest, more respectful and more humble. I now look at things and people – as well as my previous way of life and work – from different viewpoints and perspectives.

After my return from Santiago I withdrew somewhat from life around me and pursued my passion – writing. Although up to that point it wouldn't have been remotely possible for me to live off the proceeds of my writing, I made up my mind to earn my living as a full-time novelist from then on. Viewed from the outside – as, for example, from my worried father's point of view – this was an idea that simply horrified some people. However, I believed in the magic of the new and put my trust in the idea that everything necessary for fulfilling this dream would turn up one way or another.

A few weeks later something did just that. As a result of my books having been mentioned in the German 'Bild' newspaper as well as the 'Bunte' magazine, the wife of a German celebrity became aware of me. She subsequently read my Andalusian thriller trilogy, was delighted with it and told her husband, who for years had been wanting to have his memoires written by a professional writer. They both came down to Spain and met with me. Two hours later we were in agreement and I was selected to write his biography.

This job is paid so well that I am able to live off it during my writing periods and even for months thereafter. After that something new will come up – or maybe even this manuscript will meet with approval.

Focus your mind on a definite goal and an invisible kind of energy surrounds you to lead you straight to your target. The German celebrity turned out to be the best example.

During weeks and months after returning from the Camino I managed to project the freedom that hiking the Way had meant for me – the free choice to hike the stretches I felt like – on to my personal Eduard's Way. I have to enjoy the second half of my life as best as possible. Anything else would be grossly negligent.

One of the most pleasant aspects of being an author is being able to work regardless of the location. Right at this moment, as I am typing the last pages of this book project into my laptop, I am looking around outside in the light of a full moon and can see nothing but water and white waves as far as the horizon. I must hold on to my teacup, however, to stop it from sliding off my swaying makeshift 'desk'. It's three o'clock in the morning and I am keeping night watch somewhere between Sardinia and Sicily on a twelve-metre yacht, which my pal, Andreas, and I are sailing from the South of Spain via Majorca, Sardinia and Sicily to Athens.

A force eight to nine gale is blowing outside and I am cowering in a corner of the cockpit, which is halfway protected from the waves. If I hadn't spent months and even years on ships, I might have been rather frightened. Instead as I watch the rolling waves I am quite at peace with myself. For this sailing trip is also a kind of by-product of my new life circumstances. The sailing ship – a 'Bavaria 40' – belongs to a German who commissioned us to sail it to Greece for him as he didn't dare to do it himself. So I can pursue my hobby at the same time as finishing my manuscript – and get paid for it.

It's not the first time that Andreas and I have been sailing together. Four years ago we sailed through the Mediterranean with his son Marc. Father and son had planned to circumnavigate the globe and for this purpose had purchased a steel yacht in Croatia, which we then transferred from Rovinj to Spain.

After two years of restoration work, the 'tub' was ready to set sail for its great adventure – and I was to be part of it with Andreas and Marc. From the South of Spain we sailed towards the Canary Islands, from there for three weeks across the Atlantic and after that for two months in the southern Caribbean. A fantastic time. But for completing our world tour from West to East in one go we lacked the necessary funds. In addition, we still had strong sentimental ties to our homeland in the form of children and our wives or partners, which made an absence of more than three months virtually impossible. Our sailing yacht, the *Reliant*, was in dry dock in Trinidad and any further trips were still hanging in the balance for similar reasons.

Yesterday, however, we agreed to continue our voyage the following winter, starting from Trinidad and thence to a total of sixteen countries including St. Lucia, Martinique, Antigua, Puerto Rico, Jamaica, Nicaragua and Costa Rica as far as the Panama Canal and to complete our circumnavigation in stages over the years to come. That had also been a long-cherished dream of mine since the days of the *Orion*, which now seemed as if it could be fulfilled fairly soon.

Besides sailing I had discovered the pilgrimage and/or long-distance walking in general. I dream of greater challenges like the Shikoku, or Eighty-Eight-Temple-Way in Japan, the Olav's Way through spectacular landscape in Norway or even the Pacific Crest Trail, which takes five to six months of hiking through the Californian Mojave desert, across the snow-covered mountain massif of the Sierra Nevada to the north into the Oregon woodlands, where one has to look out for grizzly bears. Due to a lack of normal infrastructure, overnight accommodation is in a tent and it is important to draw up a detailed plan of provisions in advance, as it might be days before the next supply station is reached.

At the moment, however, this outdoor adventure is not listed at the top of my to-do list of dreams to be realized. However, it is always the same with things I am longing to do: I have to fulfil them some time in the near future or else I become stuffy and fusty like old pilgrim's socks.

And that is just how it had been with the Camino. After it had taken twenty years from the original intention that "I am going to walk the Way of St. James one day" until the fruition of the project, it took much less time to put my second attempt into effect: only four months after receiving my first Compostela, I set off on a second pilgrimage taking the Portuguese Way from Lisbon to Santiago. In the course of it I made a detour to the pilgrimage site of Fátima. In Santiago I even went beyond my objective and walked on to Cape Finisterre – a total distance of eight hundred kilometres. And this certainly wasn't my last Camino.

Next, I'd like to walk the Camino Mozarabe from my home village of Almuñécar in the province of Granada to Merida in western central Spain and from there on to Santiago along the Via de la Plata. This is going to be my longest Way of St. James covering a distance of one thousand two hundred kilometres.

But there's no rush – in two to three years maybe. At the moment I'm still mentally feeding on the impressions and experiences of my first two Caminos. The pilgrimage in Portugal was spiritually less intense than on the French Way, which was also due to the fact that I hiked the four hundred kilometre section from Lisbon to Porto alone, as I simply didn't meet any other pilgrims en route at all. However, on the other hand, the Portuguese Way turned out to be a lot more adventurous, as the following account of one of the stages will clearly show...

Chapter Thirty-Six

Santarém – Fátima

Compared with the Portuguese Way, the French Camino was a sheer wellness vacation. I had left Santarém at half past six in the morning. I hadn't been able to get hold of any detailed information for my planned detour via Fátima – other than a map with a 1:500 000 scale which had been handed to me by someone in the Santarém tourist information office and included a list of six hostels along the route to Fátima.

According to this map the village of Monsanto was located at about the halfway mark, that is after four out of a total of six millimetres, and since there was a hostel there, I made Monsanto my target for the day.

I kept walking at a brisk pace without dawdling until around eleven o'clock, when I came across a recluse standing beneath a ramshackle wooden shelter. He stamped my pilgrimage pass and I treated him to a one Euro tip. He then allowed me to 'immortalize' myself in his guestbook – as the seventh pilgrim this year. Wow! The man must be making as much annual turnover as I did at the time with my real estate company. I asked him how far it was between there and Monsanto.

"Fifteen", he replied. Well, that was nothing at all. As a kind of reward I indulged in an extensive lunch. There was Internet at the inn as well as an open fireplace, so I took my time. After I had paid my bill, I asked the waitress how far it still was to Monsanto.

"Twenty-five kilometres", she said. Come again? That couldn't be true. Just to be on the safe side, I asked another guest about the distance.

"At least forty kilometres", he answered.

At five o'clock in the afternoon I still hadn't reached my target. Fortunately I discovered a sign at a crossroads indicating that there was a hotel after two hundred metres. I walked five hundred metres in the direction the sign had pointed and came across another sign-board: "hotel one hundred metres". The Portuguese obviously didn't take it so exactly with distances.

After another five hundred metres I finally arrived at the hotel. It was closed. I hurried back the one kilometre to the first sign and tried in vain to pull it out of the ground. After walking more than thirty kilometres and then an additional two senseless kilometres on top of it had just made me furious.

The trail continued through a forest. It was raining, I was drenched, felt cold and dawn was already breaking. I was just preparing for the worst, when I noticed a sign nailed to a tree saying: "hostel one hundred and fifty metres". An arrow pointed down a steep forest trail. It didn't really look as if there was any kind of lodging, but at least I had to find out.

I followed the descent for about a kilometre, but nothing materialized. Gasping, I dragged myself back uphill again. Another two fruitless kilometres. This was enough even to make the Pope run amok. I wasted my last strength demolishing the sign.

At eight o'clock in the evening I arrived at Monsanto after having walked the full forty kilometres. Along the only street there was no-one to be seen. So I rang on someone's doorbell. An elderly lady opened the door. I showed her the printout with the hostels marked and pointed to the only one in Monsanto. She shrugged and said that it was not a hostel, but the town hall, which every now and then found private rooms for travellers. But by now it would be closed anyway. Great!

The woman sent me down the street towards a bar that apparently had a guest room available. My very last hope. The next village lay many kilometres ahead and in Monsanto there wasn't even a sheltered bus stop, where, at a pinch, I might have managed to hold out overnight.

My hopes were dashed rapidly. The bar owner told me that he had been using the room for a long time as a junk room. I then enquired if there was any other accommodation in the village.

"Não."

I looked around. A group of locals wearing berets were shaking their heads synchronously.

Slowly but steadily I had had enough for the day.

"Is there a church in town?", I asked the barkeeper.

"Just keep on going down the road, but it's closed and locked."

"In that case would you please call the priest", I said. "He should unlock it for me. I am a pilgrim on his way to Santiago and therefore enjoy certain privileges. The church has to grant me shelter in case of need!"

"We don't have our own priest", the barkeeper explained. "Every now and then a cleric from a neighbouring village comes around."

I spread out my arms in desperation. "Am I supposed to freeze to death out there? As a pilgrim in the middle of Monsanto? Then you can be sure that no tourist will ever set foot in Monsanto again!" I threatened the locals by sketching a worst-case scenario.

"Well, up to now no tourist has ever come here anyway", a toothless old guy with a toothpick in his mouth remarked. Point taken.

"Would you like something to eat? There are sandwiches with fresh bread from the day before yesterday", the barkeeper tried to calm me down.

"No way!" I stood up and ostentatiously folded my arms before my belly. "Thanks to the intolerable humanitarian circumstances in Monsanto, as of immediately I am going on hunger strike", I announced, asking myself at the same time whether I was perhaps going a bit too far – after all I was ravenously hungry.

Nevertheless my action seemed to work. The 'village elders'

deliberated on what to do with the troublesome pilgrim. Eventually the toothless one with the toothpick told me to proceed to the church and wait for him there. He would have to get the keys first. A little later, sure enough, the old man unlocked the annexe to the church. It turned out to be the kindergarten with a classroom for catechism lessons.

"You can sleep here", he said. "But at eight o'clock you'll have to be gone. That's when the children arrive."

"*Muito obrigado*", I replied and asked him where the beds were.

"There are no beds here."

"I see! And the showers?"

"No showers."

"Wi-Fi?"

"What's that?"

"Is there at least a restaurant somewhere around here?"

"Didn't you go on hunger strike?"

"Fucking hell!"

"You're in a church, don't forget!" the old boy ranted.

He had hardly left when I started to put on all of my still available dry clothing, slipped into my sleeping bag, laid down on a child-sized gymnastics mat and immediately fell asleep from exhaustion.

The following day I arrived in Fátima at around four o'clock in the afternoon. I managed to get shelter in an austere hostel against a voluntary donation and stayed for two nights. I decided to treat myself to a day's rest and to visit the pilgrimage sites. My pilgrim's heaven had brightened up once again.

That's all fair enough, some of my readers might say, but what on earth happened to pilgrim sister Sandy?

Well, from Porto onwards hiking became really special again – not because of the improved infrastructure or the delightful scenery. No, but from there, namely, I was accompanied by pilgrim sister Sandy!

Together, we continued the rest of the pilgrimage – this time to Cape Finisterre, to the end of the world.

Acknowledgments

Professionally, my thanks go to the Allitera publishing house in Munich, above all to Alexander Strathern, Vanessa von Proff and Lisa Heller. Also for this project I am particularly grateful to the editorial office of Dr. Annika Krummacher for the German version. *Muchas gracias* for the cooperation conducted in a most constructive spirit.

I am especially grateful to Andrea Dutton-Kölbl and Joachim Paul Fehling, who successfully tackled the task of translating this book from a combination of Austrian and German into the English language.

From a personal point of view I would like to express my special thanks to all of my Facebook friends. Hundreds of you followed my pilgrimage, kept motivating me, inspired me and ensured that surrender never became an option for me. Even the idea for writing this book is based on the impulse of some of my virtual 'amigos' on Facebook. The text itself is based on true occurrences, the names of some of the parties involved, however, have been altered.

Last but not least it is my sincere pleasure to extend my thanks to you, dear reader. I am still happy about every single copy of my book that is being read and I feel it is a special honour that you devoted your time to my work and thus to part of my life story. After having read *How I Strayed From the Path to Stop Falling by the Wayside* you should in fact know me quite well, even though I have probably never met you in person. But I would indeed like to get to know you. Why don't you simply write to me and tell me how you came across this book and whether you liked it? I shall answer you whatever the case. And if you should ever come to Andalusia, just contact me for a glass of Sangria and have your personal copy signed.

Since I am quite often on the road – whether hiking, walking another pilgrimage or sailing – the best way to get hold of me would be via email at:

info@freundlinger.com

or via Facebook:

www.facebook.com/EduardFreundlinger.Autor

I hope the contents of this book managed to reach your soul and perhaps made you think a little more deeply about the "Way" of your own life.

Your,

Eduard Freundlinger

Printed in Great Britain
by Amazon